A Bad Boy Stole My Heart 2

Londyn Lenz

©2018

Published by *Miss Candice Presents*

Where we left off...

Dreka texted me and asked me to come over. I hit Cassidy up, but she didn't answer. I wanted her to come over so she could dish about her date. Painting with my dad was so fun and relaxing. I needed to finish that Monet for my second job. I was so ready to put that grand in my bank account. Speaking of bank account, my dad surprised me with fifteen grand! I almost jumped through the roof when he gave me that much fucking money. He told me shit was going good and he just wanted to give it to me. I hugged him so tight and thanked him. I was truly a daddy's girl for life.

I texted Kenyatta, but he didn't answer. I just figured he was busy with his son.

"Why are you sitting on the porch like you lost your best friend?" I asked Dreka as I closed the door to my car.

She was looking so sad sitting on the porch swing.

"Cause I fucking did and I'm beating a bitch ass as soon as I catch her!"

I sat down next to her, ready to talk.

"Oh Lord, what happened?" I asked her.

Dreka began telling me about what happened at the shop. Her calling Z in front of everyone and them basically outing their relationship. That part made me smile. Then she told me how Tia's ugly ass was hating and they almost got into a fight. I was ready to go look for that dusty hoe when she said the bitch flattened one of her tires.

"That shit foul as fuck, Dreka. We beating that bitch ass on sight," I said to her.

"Wait a minute though cousin because the shit gets better."

She began telling me about Tia calling Z and saying she was pregnant.

I didn't react right away because Kenyatta's big ass Lincoln Navigator almost fucked Dreka's lawn up. He hopped out. He looked pissed off and held what looked like some papers.

"You a fucking grimy ass bitch!"

I jumped up along with Dreka.

"WHAT!" we both said in unison.

"You did all this shit just to set me the fuck up! Getting close to me and even giving up your fucking virginity!"

Now I was off the porch and he was in my face looking like a psychotic person.

"Kenyatta, what the fuck are you talking about, and why are you calling me out my name?!"

I was pissed off now.

He shoved some papers in my chest.

"THAT'S YO' FUCKING BROTHER AND HIS FAT ASS DADDY! THEY JUST ARRESTED MY FUCKING UNCLE! THAT'S WHAT THE FUCK I'M TALKING ABOUT!"

I heard him yelling and cussing, but I was too busy looking at the pictures of Jamie and who I guessed was his father. His dad was a fat guy who looked like Uncle Phil from The Fresh Prince of Bel-Air. They were talking and laughing together.

Then there were pictures of me and Yatta in public together. I saw pictures of his uncle and some other man who I assumed was his uncle's friend because they were dapping each other up.

I looked at the pictures and my eyes started to water. I couldn't believe Jamie used me to get to Kenyatta's uncle. But why? Why would he do that and what was Kenyatta's uncle doing to get investigated? I had question after question going on in my head.

"You ain't got shit to say? You just gone stand there and cry like that shit supposed to mean something to me?!"

Kenyatta was still yelling.

I looked up at him with tears falling from my eyes.

"Kenyatta-----"

"Naw fuck that bitch, it's Yatta to yo' ass just like the rest of them bitches. Except you not even like the rest of these bitches. You a fucking op so you don't get to call me shit!" he yelled in my face.

I was looking at him and all I saw was hate.

"Yatta or whatever the fuck yo name is! You better get the fuck out of my cousin's face. She would never play you like that!" Dreka yelled.

Kenyatta stayed nose to nose to me just looking in my wet eyes.

"I would never do that to you. I don't even know what's going on," I said as my voice cracked.

He still looked at me with hate and anger.

"Stay the fuck away from me and hope I don't fuck yo' ass up," he walked away.

Before he got in, he stopped and said, "Oh, and the shit you probably heard from your cousin is true. Cleo is having my baby again and a nigga couldn't be prouder," he smiled at me with a malice look and jumped in his truck.

I felt as if he had pulled my stomach out and dragged it down the street.

I broke down and Dreka was right there consoling me.

I knew I should have stayed far away from Yatta. He was nothing but a bad boy and I had still given him my heart.

Josey

"You had the easiest job out of all of us and you fucking FAILED ME!"

SLAP!

I slapped the fuck out of my failure of a son, Jamie Morrison Braxton. Ok, I was just mad at the moment because my son was the farthest thing from a failure. He was nothing like that first mistake I gave birth to.

"Mommy, I swear I tried to put the chip on Erin's phone but her thug boyfriend showed up," he looked at me with tears coming from his eyes.

I softened up and hugged my sweet baby boy.

"Mommy, you weren't there when her thug of a boyfriend came and slammed me on my ass. Oh my God, Mommy I was so scared. He wanted to really freak me up and Erin didn't even defend me!"

He was hysterical.

I soothed my baby boy to calm him down. Jamie may have had the look, but he was the farthest thing from a low life thug. I raised him to understand he was better than the color of his skin. I always told him every black guy in the hood was nothing and would always be nothing. Jamie was my prize child. My one and only accomplishment after that mistake I gave birth to twenty-one-years ago.

"Shhh. Mommy knows, my baby boy. Them nasty thugs are all around in that area you were in. I'm sorry for putting you in that situation, but it's what needs to be done. I hate you in these ghetto ass clothes too," I turned my nose up at his street attire.

Jamie wore nothing but suits, slacks, and dress shirts. It had been like that since he started pre-school.

"I hate them too, Mommy, and I am really sorry for failing you. I will try harder but that thug guy Yatta is going to be a problem."

My baby boy looked so scared.

"Thurgood, he can't go back down there. Can't you see he is scared?" I looked at my husband and said to him.

He was leaning against the wall finishing off a whopper from Burger King.

I rolled my eyes because all his fat ass did was fucking eat.

"Josey, he is being a baby and you're letting him play you. He has the easiest job out of all of us. Get the bitch's phone and put the chip in the inside. Simple."

He wiped his greasy mouth with his hand, looked at Jamie and said, "Get your ass back down there and get the job done. We won't be able to hold Lonell Bailey for long and we need something more concrete. Don't you want to please your mommy?" he asked.

My handsome baby boy looked at me and smiled.

"Yes, I do. I will get it done tomorrow Mommy, I promise."

With that, he kissed my cheek and walked away. I smiled at my son and ran my hands through my curly hair.

"He better do it Josey or its back to the basement for him, and this time you won't be able to save his ass."

"Thurgood, you are too hard on my baby boy but I really want this to happen so I understand. Just make sure you don't mess his face up. I want grandchildren someday Thurgood," I smiled and kissed him on his thin lips.

"If you're a good boy then I'll use the strap tonight," I told him and his face became flushed.

I reached in his pocket and pulled out his wallet.

"I'll take this and I'll see you tonight for dinner," I seductively looked at him and bit my lip.

Kissing him, I could taste the burger he had just ate. I put his wallet back in his pocket and smirked at him.

Thurgood was so easily turned on that it was so funny. Looking at him, I saw that his eyes were closed tight, he was sweating and his breathing was fast. It looked like he was about to have a heart attack. Not to mention his little six-inch dick was so hard.

"Oh God Josey sweetie. I need it now, let's go in the bedroom now. I'll get in position and you strap up. Please, I need it," he was breathing faster and faster.

Sweat was forming more and more. I could see pit stains under his white button-up dress shirt.

"Calm down, Thurgood. I need some retail therapy after our son failed us. I'll be back and more in the mood," I kissed his lips again before walking away, laughing.

Men were always so easy to play and because of my good looks and still nice body, I could play them better than lotto. My mother and grandmother had the same talent in that field and it was passed down to me. The only difference was my daddy spoiled me so bad that it literally made me rotten. You know the saying 'spoiled rotten', well I was indeed a rotten apple. I was the only thing that mattered. My feelings, my happiness, and my way. All the time, non-stop, and if it wasn't that way then I would make it that way by any means necessary.

I was the only child until my mama had another baby. A girl named Lillian and she was nine years younger than me.

I hated that fucking girl and tried many of times to get rid of her but I always chickened out. I guess I wasn't that damn hard to kill somebody.

Lillian was a fat girl though so immediately I knew she was no competition. I mean what fat woman walking the earth is competition? Not one, so I never took them seriously. Fast forward all the way to my adulthood. I had been getting by on my good looks and body. I had long sandy brown curly hair, full lips. Honey color skin, and even though I had a few wrinkles and creases now because of old age, my body was still curvy and toned because I did yoga every morning.

There was definitely some miles on this pussy but it had gotten me any and everything I had ever wanted. Whether it be a woman, man, black, white or Chinese. I could work the fuck out of them and get what I wanted.

Shit changed when I met Emmanuel Hudges, or Manny, which was the nickname I gave him in 1988. I was born and raised in Detroit on the Westside. Puritan and Cherrylawn was my area. One day, Manny was outside selling dope. I saw him beat the hell out this nigga who owed him money. He had his brother Delon and their best friend Lonell behind him cracking up.

It was love at first sight, it was something I had never felt. Although all three of the guys were fine and boss like, I wanted Manny to myself and was determined to get his hard ass.

It took me four months to get him to notice me. Hell even when I did it took me another three months for him to even take me on a date. We'd fuck, but Manny told me that he heard about how I used niggas. He wasn't trying to fuck with me on that level. That made me want him even more and I knew I was in true love. I cut all the guys I was talking to off and only focused on him.

I went to Oakland University in Rochester, MI for Nursing, even though I didn't plan on ever putting my degree to use. My parents forced college on me, so to shut them up I did it. Anyway, I went to school, came home and spent time with Manny. He finally gave in and made me his woman.

I fell even more in love with him when he shared with me his passion for art. He showed me his paintings and drawings. I shared with him my work and how I would have loved to see some of the world's top museums. I told him art wasn't talked about in my house because my parents didn't think it was a steady career. They took it as a joke so I hid it from them.

Manny and I started painting and drawing together. It was such an aphrodisiac and every time we did, it my soul felt free. Like a zing went from my head all over my body and around my heart. I knew he was my soulmate and at that moment we were tied together forever. We traveled in the country, out the country and we moved in together.

Things were great until I found out I was fucking pregnant. You see, Manny had always told me he wanted to settle down and have a family. I never wanted that because I never wanted to share him or his love. I wanted it all to myself and I loved our carefree life together. I made sure to always take my birth control when he wasn't around. I fed him some bullshit about if God wanted us to have children then we would. He brought the crap I was talking and we never really talked more about it. Then, my stupid ass fucked up and missed a few days of my pill and got knocked up. I told him if he wanted me to get rid of it then I would. That crazy fool chocked me up and threatened my life and my parents' life.

I tried to do everything to get rid of the baby but no matter what, every doctor's appointment the baby kept growing and getting healthier.

Finally, I was ok with having a child if I was having a boy. Men are never soft with boys, and with two of my men in the house I was definitely going to be the center of both of their worlds.

Me and Manny decided to wait until I gave birth to find out the sex. In the meanwhile, I was in a good space about being pregnant. Me and Manny were still going strong as hell. His brother Delon and friend Lonell hated me from the beginning, even with me being pregnant. They still hated me and always called me an opportunist. Little did those two-low lives know I really did love Manny.

Fast forward nine months and I gave birth to a healthy 8lbs 7oz baby girl. I could have thrown that bitch across the room when the nurse put her in my arms. I broke down when I saw how Manny was looking at her. I had lost him forever at that moment and I knew it. The nurses thought my tears were tears of joy. Hell no, they were not! I was livid and wanted her to just disappear. Manny kept looking at her in a way he never looked at me. He even named her without asking me how I felt about it. He named her Erin Khila Hudges. The name pissed me off because it was another level that they bonded on. I hated my own daughter and wanted her to just go the fuck away.

By the time the bitch turned one years old, everybody loved her. All of Manny's friends, his brother, even my parents, loved the ground she walked on.

Then get this, for me to have carried her she was a spitting image of Manny. She had his light caramel skin, his chestnut color eyes, and his smile. She only had my big curly hair and that was it. Manny was more in love with her every single day and it pained me. We didn't paint together as much, the traveling stopped and he was at her beck and call. We'd be in the middle of fucking but if he heard her he would jump up like I wasn't in the middle of riding his dick.

Every fucking thing was Erin and I was just fading in the back! It was if I didn't carry that little bitch. Finally getting fed up, I started cheating and getting my needs met elsewhere. I knew how dangerous that was because of Manny being a loose cannon. But hell, I had needs and feelings too and he was neglecting me. Even though I was messing with other men I still wanted Manny. Nobody would ever do me like that man. Sexually, spiritually, mentally or emotionally, Emmanuel was all of that for me and the other men were just toys.

Erin had just turned two and I told him I was working late and couldn't make it to her birthday party.

I was with Thurgood at a motel on Michigan Avenue where prostitutes went. We were in the middle of fucking when Manny barged in with Delon and Lonell. They beat the fuck out of Thurgood and Manny did a number on me, too. He put both of us in the hospital for almost two weeks. To make matters worse, Manny didn't visit me once. He put the word out to my family about what happened, and out of fear of him, me nor Thurgood pressed charges. We told police that it was some senseless young dudes trying to rob us. The shit was swept under the rug and we were discharged. Manny put me out the house and all my shit was thrown away. My car was sat on fire, along with all my artwork. I lost painting and drawings I had done from when we used to go on our trips.

I was broken and depressed for so long. Thurgood was right there and came from money. I settled for him to take care of me. He was soft and let me walk over him. Thurgood was a fat, lonely, wealthy man who was into being submissive. I figured fuck it, I was out of options. I made it work with him. Fed his weird ass sexual desires of me fucking his fat ass with a strap-on. He gave me any and everything I wanted and he loved the ground I walked on. He would lick the bottom of my heels clean. I knew this to be true because he had before. His ass was into all kinds of kinky humiliation shit that I was proud to do to him.

As time went on, I got pregnant and was happy as hell that it was a boy. Jamie was love at first sight and I couldn't have asked for a better son. He had that weak response to please me just like his dad. My two men loved me the way I deserved to be loved.

As time went on, I stayed in touch with Manny. I watched Erin grow into a gorgeous young woman. Shit pissed me off how flawlessly beautiful she was. His passion for art was even in her and from some of the pieces I saw the little bitch was better than me. I would never tell her that though.

I just hated her. Her beauty, her artistic ability, and her heart. It was pure and selfless, shit made her better than me.

Manny loved her so much and didn't even blink twice when I didn't raise her. His grey-haired ass mama raised her along with her uncle and his daughter he had a little after Erin. I was hoping she would get pregnant at a young age. Drop out of high school, start stripping or even become a hoe. Something to disappoint Manny and everybody else who was team Erin. But I got nothing, the little bitch was smart, beautiful and had endless talent. I hated her and tried my best to ruin her life from afar. No matter what I did the little bitch just kept winning.

Then Thurgood came home crying saying his best friend was murdered by some young thug. The case was looking like it was going to be another cold case. Thurgood's friend was known for getting high off dope and gambling. He did some illegal shit with some dudes in Detroit.

As Thurgood rambled, I was rolling my eyes. I didn't give a fuck until he said a name that made me pay attention. Lonell Bailey! Thurgood told me his best friend used to sell shit for Lonell and he would always give Thurgood a cut. Even though Thurgood was a cop he still was into some dirty shit. Any cop who lived the high life was usually in some dirty shit. I don't give a fuck who you are. A cop's salary wasn't buying luxury cars, big houses, and expensive trips.

Thurgood had his best friend in all kinds of illegal shit. It was to protect his own name. If shit went bad, he could just put it all on his best friend. Brilliant, right?! This was why I married him, he was smart.

Well, Thurgood told me he thought Lonell sent his nephew Yatta to kill his best friend. I knew that damn name from my stinking ass daughter. I followed her on Facebook and Instagram under a fake account. I had been doing that since her tenth-grade year of high school. Her father always made sure she knew the truth about me so Erin didn't really talk to me like mothers and daughters would. It was so robotic and seemed forced. With me not giving a fuck I never tried to fix it.

I just started spying and being a part of her life in other ways. I was able to see her friends, what they did for fun and who they hung out with. Erin never posted much about a guy unless they were famous. I knew she was still a virgin, even though we never talked about anything personal. I had been in the game a while and I could sniff out a virgin from a mile away. That annoyed me even more.

Anyway, I knew the name Yatta and told Thurgood all about his uncle Lonell. Thurgood came up with the idea of letting Jamie get close to Erin so we could spy on her. Thurgood wanted to frame Yatta of all the crimes that his dead best friend was into and his murder.

All Jamie had to do was put this chip on Erin's phone that would allow us listen to her conversations and the ones that went on around her. I wanted Lonell and Yatta to get locked up because I knew that would hurt Manny and Erin.

About two weeks ago, I saw on her Instagram that she was with that thug, Yatta. He had pictures of him and Erin on his page and so did she. I knew if I could make it so her little thug of a boyfriend went to jail for a long time, that would break her fragile ass heart. But Jamie failed and wasted time! I swear if he was starting to like Erin I was going to disown his ass.

This needed to happen because I was tired of Erin's ass winning. She came along and took my perfect life I had with Manny. My one true love and happiness that I have ever known was stolen from me. Now I was married to Thurgood's fat nasty ass and stuck in this marriage. All because of someone who never should have been born in the first place. I may not have the balls to kill her but I will destroy her life as many times as I could. I just hated that bitch!

Cleo

"Yatta, you been sleeping on my couch for three days now. Just come into the bedroom, it ain't like you haven't been in my bed before," I stood on the side looking down at my sexy ass baby daddy.

He was laid out on my couch with his jeans on, no shirt and that 'Yatta' chain all iced out on his sexy chest. His dreads were half up half down, and his goatee was a little fuller than usual. He still was fucking on point. I wanted him to come in my room so bad and just dick me down, but he wasn't cooperating.

"Cleo, get the fuck out of my face. I can hear ya hot pussy callin' my name from where you standin'. I ain't fucking you, ma."

He didn't even give me the courtesy of looking at me. He just went from looking at his phone to Sports Center on TV.

I got pissed off and stomped away to my room like a child, slamming my door.

Ugh! All I wanted was for my baby daddy to lay it down on me. This shit was ridiculous. There was some hard dick feet away from me and I couldn't have it. I know from book one y'all either don't like me or think I'm stupid for dick riding Yatta the way I do. But guess who don't give a fuck?! Yatta was mine and has been since my first day of Central High school. It was many other niggas taller, with more money and willing to be with me. That shit meant nothing to me compared to Yatta. That nigga had mad poise about him that made a bitch drop to her knees.

It was as if he wasn't with our generation, he was in a league of his own. His voice, looks, even how he wore the basic jeans and white t-shirt was so commanding and sexy. Oh, my God, my pussy was just screaming for him as I sat here and thought about it. He just had it, whatever the fuck 'it' was. Yatta had it and I wanted it and him to be mine. I swear I wouldn't pop no pussy or suck another nigga's dick if I could just get Yatta to be with me. I fucked up when he was in jail and was fucking with one of his homies. But shit, a bitch was mad as fuck and lonely.

I thought when he got out he, K.J., and I would be a family. But salt was thrown all in my water when this bitch Erin came back from New York. When I tell y'all I hated that hoe, I really hated that hoe. Let me start from the obvious of why I hated her.

The bitch was from head to toe fucking beautiful. I knew because I saw the bitch naked a few times when we were in the locker room in high school. Her body looks the same as it did in high school, except her hips are spread a little more.

Her hair was fucking big and curly as fuck. It reminded me of the twins from that show Sister Sister. This bitch's face, eyes, and skin was flawless with a pretty ass smile to match.

Get this shit though, she was smart, sweet and had an innocence about her that made me believe the bitch was a virgin. Now, I was a bad bitch! Nice body, sexy brown skin, and nice lips. I was a bitch that I was sure every Detroit nigga would want on their team. But Erin was the type of bitch niggas wanted to wife and I wanted to kill that bitch. I wasn't her soft ass mama, I'd drop a bitch dead if they stood in the way of what I wanted. And Erin was in my fucking way! Yatta had been wanting her since our freshman year in high school. He had never fucked with her on that level, but I still used to watch him gawk over her weird ass.

That bitch used to sit in class and draw some ugly ass pictures. You give me one bitch in Detroit walking around drawing and painting?! Who the fuck does that lame shit?! Erin wasn't on none of the club scenes, she was lame as fuck and green to anything poppin'. Her and Yatta together didn't make sense at all. That nigga was hood and everything that was fly. He needed a bitch like me on his team. I could handle the hoes that dick ride Yatta. Whatever his hustle was I could handle him out all night making money. I also could handle his dick game, all ten-inches of that thick pole. Erin's soft ass was just that, too fucking soft for him.

If she knew any better her and that fat ass Dreka better stay the fuck away from me and Tia's niggas. I don't know how far Tia was willing to go to keep Zamir, but I was willing to go beyond far in order to keep Yatta away from Erin.

Look at God, he was on my side because Yatta had been at my apartment for three days now! A bitch was two-stepping on the inside! I didn't know what the fuck happened between him and Erin and I didn't care. All I knew was he was mine and I was going to keep his ass this time. I swear if he thought he was going back to her he had another thing coming. Yatta was going to be with me and K.J, we were a package fucking deal.

Speaking of my son, I figured I should get up and go get him from his crib. Yatta loved our son so much and always wanted to be with him. Maybe if he saw K.J. in my bed sleeping then he might want to lay with us. I loved my son dearly, but he was a way into Yatta's heart. I swear I praised God for months straight when Yatta fucked me without a condom. Another thing that was sexy about my baby daddy was him never being pressed for pussy. He strapped his dick up on a hoe twice and made sure he was tested every six months. He would leave yo' ass high and dry if you wanted to fuck him without a condom.

He would put his hard dick back in his jeans and dip out on yo' ass with no argument, no debate and no explanation. Pussy was never-ending for him so he was never pressed about a bitch, no matter how bad you were. He didn't care how thick someone was or how wet the pussy was for him. He'd have another bitch on his phone waiting for him by the time he made it out the door. My baby daddy was just that fucking nigga!

So when he popped up at my crib, put some lame nigga I had here out my shit and fucked my brains out without a condom, I was so happy and prayed I was pregnant. Lo and behold, I gave him his first child.

I would give Yatta as many kids as he wanted as long as he committed to me and only me.

I kissed my baby on his chubby cheeks and got him comfortable in my bed. It was only around eleven at night so I knew for sure Yatta would be getting up around midnight to check on our son. When he saw him in here with me sleeping peacefully he'd for sure want to join us.

"Don't worry K.J, Daddy and Mommy will be together," I whispered in his ear and laid down next to him.

Sleep came in no time.

***

"Bitch, you still hiding from Z's big ass?!" I looked at my best friend Tia and asked her.

My two sisters Capri and Nay came over with Tia this morning. I woke up to these hoes knocking at my door loud as fuck.

My little plan didn't work last night. Yatta was gone when I woke up and K.J was in his crib. I was so fucking mad that I called my baby daddy nine times. He didn't answer or return my texts. I started to say something was wrong with K.J but I didn't feel like fighting with Yatta about that shit. I knew he'd be back though because his hygiene stuff was still in my bathroom. That made a bitch happy as fuck.

"Hell yea I am. I pissed Dreka off and made her ass dump him. I been laying low at my grandma's house. Ducking and dodging his ass hard as fuck. But its been three days so I'm sure he has cooled off by now. Plus, all I gotta do is get his big dick in my mouth and all will be forgiven," Tia said, laughing and eating her Burger King breakfast.

"I don't know why you fuck with his scary looking ass. He puts his hands on you and he don't be dropping no bands on yo' ass. Hell naw, I gotta at least get some money outta a nigga if I gotta sport a busted lip," my stupid ass sister Nay joked.

Capri and I laughed loud as hell and both gave Nay high fives.

"Ya' feels me, bitch! Like he too fucking big to be smacking any fucking body. And yo' stupid ass keep chasing him around like a desperate puppy. I would beat Yatta's ass!"

I was putting K.J's socks on while he sat in Capri's lap.

"Wait a muthafucking minute! How the hell you coming for me when Yatta wifed a whole bitch up? He all on Snap and the 'Gram posted up with Erin's weird ass. That nigga straight curved you like Safaree's dick curves tha pussy! Yo' stupid ass still trying to play 'Family Guy' with him. Bitch, he probably eat Erin's pussy and fuck her without a condom!"

When she said that I got pissed off. I took my cup of coffee and threw it on her white maxi dress. My sisters cracked up and I did to.

"BITCH WHY THE FUCK WOULD YOU DO THAT!?" Tia jumped up, screaming and crying.

"Cause bitch, you talk too much! You better be lucky the shit ain't hot no more!" my sisters and I cracked up when she ran out the kitchen to the bathroom.

"That was bold as hell, Cleo. You wrong as fuck for that," Nay's soft ass had to put her two-cent in.

I smacked my lips and waved her off.

"That's my best bitch. She know all she gotta do is go in my closet and get something else to wear," I started, cleaning up my kitchen while Rocky Badd's "With You" song played through my Bluetooth speaker.

Minutes later, Tia walked back in with one of my cute maxi dresses on.

Told you!

"So, since you had to quit the job at the shop because you're hiding from Z, why don't you make some extra money from me by babysitting K.J? I'm trying to pick up some day shifts at Sphinx and Yatta not gone sit in the house all day," I looked at Tia and asked her.

She smiled and agreed.

Sphinx was a strip club that all of us danced at. I fell back on it after I had K.J, but now I was ready to get my coins together. Yatta only bought shit for K.J and kept all my bills paid. A bitch like me needed money for clothes, bundles, and shoes. Until Yatta was ready to make me his woman, I had to get my own bread.

"Bitch fuck that, you betta get you a baller," Capri said as she walked out to lay K.J down in his playpen.

He had fallen asleep on her big ass titties like he always did. Both my sisters were fine as fuck. Slim thick, thirty-inch straight blue bundles touching both their asses and they stayed in designer clothes. But they both had old ass niggas taking care of them.

Tia was bad as fuck to with her thick ass. She always wore long ass box braids that were black and pink and her light skin was flawless. That was why I didn't understand her dumb ass letting Z hit her. She always healed good and kept makeup on her face. Still, he wouldn't be fucking my pretty ass face up. It worked for her though because Tia always loved all that heavy makeup shit.

"Why would I fuck with someone else, dumb bitch? I just told you me and Yatta about to make this family thing work."

These hoes thought I was playing about changing my ways.

"What about you?" Nay asked, pointing to Tia.

"You losing yo' nigga to that fat bitch Dreka?! You might as well let me hook you up with my nigga's brother. He lives in Northern Michigan by himself and he paid. His wife died last year so he lonely as fuck, bitch," Nay smiled while convincing Tia.

"I'm down with that, but before I do anything I gotta get this bitch Dreka. She got that shit coming to her for coming between me and Z. Ol' big bitch need to get between some Slim Fast and a gym membership," Tia joked, making us laugh.

I sat down at the kitchen table with them with some Chardonnay wine and a few glasses.

"Bitch, I feel you and you know we down with you on whatever you want to do. If Yatta wouldn't have dumped Erin then I would have fucked that hoe up!" I said while opening the bottle of wine.

"What the fuck happened between the two of them anyway?" Tia asked me.

"Shit, I don't know but the both of them cleaned their social media up with all their lame ass pictures and videos. All I know is I got my man back and I'm never losing his ass again. You know how niggas gotta test the waters first before they settle down. He probably realized that Erin slow paced ass ain't for him. I'm more of his speed and can handle how he lives," I told them.

They nodded their heads in agreement.

"Well, I wish Z would drop Dreka's big ass on her stomach. I'm still seeing him post statuses about her annoying ass. She ain't been liking shit or watching his shit though, so maybe my little outburst worked."

Tia's wild ass started sticking her tongue out and laughed.

"Oh yea, thank you, by the way bitch, for dragging my name in that shit, too! Yatta was pissed off. He was looking for yo' ass, along with Z. He didn't say shit about you saying I was pregnant though. I think he knew that was a lie," I said while I took a sip of my wine.

I thought Yatta would have clowned me about what Tia said. This crazy bitch called Z lying saying she was pregnant by him and I was pregnant by Yatta. She knew Dreka would run her big ass back telling Erin.

"Bitch, maybe that's why Yatta and Erin not together anymore. Erin probably got word from Dreka about you being knocked up and dumped Yatta's ass," Capri said to me and I shook my head.

"Naw, he been wanting Erin since high school. Some shit deeper had to have happened," I got annoyed even thinking about how I knew Yatta wanted Erin.

It was as if he was in love with her plain ass.

"Anyway, all that shit doesn't matter. I got my nigga, and bitch you need to get yours if that's what you want," I said to Tia while she lit her cigarette.

"I do want Z, bitch. I was here first before that wide hoe came and pushed me out the way."

My sisters and I looked at each other and then at Tia. My best bitch was really sad about not having Z.

"Well, bitch we gotta step our game up on making sure Dreka stays the fuck out of your way," I looked at her and smiled.

After that, we started making our moves. Yatta and Z were off the market and it was time these hoes understood that shit.

Alaric(Ric)

Three days before

"Well ain't this some cute shit!"

Cassidy and I jumped up when we heard a loud voice in my room. I looked up to my dad on my dresser with his two boys in my shit.

"What the fuck you doing, Dad?"

I pulled the cover over Cassidy's body to make sure she was covered. We both were naked as hell.

"I'm here to see my son. My one and only son who has been dodging the fuck out of me like I didn't put his ass inside of his mama."

He was pissed off.

He looked at Cassidy and licked his lips.

"Well damn, I see why you been laying low. She fine as fuck, son! My fucking boy!"

He started clapping his hands and laughing. He was sitting on my dresser with his all black and beanie cap on.

"Dad, could you and your niggas get the fuck out?! I'll get at you later."

When I said that he started cracking the fuck up.

"Nigga, you don't dismiss me! I'm YO' fucking father! Now, I saw how you laid up with this pretty thing. She got you acting different, like you in love. I can't have that."

He pulled his gun out and my eyes got big as fuck. He nodded at his men and they both grabbed my naked ass up and pinned my ass against the wall. Cassidy screamed and started crying.

My dad walked over to her, licking his lips.

"Dad, I swear to God!" I yelled.

He stopped walking and cocked his head to the side, looking at me.

"You swear what, nigga! What the fuck you gone do to me?! I will whoop yo' muthafuckin' ass in front of this bitch!"

He looked back at Cassidy. She started crying and trying to move. He snatched the cover off her, exposing her naked body.

My dad's two friends looked away. That told me they really didn't want to do this.

"Come on, Dad! I'm begging you not to fucking hurt my girl!"

He looked up at me, smiling.

"Yo' girl, huh?"

He put his gun to her head, making her scream. She closed her eyes and started to cry. That shit broke me and I felt my tears fall.

"Nigga, this bitch got you crying for her! Like I raised a fucking pussy ass nigga! Naw, she gotta go!"

I watched my dad's face as he pressed the gun harder to Cassidy's head.

"NO!" I yelled.

When I heard the gun go off, I closed my eyes.

PHEW!

Opening my eyes, I saw that my dad had shot a hole in my ceiling. He was smiling and looking at me. Then, he looked at Cassidy and smiled.

My Cass love was crying hard with her hand over her mouth.

My dad lowered the gun to between her legs. The smoke could be seen coming from the end of his silencer.

"What's wrong, Lil Mama? Don't you like hard shit going inside that pretty pussy? All I'm trying to do is make you feel good," my dad said to Cassidy, smiling.

I was trying to break free of the two big niggas that had me pinned against the wall.

"Dad, yo' beef is with ME! What the fuck are you messing with her for?!"

I was so fucking heated at this nigga. It was as if I didn't know who the fuck he was right now.

"Because, nigga she got'chu acting like a straight pussy and I had a fucking boy! Now, listen to me clearly. You're done with this soft shit and with them lil niggas you running around with. Come work for me son, like it always should have been. I'll set you up in a nice ass crib, all the bitches you want and the money will be never-ending," he looked in my eyes as he spoke promises.

I looked at my dad like he was crazy.

"Now, you might wanna watch how you answer me," he said as his hot gun went closer to Cassidy's pussy.

"I will shove my steel up this hoe's pussy and blow her fuckin' clit off."

Looking at him and then at Cassidy broke my fucking heart. Her eyes were closed and tears were coming down her face fast as fuck.

"Naw Lil' Mama, look at'cho new daddy while my son chooses you over me," he looked at her and said. Cassidy slowly opened her eyes and was face to face with my dad. He smiled at her and then looked back at me.

"What's it gonna be?" he asked me.

I looked at Cassidy again and her eyes met mine. They were red and puffy. Even though her life was on the line, she still looked at me and shook her head no slowly. My dad didn't catch it because he was still looking at me waiting on an answer. I swear I didn't want Cassidy to die but something was telling me that my dad was not about to kill her.

"I'm not coming to work for you. Fuck you, Dad!" I said that shit with my heart and soul.

This nigga was now dead to me. With his eyes turning more menacing, he held his stare. I did the same, not blinking, I didn't hesitate to look like I was scared because I really wasn't, at least not of him. If anything, I was praying that I wasn't wrong and he wouldn't kill Cassidy.

"You ungrateful son of a bitch. You came from my golden nuts and you would choose this bald-headed bitch over me?" he asked calmly.

Before I could answer, he quickly hit Cassidy in the face with the end of his gun. I saw blood come from her face and her head go back.

"Beat that nigga's ass," he said to his boys.

The next thing I knew I was getting my ass whooped by my dad's two niggas.

I didn't take that shit down. I was able to steal a hit from one of his big niggas. It was two against one, and soon enough I was on the floor getting punched and kicked like I was a bum on the streets.

I felt my ribs crack and each hit was harder and harder. My blood filled eyes looked at my dad who was smiling while looking down at Cassidy.

She had her hand on her mouth with blood coming from it. When I saw that nigga undo his pants, I lost it. I headbutt one of his niggas and hit the other one in his nuts.

The minute I thought I had an advantage to get to Cassidy I was grabbed from behind and slammed against the wall.

"Tape that nigga up and keep him standing," my dad said.

One of his boys hit me in my ribs hard as fuck again, making me cough up blood. My eyes were blurry from the blood coming. I was duck taped around my mouth and my risk were taped together. My whole body was burning while these muthafuckas pinned me against the wall.

"Don't scream Lil Mama or I swear I will kill you, this pussy and your fucking big ass brother," he looked at her and said.

Dropping his pants, he started stroking his dick. Cassidy tried to sit up and my dad slapped her hard across her face, knocking her out cold. He climbed between her legs and started licking and sucking her titties. His nasty ass mouth was leaving slob everywhere he kissed and licked. He went from her titties to her neck and back again all while looking at me. He stuck his middle finger in his mouth and sucked on it. Bringing it to Cassidy's pussy, he inserted it inside of her. She still was out cold while he finger fucked her for a second.

Pulling his finger out, he sucked on it.

"Damn son, her pussy taste good as hell. She a little tight bitch, just like I like it."

He kept eye contact with me as he got on top of Cassidy and fucked her.

Her body didn't move and she stayed out cold while he pumped into her. I know I probably should have closed my eyes, but I needed to see this shit, at this moment. I knew I was going to kill my dad and his fucking niggas. I was even killing his fucking wife and her fucking family. All these muthafuckas were dying for this shit.

Fuck me, fuck the ass whopping I got, and my broken ribs. My broken nose and my fucked-up face. He hurt Cassidy, my heart, the first and only girl I will ever love, next to my mama. We had just got our thang right after me fucking up and now this shit.

Naw, I was killing this nigga that I called dad. As a matter of fact, I ain't got no fucking dad. German Bell was no longer my dad and I swore on my life that I was killing this nigga.

"Arrghhhhh! Yeaaaa bitch!"

He was putting his kids all on my Cass love's stomach. I swear to God I would have died if she was awake and had to see this shit. I know this would have fucked her up not saying this wouldn't but still. I could feel blood and tears coming from my eyes.

My dad got himself together, picked up his gun and walked over to me. He snatched the tape from my mouth and stood face to face with me.

"You will come work for me, nigga. Or I swear I will kill that hoe, those punk ass niggas, ya mama and them little bastards that came out of her disloyal ass pussy."

He looked at me and then to his niggas again. Within seconds, they were beating my ass again until I blacked out.

⁇

***

Present day: Three days later

God damn! This bright ass light in my fucking eyes was burning like a muthafucka. I swear Cassidy was always opening up all the blinds in her apartment. I wished her microwave would shut the fuck up beeping.

After rubbing my eyes slowly, my vision cleared up. All I saw was a white ceiling and a mounted TV. My head was kicking my ass. What the fuck happened last night?

Closing my eyes, I tried to remember the last thing I did. Cassidy popped in my mind first. Her sexy ass was looking so good last night in this tight ass dress that hugged her slim thick body.

That sexy ass short haircut she rocked was short in the back and on the sides. Her grade of hair was so pretty. She kept a little of her long hair on the left side of her face and it covered her eye.

Her smooth caramel skin was glowing and those brown eyes just looked good in the summer night sky. The dress she wore showed her perfectly sculpted legs that I missed wrapped around me. I already knew her nails and feet were on point because that was just the type of woman she was.

Plus, Cassidy did nails as a side hustle so she kept her own shit up. These sexy ass heels she wore completed her outfit. My dick was getting hard as fuck at just watching her walk out her door from her apartment complex. She didn't have on any makeup because she never needed it. She only wore some gloss shit on her full sexy lips that I could see shining from my truck.

As she walked, I noticed she wasn't walking towards me.

What the fuck! Who the hell car is this she getting into?!

My heart was racing and I swear I wanted to grab my .45 and kill whoever the fuck was on the driver's side. Then, I remembered that me and Cassidy were done. She walked away from me because I played her at Yatta's party. I had a bitch suck my dick and let the hoe sit on my lap. Instead of me owning up to my shit, I played games and hurt my Cass Love. Now she had moved on and was putting me behind her.

Hell no. I can't have this shit.

I remembered going to the restaurant she and this lame ass nigga were at. I put all my feelings on the table and she still didn't want me.

Getting put out the restaurant, I went to my truck to figure out my next move. Then, my passenger door opened and Cassidy got in.

A nigga was happy as fuck. I remember making love to her all damn night. All my rules went out the window for this girl. I didn't give a fuck about what bitch threw pussy my way. I wasn't catching that bullshit. I had the baddest, sexiest, smartest bitch in Detroit. With that alone, a nigga was complete. At twenty-one years old, I had found who the fuck I wanted to be with forever. Shit would be smooth from here on out.

What the fuck? Why is my dad standing at the end of my bed clapping his hands?

Shit started coming back to me. Him giving me an ultimatum, his threats and then his niggas fucking me up.

Cassidy! This muthafucka hurt my Cass love!

I sprung up from where I was laying, and I swear I felt like someone took a sledgehammer to my chest.

"AH FUCK!" My ribs and chest knocked my ass back down in the bed I was laying in.

"Nigga, what the fuck are you doing? Trying to fuck ya shit up more?"

My eyes were bucked as I looked at Z standing on the side of me.

"Where the fuck is my girl?! That muthafucka------"

"Calm down, Alaric man. Cassidy is good, nigga and she already told me what was up. I swear my nigga she's safe, but I need yo' ass to calm down so we can talk before the nurse and doctor come in," Z said to me before he pulled his phone out and made a call.

He talked for a minute and then gave me the phone.

"Ric babe, you're awake."

I swear when I heard Cassidy's sweet voice, my punk ass eyes watered. I thought the worse happened to her after I blacked out. All the horrible shit that muthafucka did to her came back.

"Boo, I swear I am so sorry for this shit, man. Like on some hunnid shit, I promise you—"

"Calm down babe, it's ok. I'm on my way up there to see you and we can talk. I love you."

I closed my eyes when she said that shit.

"I love you too, Ma."

She hung up and I gave the phone back to Z.

He grabbed the chair and sat down. I didn't know what the fuck he was thinking or how much he knew but I did know that my nigga didn't play when it came to his sister.

"You know your dad has to go, right? You my day one nigga but the shit he did," his nostrils flared and he shook his head.

"Look Z, you saying shit I already know. I get Cassidy told you what happened and I'm glad she did. But my nigga, I saw the shit. I had to watch the shit, as a fucking man I feel defeated as fuck. This ain't no game to me and that muthafucka is not my fucking dad. You don't have to tell me shit about what has to happen."

I looked my nigga dead in his eyes.

"I know what the fuck is going to happen. You're not the only man in Cassidy's life that loves her anymore. I swear on my fucking life I'm killing him for this shit, even if I have to die with his ass. He violated in the worse way possible."

Z kept his eyes on mine as he nodded his head.

"As long as we clear. That's baby sis my nigga and she didn't deserve that shit. I know how ya pops move. I'm telling you now we're doing this shit together. He touched my fucking sister in a way that will never make her the same again. I want in on this shit."

I told him I agreed with him.

He dapped me up and gave me a brotherly hug. The nurse and doctor walked in just as we finished up.

The both of them checked me out. I had been out for three days. My ribs were broken and my shoulder was dislocated. I had to be careful with everyday activities. For a while, I wasn't going to be able to drive and I'd need help getting dressed.

While they were talking to me, someone knocked on my door. Yatta walked his ass in, grinning and shit.

"Damn bitch, you was trying to check out on us and shit?!" His p,unk ass talked shit as he dapped me up and gave me a hug.

"Fuck you nigga. Let's see how you take having broken ribs and shit," I joked back with him.

My white doctor shook his punk ass head as he walked out.

Fucking cracker.

My damn nurse was young and black though. Her damn eyes were glued on my nigga Yatta. She was fine as fuck with a thick frame. Too bad that nigga was gone on Erin.

"Aye, I heard what the fuck went down. You know we got you, right? Yo' pops wild as fuck for this shit," Yatta got serious as fuck when he said that.

I nodded my head letting him know I agreed. I was going to talk more to him about it when my nurse left the room. Right before she was about to dip Yatta stopped her.

"When can I get an oral exam from you, Ma? I know you down from the way you keep staring at a nigga."

This bitch blushed and wrote down her number before she walked out.

"Damn my nigga, you just gone play Erin like that? I mean that bitch cute but she ain't got shit on Erin," I said to him as I took a sip of water my nurse left for me.

My mouth was dry as fuck.

"Man, fuck that rat bitch."

When Yatta said that shit, I almost spit my water out.

Z shook his head and mumbled, "This nigga."

"I know I been out for three days but somebody gotta catch me up on what the fuck is happening."

I looked from Z to Yatta and nobody was saying shit. Finally, Yatta spoke up. The shit he told me had my head hurting more.

"Hold the fuck up. The suit that's been fucking with you and Z is Erin's brother's pops!? Then her half-brother is a D.A.?! They got pictures of you and her and you think she been setting us up for them to lock up Lonell?!" I looked at Yatta like he was fucking crazy.

"My dude, you ain't fucking deaf. You heard right so like I said fuck that bitch."

I've known this fool all my life. He didn't mean shit he just said.

"I gotta agree with Z, nigga. I don't think Erin would do some shit like that. I get where you're coming from and how it looks. But come on now, really think about this shit. Her fucking pops fucks with Lonell heavy. He also fucks with our operation heavy as hell. Dreka's dad is down with us and all. You mean to tell me Erin would fuck all of that up? What the fuck would be her purpose of doing it? You just said yaself that she had never even met her brother until a few weeks ago. You straight tripping, my nigga," I told his ass straight up.

This bitch nigga gave me and Z the stink face.

"Naw, y'all two just letting pussy cloud ya judgement, but not my ass, I'm done with Erin. Like I said, fuck that bitch."

Z and I just shook our heads at this fool. He was on some other shit. This fool needed a minute to really think about this shit. I would bet my fucking savings that Erin wasn't dirty like that. I understood the world we were living in and that people did some fucked up shit but I just don't see Erin being that way. Neither did Z and truthfully Yatta's stupid ass didn't either. He was just being a bitch and was in his feelings.

We changed the subject just as my door opened again. I smiled big as fuck when Cassidy walked in looking so fucking good. She had Dreka and Erin with her.

Leave it to chicks to be girly as fuck. They had stuffed animals, balloons and shit with them like a nigga just gave birth or some shit. Cassidy put her balloons and bear down.

She came to me and gave me the biggest kiss. Her tongue was sweet as hell. It tasted like she was eating Starburst or some shit. She smelled good as hell and the long dress she had on had her whole back out. My hands was on her soft ass skin.

"Break that bullshit, man. Cassy, sit'cho fast ass down," Z's big ugly ass said, looking at us like he was disgusted.

Cassidy smacked her lips and waved him off.

I moved over so she could sit in the bed next to me. Dreka and Erin gave me a hug and tied their balloons to the front end of my bed. Yatta was being a bitch. He was all in his phone with his nostrils flared. I noticed Dreka didn't say shit to Z either.

What the fuck was going on with my niggas and their girls? I know damn well I ain't the only one with some solid shit?!

These niggas had they shit on point with Erin and Dreka before me and Cassidy got right.

"I'm outta here, my nigga," Yatta stood up and walked over to me.

I saw Erin look at him but he didn't even pay her any mind. He dapped me up and gave me another brotherly hug. Then, this nigga did some corny shit.

"I'm about to go play with that sexy ass nurse you got," he laughed as he was about to walk out.

"You so fucking lame for that shit! You see my cousin right wit'cho loose lips ass!" Dreka was on that shit.

Me and my niggas had known Dreka and Erin since ninth grade. We had been out of high school for three years now. Dreka never played about Erin and constantly fought bitches over her, so I knew she wasn't scared of Yatta and his smart ass mouth.

"Yo bitch ass cousin fucked us up so talk shit to her ass."

"Nigga, fuck you and yo' stupid ass thoughts. I didn't fuck shit up but you're too damn stupid to even hear me out. Believe whatever you want but I ain't gone be too many more bitches. You're the true bitch."

Dreka and Cassidy fell out laughing and I couldn't even hold my shit in either. I never heard Erin's good girl ass talk like that. Yatta was blown the fuck back himself, but with him being the true asshole he was, he tried to play it off.

"I don't have time for this shit. I got a family to get home to," Cassidy smacked her lips and Dreka looked like she wanted to ram that nigga in his ribs.

They wanted to have his ass lying next to me in a hospital bed.

Erin laughed and shook her head.

"You do that Yatta, I got some new dick that I need to get home to!"

Yo, my nigga's face lost all color. This fool charged towards Erin, and if Z wasn't here, I don't know what the fuck he would have done.

"WHAT THE FUCK YOU JUST SAY! SPEAK THAT SHIT AGAIN, ERIN!"

"Aye nigga, calm yo' ass down! You ain't about to put yo' hands on her!" Z's huge ass stood in front of Yatta.

That nigga was red as fuck and Erin looked like she wasn't scared at all. Shit, they were perfect for each other because now she was being petty.

"Dick! Dick dickity-DICK! That's right muthafucka, you may have had it first, but you won't be the last! Go home to your rat and the baby rat in her stomach!"

Dreka must have known Erin was tripping now because she stood in front of Erin and put her hand over her mouth. Cassidy and Dreka pulled her in the bathroom in my room.

This shit was like a movie. Z had to hem Yatta against the wall. For this nigga not to give a fuck about Erin, he sure was pissed the fuck off.

"Nigga, calm yo' ass down before these white people lock yo' ass up," I told his ass.

I hated that I couldn't get out my hospital bed without help. Z's big ass was having a hard time getting this nigga not to go through the bathroom door.

"Naw nigga, she flapping her gums talkin' cash shit! Fuck that, my nigga! Yo, I swear I will kill her ass and whoever the fuck she thinks she about to fuck! That pussy is MINE!" his ass yelled loud as fuck at the bathroom door.

I threw my head back when two nurses and security came in my room.

"Excuse me! Do we have an issue? We are getting complaints about arguing coming from this room," the security guard turned to Yatta.

"Sir, you're going to have to calm down or leave."

Yatta finally chilled out and then stormed the fuck out, knocking the same nurse who gave him her number flat on her ass. That nigga was pissed the fuck off. Shit was wild as fuck.

***

"I cannot believe the drama that went on earlier. Now you're on the damn monitor visits list. I should kick Yatta's ass."

Cassidy was laying in my hospital bed next to me. Everyone left a little after the shit with Erin and Yatta. My mama and brothers came up here after that.

I told her the same shit me and Cassidy told the police. I had a few friends over, shit got bad and they jumped me. Z told Cassidy not to say shit about being raped. When that muthafucka blacked my ass out, Cassidy came to and the first thing she did was call her brother. Him, Yatta, and Lonell came to my spot. They took me to the hospital and had Cassidy fixed up. She only had a swollen lip and a bruised nose. Her face looked good now, but because she was a light caramel, there was a noticeable little bruise by her nose.

She was still flawless in my fucking eyes. I didn't want my mama or anyone to know what went down. I was handling this shit myself.

My mama came and babied my ass for about three hours. I told her I was good; I was just a little sore. Her and my brothers finally left after the doctor said I could go home in two days.

Tomorrow, I had to try and walk around a little. I got all the instructions on how to care for myself while I recovered. Cassidy wanted me to stay at her crib while I healed.

I didn't want to have her responsible for this shit, but she wasn't about to let me tell her no. Now, she was staying the night with me crammed in this little ass hospital bed, but I swear I was comfortable as fuck with her next to me.

"Fuck what went on today boo, I wanna talk about me and you."

She looked up at me and sat all the way up. I could see the fear in her face and how uncomfortable she was.

"Cassidy, you don't have to be scared to come closer to me. I'm not going to break," I said to her while pulling her closer to me.

My chest and ribs were tender as fuck, but I was a grown ass man. I could handle a little pain for her.

"Ric I'm fine, really. I understand what happened and I know you and my brother are going to handle it."

She wouldn't even look at me when she spoke. I could see her eyes getting watery as she tried to focus on the TV.

I grabbed the remote attached to the hospital bed and turned the TV off. I needed her undivided attention.

"Cassidy, look at me!"

She rolled her eyes and looked up at me.

"I'm sure this shit is hard as fuck for you. I swear if I could make this shit go away I fucking would, but we are not about to act like my fucking dad didn't rape you."

She looked down and her tears started falling. I didn't mean to sound harsh but I needed to get this shit off my chest.

"Come sit in front of me," I told her.

Cassidy got up and sat between my legs. We were face to face, but her head was still down.

I lifted her head up by her chin, making her look at me.

"I cannot let this shit go. I gotta kill him either way, Cassidy. Even if he didn't touch you, I still wouldn't have a choice. That muthafucka won't let me tell him no and be with you peacefully. Shit is deep as fuck with me and him. He believes no fucking body walking this earth can be loyal. He got played by the only woman he loved and then my mama played him. Love is a weakness to him and he won't stop until I'm dead along with you, Yatta and Z. I can't have that shit. I promise I will make it out of this shit and so will Z. A'ight?"

I pulled her to me and hugged her as tight as I could. My fucking body was a blaze but I didn't care.

"I'm so fucking sorry this happened to you. I apologize for having you caught up in this shit. No woman should ever be violated the way you have. I swear to you Cassidy, all of their asses will pay."

I rubbed her back and kissed the side of her face while she broke down. We sat in silence for about ten minutes. I was just letting her get out as much as she could. I swear every time I blinked, I saw what the fuck that muthafucka did to her. I saw her fear over and over in my head. Shit killed me.

"Do you still want to be with me? You know, after what went down?"

Shit, she was trying to break a thug down by asking me some shit like that.

Her face was so sad and her eyes were red and puffy from crying. I looked at her pretty face and rubbed the side of it gently. I put that same hand on the back of her neck while pulling her face to mine. I kissed her soft and then deepened it, almost swallowing her pretty ass.

Cassidy was so sweet and even the inside of her mouth tasted good as hell. I was trying my best to answer her question through this kiss. She stayed in the same position between my legs and my right hand stayed around the side of her soft face. All that could be heard was the sounds of our kiss and her soft moans.

My dick was about to fall off and I knew her pussy was wet as fuck, but I had to push that shit out my head because there was no way would I be able to make love to her right now. It wasn't even because I was fucked up. It was more so of how Cassidy might feel about being physical after what happened three days ago.

I wanted her ready. I wanted to take my time with loving on her and showing her body all it deserved. After kissing the fuck out of Cassidy for a while, I pulled away slowly. Her eyes were still closed. I kissed her cheeks, her nose and then pecked her sweet lips again. Her eyes opened and she gave me a small smile.

"Cassidy, I will always want you, boo. I don't feel any type of way towards you. I never want you to think that. I never want you to think you're at fault for what happened. I never want you to feel I will ever regret choosing you. I love you and I swear I meant what I said when we were having sex. I'll kill ya ass if you tried to leave me again."

I bit my bottom lip while looking at her. She blushed and smiled bigger.

When me and Cassidy had make up sex before this bullshit with German, I told her ass while I was drilling that pussy that I'd kill her ass if she left me again. I meant that shit; she was stuck with me.

"I love you, Ric," her sweet voice said to me.

"Say it again," I told her while I pulled her towards me slowly.

"I love you," those words left her mouth again.

I kissed the side of her neck and her ears.

"Again," I whispered to her as I kissed and licked her lips.

I could feel her breathing changing.

"I love you," she whispered, low and sexy as fuck.

I needed to chill on getting us horny because I knew we couldn't fuck. Hell, I couldn't even eat her pussy.

I kissed her cheeks and got to them pretty ass lips.

Looking her in her eyes I said, "Again."

Just when she said I love you again, I kissed her deep as fuck once more. We made out for a while, getting all hot and bothered.

We ended up watching Law & Order until we both fell asleep. I dreamed of how I was going to kill German Bell. That shit made my fucking dick brick hard, thinking about how I was going to kill all them muthafuckas.

Kenyatta(Yatta)

I had never been so conflicted a day in my life. This shit was fucking with a nigga mental. Bitches do fucked up shit like set niggas up to be robbed, killed or put in jail. I just never thought I'd be in a situation where I might have been set up. What was bad wasn't even being set up, it was who might be behind this shit.

Erin had always been something I wanted. I lowkey watched her when she didn't think anyone was watching. Being in Detroit, going to Central High School, which was dead smack in the hood had bitches on their phone, talking shit with their friends. They stayed putting on makeup or trying to get a nigga like me to notice them.

Not Erin though, she was drawing. If she wasn't drawing or painting, then she was daydreaming. She didn't even daydream like a normal person. It was as if whatever she was thinking about or picturing was bringing her joy. It put her body at peace and it gave her such a beautiful expression on her face.

I wasn't a deep poetic nigga, but I swear when I watched her I understood all the bullshit that are in the corny ass movies women like. After she was done daydreaming, she would always start drawing. It made her completely oblivious to the dumb ass high school life around her.

It also made bitches and niggas think she was weird. I used to hear dudes talk about how fine she was but how she was off as fuck. Then, her pops was a fucking narc, which was what they called a cop, so that made everybody stay clear of her.

Not me though, her pops was homies with my uncle. My nigga's sister was Erin and her cousin was Dreka's best friend, so I spent a good deal around her. I didn't meet her until high school because we never went to the same school. Hell, I didn't even know Emmanuel had a daughter until high school. We used to all joke around, hang out and chill together, but I never made a move on Erin. I wasn't scared or any if that bitch shit. I just knew she was destined for great shit. Shit that would take her all over the world. Her paintings and drawings that she would show were good as fuck.

They were always nature drawings, paintings of buildings throughout the city, or a bunch of abstract colors. I never seen any drawings or paintings of people. I'm sure she did them because she was that damn good. I knew she wouldn't be bound to Detroit for the rest of her life.

Getting fast money was what I was good at in high school and even out of high school. I was book smart as fuck, thanks to my auntie, but I didn't have a gift like Erin did. I wasn't about to stand in the way of her reaching her fullest potential. So, I kept her as one of the homies. If I wasn't fucking up her shine then neither was any other nigga.

The shit I did to keep niggas at bay from her would put my nigga Z to shame. He was blocking niggas from getting at Dreka as well. I just went to the extreme with my shit.

There was one nigga named Lanard who was in our French class. He was feeling Erin tough as hell but he was Central's top hoe. That nigga fucked anything and anybody. He even gave a bitch the clap. Erin was green to a lot of shit because she didn't hang out or involve herself in drama. When I saw that she was next on Lanard's list, I wasn't having that shit so I deaded it.

Lanard smoked weed, hella weed. His weed man was one of my old homies. I laced Lanard's shit with heroin. I knew that shit was extreme, but to be fair, I warned him about Erin.

Lanard was a cocky big mouth ass nigga. He was spoiled as fuck and parents were always fighting his battles. His pops was principal of another high school in the suburbs. Lanard swore he was a street nigga so he lived in the city with his mama.

Anyway, when I told him not to step to Erin he took my threat as joke. Now, he was strung out, and the shit got so bad that he dropped out of high school. Ask me if I felt bad, hell NO! I still got my full sleep and as far as everyone knew Lanard was just another sad story of a young boy hooked on drugs.

There was another dumb ass named Tamaj. Like Lanard, he didn't take my warning about staying away from Erin either. So, I beat that nigga's ass when he was leaving a house party. I was a little drunk so he was able to get a hit in. I still fucked him up and I stomped on his left hand, which he used to throw touchdowns on the football field. Little bitch nigga never threw a ball again. He knew better than to snitch, so his mama sent him to Arizona to live with his peoples.

The shit didn't stop there but that was just a taste of what the fuck I had done to keep niggas away from Erin. I knew I couldn't keep'em all at bay, but I did my best for the ones who tried to make it a mission to get her.

Now at twenty-one, I was ready to have her as my own. We made shit official and sealed our deal by having sex. I found out she was a virgin, which threw me all the way back. I was happy as fuck that I would be the first nigga to be inside of her. I made it clear to Erin that I would forever be the only man inside of her. We were sealed for life and she agreed to the shit. We were good and just getting our thing started.

Then, this bullshit came up! This shit was suspect. Me, my uncle Lonell, Z, Alaric and my uncle's right-hand Havoc were into the thieving business.

The shit gave me a fucking thrill ever since my uncle put me and my two niggas on when we were fifteen. Z and Alaric been my niggas since our sandbox days. My uncle and his wife took me in after my mama did a murder-suicide on my pops and herself.

I grew up loved and spoiled as hell. I figured since both my uncle and his wife Juziel had degrees and shit they both had some good ass jobs that paid for the life we lived. We went on trips and had nice cars, too nice to be living in the hood of Detroit. Our house was big, and even though it was in the city, we were in a good area of Detroit.

I kept every toy, designer clothes and shoes, electronics and video games that I wanted.

My uncle Lonell finally came clean about what him and his right-hand man Havoc did for a living. My two niggas and I wanted in so my uncle trained us and put us on. Shit has been sweet as fuck ever since. We even had my uncle's other best friend Emmanuel and Delon in on the shit. The three of them used to run Detroit back in their day.

Emmanuel and Delon got out the game when they had Dreka and Erin. Even with legit jobs, they knew the real money came the illegal way. Anyway, we had our shit locked and were careful about how we moved. My uncle made sure me, Z and Alaric had jobs of our own to fall back on. We weren't flashy, loud or in and out of trouble.

That was why when a suit started fucking popping up on me and Z, I was thrown off. Emmanuel looked into the shit but came up dry. No cop was investigating us at all. He told us to fall back on doing hits in Michigan until the suit stopped fucking with us. We agreed and decided to only take the hit we had lined up in D.C.

We had a plan and all the shit fell apart three days ago. The shit happened so fast that I didn't have time to react. I was at my uncle's house chilling before I had to go to the tattoo shop I worked at. That was my legit job. I did tattoos and piercings at two shops. One was on the Westside and the other was in Inkster. I was good as fuck at my craft and kept clientele because bitches loved ya boy!

My uncle's phone rang with Delon yelling that Emmanuel found out that the cop that was fucking with me and Z was Erin's mama's husband. He was giving my uncle the details and said he was on his way with some shit that Emmanuel found out.

While he was talking, someone knocked at my uncle's door. My auntie Juziel answered it and the suit nigga showed up with three other cops. They had a warrant for my uncle's arrest for a murder.

The fat Uncle Phil looking nigga gave my auntie the warrant, and his nasty looking ass winked at me.

When they said the name of the person my uncle was accused of killing, I tried to dead that shit. I recognized that name from the nigga I shot in Grand Rapids. Lonell had beef with the fool. He owed my uncle some money and the bitch ass nigga was dodging. My uncle and I went and paid him a visit. That fool started threating us, saying his best friend was a detective. He could have us arrested for some stupid shit. So me not taking too kindly to threats, I popped his ass in the head. Lonell wasn't mad at all. The shit had to be done, although he would have done it in a cleaner fashion.

The lame nigga fucked with dope and had a bunch of stolen shit in his place anyway, so we knew the police was going to assume the crime was drug-related. We didn't leave shit behind or anything. Nothing could have tied us to the crime scene, so I didn't know how the fuck this shit was happening. I just knew my uncle wasn't about to go down for some shit I did. I tried to speak up, but Lonell told me to close my fucking mouth. My auntie Juziel was already on the phone with our lawyer.

As soon as the two cops walked outside with Lonell handcuffed, Suit walked up to me and shoved an envelope in my chest.

"You think Erin is loyal to you? You're a fucking hoodlum, fool."

He looked at me and smiled before walking out of my uncle's house.

I opened the envelope and saw pictures of me and Erin. We were at the mall, on our first date at Andiamo downtown and some other places. There were pictures of my niggas, my uncle and of us meeting up with those Flint niggas.

I swear, I almost pulled my gun out and blew this fat ass nigga head off. I watched him and the cops pull off. My uncle was shaking his head and saying something, but I couldn't hear him.

I rushed to my truck and knew where the fuck I was going. I was going to snatch up this bitch, Erin.

I couldn't believe she would do a nigga like this. Even if me and her never got together, she had known me and my family for a while now. Hell, we hung out because her best friend was one of my best nigga's sister.

My drive to her spot was so blurry because I was that fucking heated. I had a lot of street smarts instilled in me. I had fucked up my share of set up bitches. I did that shit with not a care in the world, but Erin was different; this was my cutie pie. The fucking girl who I been wanting for so damn long. There was a voice in my head telling me some shit wasn't right. Erin would never play me this way, but my anger was pushing that shit further and further back.

Before I knew it, I was at her place cussing her ass out. I wanted to fuck her up, but I chickened out. I was heated, but I still couldn't bring myself to put my hands on her. The look she gave me let me see that I was breaking her heart. I didn't give a fuck though; my uncle was locked up. The shit was all too much of a coincidence with her nerdy ass brother being a D.A. lawyer and his pops being a cop. All the pictures that were taken of us, what the fuck he said about Erin's loyalty. All of this shit had my head spinning and I just went the fuck in on her.

Z had already called me about the drama with him and Dreka. He told me Tia made a scene saying her and Cleo were knocked up by us.

He was telling me so I could have a heads up if Dreka went and told Erin. All the shit happened in the same breath of my uncle getting arrested, so I said some hurtful shit to Erin about how I was happy Cleo was pregnant again with my baby. On God, when I said that shit, I could feel Erin's heart shatter. Shit, on some low-key shit, my heart shattered right with hers. Then, she still tried to reach out to me and explain. I just didn't and still don't know what the fuck to do. I couldn't let pussy cloud my judgment. Hell no! But on another hand, I was so fucked up not having Erin. Then this shit with Alaric and his punk ass dad. I knew we were handling that nigga and I was ready.

All I wanted was to be under my girl at night. I wanted to be inside of her, too. I wanted to smell and taste her sweet ass body. Hear her voice and wake up to my apartment smelling like her good ass cooking. Now, I was on some creep shit sitting in her room on her desk. Yea, you read that shit right.

When her and I fell out in Alaric's hospital room and she made that 'dick at home' comment. I lost it, I swear if Z wasn't there to stop me, I probably would have killed Erin. I didn't give a fuck, no nigga was about to know her body. Know her insides, her moans, none of that shit. Only me, Kenyatta Niemman Bailey.

Once I left the hospital, I came to her pops' house, but he wasn't home. His ass supposedly was on a mission to handle Erin's mama.

I had talked to my uncle a few times while he was locked up and he filled me in. Anyway, I broke into shit for a living so it was easy as fuck getting into Erin's house. Her room smelled just like her. Sweet and like berries. She was so neat and girly as fuck with her pink and white comforter set. She had some drawings on her wall that I knew she did because her initials were in the corner of each drawing. I swear this girl was so talented. She had polaroid pictures of her, Dreka, Cassidy and her family all on her wall also.

I got off her desk and went to her tall chocolate brown dresser. She had so much perfume on it. All expensive girly shit. I swear I knew the days she wore each bottle.

Opening her drawers, she had all her pajamas folded neatly. Her socks were all rolled up and color coordinated. Then I got to her panty and bra drawers. God damn, she had so fucking many. I thought I was bad, but Erin had me beat.

I picked up a sexy red thong. I got hard as fuck picturing her thick ass in it. Yea, I was taking this pair with me. Putting it in my pocket, I closed her drawer. I'd be dammed if she was about to go be with somebody else. I swore that I was jumping out and fucking her shit all up if she even attempted. Oh, what I was going to do to the nigga she called herself being with!

Man, there were no fucking words in the human dictionary for what I was going to do to him.

I heard the front door open and knew it was her. I could hear her talking to Dreka. I parked my truck away from her house, so she wouldn't spot me. He was near what was fucking mine. He was near what I claimed and marked with my dick. I could see some headlights on the side of her window. I knew it was Erin pulling in the driveway.

I opened her big ass walk-in closet and stepped in. If she opened the far end left part of her closet, then I was busted. I wouldn't even have any shame in what the fuck I was doing.

Erin's fine ass walked in her room looking mad as hell. I knew it was because of me, but what the fuck ever. I watched her put her phone and Bluetooth on her tall dresser. She had on a t-shirt dress and some pink and black Puma's. She was looking so damn good. She pulled her dress over her head. I was pissed off because she had on a thong and matching bra. The fuck she out in that shit for and she ain't with me?! Her dress was already too fucking short!

I had to grab my dick still because I was getting rock solid looking at her body. I must have really pissed her off because she left all her clothes and shoes in the middle of the floor.

Hitting the power button on her speaker, she began playing some old school Jagged Edge. Her big ass curly hair was down so she put it in a ponytail. When she walked out her bedroom and into the bathroom, I could have left then, but I was enjoying watching her move around. I heard the shower go on and her phone started ringing.

I opened her closet to see who the fuck was calling her.

"Who the fuck is Mario?" I said to myself.

I got mad as fuck and started to answer it. I decided against it because I wanted to see what she was going to do when she saw the missed call. I wanted to see who the fuck this nigga was. I also wanted to see if she would call her punk ass brother. I had my heat on me, which wasn't a good thing. I didn't know how the fuck I was going to react if she even talked to a nigga or her fucking brother. I made my shit clear to Erin and y'all asses reading this shit from book one know that I wasn't wrapped too tight. Women never take a nigga's warning seriously when he tells them he's fucking crazy.

Now look at this shit, I was in her closet watching her naked fine ass lotion up.

Damn Erin, I thought to myself while watching her oil her body up.

She put on a sports bra and some shorts that hugged her booty. My dick was about to break out her closet and hug the fuck out of her pussy.

When she picked up her phone my heart stopped. Unlocking it with a code that I couldn't make out she saw the missed call.

When she rolled her eyes, I smiled big as fuck like a lame nigga. Sitting her phone back down to charge it up, I watched her put her wet hair in two braided ponytails.

She walked over to her desk and grabbed the same drawing pad I'd seen her with. Picking up some pencils, she got her sexy ass on her bed and got comfortable.

From the way she was sitting, I couldn't make out what she was drawing.

The music played that SWV song, "Rain." My auntie used to play all that 90's R&B when I was younger. Shit, she still did.

I looked at Erin's face as she started drawing. That calmness, peaceful and free expression. The shit made me feel some type of way in my heart. I wanted to be behind her sexy body just watching her draw. I envisioned wrapping my arms around her waist with my chest pressed against her back.

Damn.

After about twenty minutes, she closed her drawing pad and put itack in her desk.

She picked her phone and Bluetooth up from her dresser.

Who the fuck is she about to call? I thought to myself.

She sent a text out and I watched her put the Bluetooth around her neck. She cut the speaker off that was playing in her room. The TV came on, muted. She turned the light off.

I smiled to myself knowing she wasn't doing no foul shit. She didn't even get on social media. I smiled even bigger when I heard her Bluetooth play 112's "Cupid" song.

When she closed her eyes and I saw tears roll down her face that fucked me up. I still couldn't even bring myself to fix this. I couldn't do anything regarding me and Erin until I got to the bottom of this.

About an hour later, she was good and asleep. I opened her closet slowly. Her music was still playing in her ear. I walked over to her and just looked at how fucking gorgeous she was. That smooth skin, sexy ass lips, and thick frame was every fucking thing. I wanted to get in bed with her and just hold her ass. I bent down and lightly kissed her lips. It took everything in me to not do more.

"I swear I don't want to kill you, Erin. Please be real about me and you and do not fuck with no other niggas," I whispered in her ear and kissed it.

She stirred around a little but then went back into her deep sleep.

Before I walked out, I went to her desk and picked up her drawing pad. When I opened where she had her pencils saving her page I saw what she was drawing. It was my chain that said 'Yatta' and my lips. There was nothing else but my chain and lips. Shit looked just like my shit, too.

I bit my bottom lip and did a little chuckle. Putting her drawing pad down, I opened her door and left.

Erin

"I feel like fucking Yatta up for you, cousin. He got a lot of nerve showing his ass at the hospital when he started the shit," Dreka said to me while we were in my room.

I was finishing getting dressed when Dreka came over. She wanted me to go eat with her. We invited Cassidy, but she wanted to stay with Alaric. We were going up to the hospital to see him and our girl again later. That was how we started talking about Yatta's stupid ass.

"At this point, I gotta just move the fuck on. I have tried to talk to him over and over. Then he got Cleo pregnant again, meaning he lied about not still fucking her."

I started getting mad all over again.

I sat down on my desk chair and wiped my eyes. Every time I even thought about me and Yatta, I cried. I wanted that dummy so bad and wanted him to hear me out. But not only could I not force it, I couldn't ignore that fact that Cleo was pregnant again. How the hell could he just dog me that way? I mean, he straight played my ass.

"Don't cry Erin, you gone make me pull up on his yellow ass. And where the hell is Uncle E at? My dad had some cars to test for General Motors so he in Chicago for a few days," Dreka asked me as she rubbed my back, calming me down.

I loved my crazy cousin.

"He told me he had to handle some police business for a few days out of town. I just talked to him right before you came over," I sat down next to Dreka on my bed so I could strap my sandals up my leg.

"So, where you going after me and you go eat? You getting all dolled-up bitch, and I know it ain't to eat with my fabulous ass."

She tossed her hair back and laughed. I laughed, too, at her annoying butt. I didn't even have on shit special, just a grey Heather romper from Fashion Nova's website. It was so cute and hugged my body like a glove.

I wore my big hair all down in a curly state and thanks to Cassidy my nails and feet were on point.

"Shut up, I'm only going to meet up with Hayden later. And stop looking at me like that, Dreka. Hayden is and always will be just a friend," I assured her as I stood up to spray some Miss. Dior on my body.

"So, how are you after the whole Tia incident?" I asked my cousin while I put my jewelry on.

Dreka blew out a long breath when I asked her about it.

"Girl, Z blows me up every day all damn day. I love the hell out of him, but I just need a minute. Plus, I wanna beat the breaks off Tia for what she did to my fucking car. As far as her being pregnant by Z, I just don't know, Erin. Like, I cannot deal with her extra ass as his baby mama."

Dreka shook her head no.

I walked back over to her and hugged her. My cousin looked so sad while talking about this.

"How the fuck we both get nigga problems so damn quick?!" I chuckled and said to her, trying to lighten the mood.

As she was about to respond, her phone started vibrating. We both looked down at it and saw it was Z.

"I told you. I have to keep my shit on vibrate because his ass will call and text all damn day. I want to talk to him, just not right now. I'm staying the night over here so his crazy ass won't pull up on me."

I nodded my head okay as we both got up and walked out my room.

☐

***

"This nigga got some nerve calling me," I angrily snatched my phone off the table.

Me and Dreka were enjoying our food at Dime Store on Griswold Street. Their breakfast was always on point and it had an after school special type of feel.

"Who is it?" Dreka asked me while biting her breakfast sandwich.

"It's Jamie. Let me take this and see what he wants," I stood up and walked out the restaurant.

It was hot as hell outside and downtown was already packed with people.

"What is it, Jamie? You been blowing me up for two days now, but when I was calling you I got no answer," I almost yelled at his ass.

I didn't know what was going on and no one had answers for me. My fucking mother wouldn't answer my phone calls, either.

"Erin, please just hear me out. I had no idea my father was investigating anything in Detroit, let alone your friends. I know it looks weird, but if you just meet up with me so I can tell you what I know, maybe I can help," he pleaded his case.

I softened because Jamie could be in the same situation as me. He could be stuck in the middle and really have no clue what was happening. I didn't want to do him like Yatta was doing me and just shun him. I needed my dad here to help me figure out all this mess. I was so confused and just wanted to know what was going on.

"Erin, you there?" he asked me, snapping me out my thoughts.

"Jamie, I have no idea what is going on. I just know that right now I must fall back a little until I can process this. I'll call you, okay," I said to him.

My dad always told me if I was confused about anything, don't make a decision. Take some time to think more about it. And right now, I was confused as hell.

"Come on baby sister, I just need a chance to talk to you. I mean if you think about it, every nigga in Detroit is up to no good anyway. I just don't want you to think my intentions are wrong towards you."

When he said that, I looked at the phone as if it had a foul odor coming from it.

"First of all, Jamie, people do stupid shit every fucking where you go. Not just me, not just one race and not just here in Detroit. Look, I'll hit you up if I decide to see you."

I hung up and went back into the restaurant even more annoyed. I should have known he was judgmental because my mother raised him.

I felt like I needed a heavy ass drink and a fat ass blunt. Dreka and I were definitely smoking after we were done eating.

***

"Thanks for a good evening, Hayden. Jurassic World: Fallen Kingdom was good, really good."

I smiled and looked at Hayden while he walked me to my door.

I had a nice time tonight and it took my mind off things for a while.

"I'm glad you enjoyed yourself. You still owe me for knocking my buffs off my face," he laughed when he said that, but I low key felt so bad.

Before we went to the movies Hayden took my bumper car racing. I rammed his car hard as hell and his Cartier buffs flew off his face. Another bumper car ran over them. I felt so bad and I apologized the entire night. Hayden was so cool about it. His parents had money and so did he, so I knew it was nothing for him to buy another pair. But, I still felt so damn bad.

"Hayden stop saying that, I already feel so bad. I have some money saved up, let me----"

He grabbed my hand and cut me off.

"Erin, cut that shit out, a'ight? It's cool ma, I'm just fucking with you. You make the cutest face when you feel bad. But I like you smiling way better."

He pulled me to him and just looked at me.

Hayden was fine as hell and had been since high school. He was tall, athletic body, and had no tattoos or piercings. He had nice ass caramel skin and a low haircut. I knew he was packing because tonight he had on some grey sweatpants. Let's just say all night the bitches were breaking their necks to look. Hayden's only downfall was his spoiled behavior. His mom and dad always ran to his rescue. He didn't even have to go to class because he was an athlete, so he skated through school.

His attitude was stuck up at times and he was controlling. He sometimes talked shit about certain things that made me a little mad. Like tonight, he talked about the waiter at the restaurant making minimum wage. He said the shit in front of her and that made me mad.

"Hayden, you know you and I are just friends. I don't want to mess that up by complicating things," I said to him before he could try to kiss me.

"Come on Erin, fucking with me would secure your entire future. You know I'm up next to go pro in football. You could move with me to Alabama. You would look good as fuck on my arm. We could be the next Steph and Ayesha Curry," he smiled and licked his lips.

Lord, help me.

"As tempting as that sounds Hayden, I just need friendship right now. Ok?" I put a little distance between the two of us. Even though Hayden was fine, and I knew him well, I just couldn't go there with him, especially when I wasn't over Yatta yet.

"Ok, I'll respect that, but please don't get wrapped up in Yatta's bullshit. I follow you on Instagram and Snap, so I saw y'all shit. I'm trying to make you a wife and give you the life we only see on TV. Don't be a fool," he kissed my cheek and walked off my porch.

See what I mean about his comments?! Ugh!

I unlocked my door and walked in. It was a little after nine at night, so I sent Dreka and Cassidy a text. Me and Dreka went up to the hospital to see her and Alaric. He was doing well and going home tomorrow. I still couldn't believe the shit his gay ass dad did. Fucking bitch ass needed to be six-feet under. I wanted to tell my dad, but Zamir and Alaric told me not to. I figured they wanted to handle it themselves so all I could do was pray they would be ok.

Speaking of my daddy I hadn't heard from him today. I called and texted him, but he said he was busy and would call me in the morning.

I didn't know what was up with him either. I hadn't told him what went down between me and Yatta yet. I was deciding if I should because of how overprotective my daddy could be sometimes.

I took a few more sips of my Brisk iced tea in the refrigerator and wiped my mouth. Grabbing me some chips I turned the light off and headed to my room. Dreka texted me and said she was leaving the shop she worked at and was on her way here. I was happy she was still coming. I wasn't in the mood to be alone right now.

Turning my light on in my room I sat my phone and chips on my tall dresser and closed my door.

"So, you think this shit is a fucking game?!"

When I say I almost shitted, threw up, screamed and pissed on myself at the same damn time! My heart and stomach went from normal to doing summersaults.

"Yatta, what the fuck are you doing in my house?! In my room?! In my closet?! How did you get in here?!"

I was holding my chest and screaming at him. I swear I felt like I was about to pass out.

"Naw, answer my fucking question first!"

He walked up on me and pressed me hard against my bedroom door. I wasn't hurt or anything, but he did have a little grip around my neck.

"You think this shit is a game? Didn't I fucking tell you when I stuck this seasoned dick in this new pussy that I was it for you?! I made my shit clear that no fucking body would ever know you that way. Erin, you just fucked up any future that nigga had of picking up a football again."

I looked in his eyes and even though he was fine as hell, he was scaring the shit out of me. He looked like an angry bull, ready to charge. His nostrils were flared, his eyes were red and low and burning a hole through mine.

Still, how fucking dare he come at me like this!

"Yatta, get the hell off me! You broke up with me for some shit you won't even let me explain. Then you get Cleo pregnant and tell me you're happy about it!"

My tears started falling because I was a damn water sign so emotions were my thing. I was mad and mixed with anger, so I pushed his arm hard as fuck away from around my neck. He must have wanted to knock my ass out because he balled both his fists up and bit his bottom lip. His face was red as fuck, matching his eyes.

I stood by the door breathing hard with tears still falling from my eyes.

"So, to answer your question, no. It's not a fucking game to me. You will never know me like that again. And you have no right staking claim on me when you clearly do not want me. Get the fuck out of my house, Yatta. You told me to stay away from you, your ass needs to do the same," I turned to open my bedroom door.

He came behind me and slammed it back. I was back pressed against my door. We were face to face and he was looking so evil. We matched expressions because I was ready to kill his ass.

"Erin, my fucking uncle got locked up. A fucking cop was following me and my niggas. Then I find out your brother and his pops been following us around taking pictures. The fat nigga told me you were on their side. How the fuck you expect me to act?"

He was calm but talking through gritted teeth and still looking evil.

"I expect you to know me! Know that I would never do anything to hurt you, your family or Z and Alaric! Both of them mean a lot to Cassidy and Dreka, why would I hurt my best friends that way?"

I was full blown crying and screaming now. Through my tears and with my voice cracking, I said, "You never even gave me a chance to explain that I have no idea what is going on. I have never even met my mom's husband. Hell, I just met Jamie for the first time a month ago. You thought I would go so far as to give you my virginity just to set you up? I can't believe you'd think so little of me."

Yatta was 6'1 and I was 5'7 so he had some inches over me. His whole expression softened up and his eyes roamed mine. He was about to touch the side of my face, but I smacked his hand away.

"Don't fucking touch me. Just leave Yatta, and stay the fuck away from me. I know we have the same circle of friends. Let's just be cordial and leave it at that. Forget whatever the fuck we were trying to build," I wiped my face and he still just looked at me.

His eyes were locked on mine bringing me so close to breaking.

"I was conflicted as fuck, Erin. The first thing I thought about was how many niggas I fuck with could have their bitches set them up. That shit is more common then you know. At the moment when everything went down, all dirty fingers pointed to you. A nigga was hurt and ready to fucking kill yo' ass."

He got closer to me, although I didn't know how that was possible because he was already all in my space.

He looked good as hell tonight. Even in his simple white t-shirt, blue hooping shorts and white and blue Lebron James on his feet. This boy kept a pair of Lebron's on ever since I met him freshman year. Those shoulder length dreads were half up and half down, and that damn 'Yatta' chain that I loved him in completed his look. I was weakening and didn't like it.

"I understand what you're saying and I hear you loud and clear. Shit is still fucked up, Yatta. There is no trust between you and me, Cleo is-----"

"That shit is a lie. She was never pregnant by me, I swear Erin. I haven't fucked her since I put my son in her. I was just pissed off at you, so I went along with that stupid as lie. That was a bitch move on my part. I swear her or that rat Tia ain't pregnant by me or Z. He would kill that bitch first before she brought his child in the world. On God Erin, Cleo only been pregnant by me once."

I squinted my eyes and just looked at him before I lost it.

SLAP!

"THA FUCK ERIN!?" Yatta yelled when I slapped the dog shit out of him.

"So, you just wanted to hurt me so bad that you would say that bitch was pregnant! Why would you do some shit like that over accusations?"

I reached to slap him again, but he caught me by my wrist.

"Stop puttin' yo' hands on me, Erin. I fucked up and I swear on my fucking son life that I apologize. All of this shit between us is on me."

He still had my wrist as he looked in my eyes and waited for me to say something.

"Yatta----"

"Yo nigga's name is Kenyatta, baby," he said, licking those sexy ass lips.

I knew it was over for me. His lips had the sexiest shape with that dip in the middle on his top lip. God, I was weak and I know someone was smacking their lips at me. If they could understand how fine this boy was. How sexy he moved and how much swag he had. Not to mention his sex and tongue was no fucking joke.

"You done gawking at me?" his ugly vain ass snapped me out of my trance, making me smack my lips.

"I don't have a nigga Yatta. I'm single as a dollar bill."

He squinted his eyes at me this time and that hand went back around my neck.

Biting his lip and locking eyes with mine again, he said, "You not fucking single, Erin. You never were, so stop fucking playing with me."

Before I knew it, his lips were on mine. I melted like a fucking sundae left out in the heat. His breath smelled so good and his lips were soft as hell. His tongue felt so smooth and silky swirling with mine. As good as the kiss felt, I had to break away.

"Don't do this shit with me. I'm not a wind-up toy you can play with and put down when you're pissed or some shit is told to you. I want someone who knows me, even if someone tries to tell them different. If you didn't, you would at least give me the respect of coming to me. Not just leave me high and dry."

I walked away from him and stood in front of my tall dresser. That still didn't stop him from walking back in my personal space.

"I apologize, Erin. I'm dead ass serious right now. I swear if you fuck with me again, I would never let no fucking body get in my head again about you. Forgive me cutie pie and let's start over."

I shook my head no and this fool gave me the ugliest face.

"Aye yo, tell me no again and I swear my hand fo' God I will go shoot that nigga Hayden in both his hands!"

My eyes bucked out at him.

"Why are you dragging him in the middle of this, Yatta? This is between me and you!" I was yelling because he was pissing me off.

He fucked us up, not Hayden.

"He put his fucking self in the middle when he decided to push up on my bitch! Fuck that nigga, and stop calling me Yatta, Erin."

He pulled his gun out and cocked it.

"Now, what's it gone be, cutie pie? A lifetime with me or knowing you fucked up that nigga's future? Choose wisely."

I looked at him like he was crazy.

"You're being a sore fucking loser and right now you looking a little coo-coo. You're forcing me to decide something that you fucked up in the first place. How is that fair?"

He stood there looking at me with a blank expression.

"You're wasting time, Erin. Give me an answer or I'm assuming that you telling me no, and I can't handle that."

"You are not right in the head, I swear," that was all I could say.

"You knew that shit already and ya still fucked with me. Now, last time. What's it gonna be?"

I guess I took too long because he turned around and opened my bedroom door. He was walking so fast that I had to speed walk to catch up with him.

"Ok, Ok! Stop Yatta, please don't do this!"

I ran and blocked the front door.

Thank God, my daddy wasn't here.

"Naw, you think this a fucking game. You don't mean that shit because you still calling me Yatta. You just don't mind fucking me so I won't put a hole in each of that nigga's hands. He gone be able to really enjoy beatin his meat when I'm done with him. Get the hell out my way, Erin."

He tried to move me, but I was using all my strength to not move.

"STOP! You can't expect me to just jump back on your team after the way you did me. Own up to the shit first before you act like a child and pout! Kenyatta, you broke my heart and then tried to crush it more by telling me Cleo was pregnant. If I did you that way, you'd be ready to pop off like you're doing now," I laughed because he had me so mad.

"Don't sit here and act like you wasn't with bitches out of anger. If you can look me in the eye and tell me you didn't hook up with a girl, then I'll suck yo' dick right now."

He looked at me in shock. I had never sucked dick before but I had seen it enough in pornos to know the shit wasn't rocket science. When he didn't say shit, I shook my head.

"Exactly, so stop tripping about Hayden. We went out, but that's it. He offered more but I'm still on you and didn't want to fuck up me and his friendship."

"Ain't no fucking friendship! And what the fuck---," he started massaging the bridge of his nose.

I swear it took everything in me not to laugh at him right now.

"Yo Erin, I swear to God you straight pissing me off. Is you mine or not? Stop fucking stalling and answer me right fucking now. You can say a nigga pouting all you want. I was wrong as fuck and I promise I'll make it up to you. But right now, I need to know if you my girl or not."

His sexy ass looked at me all angry. I couldn't even hold my smile in.

Still holding his gun in his right hand, he used his left hand and pulled me to him, kissing me deep.

"Say my name again," he looked at me and demanded.

His deep voice was low and just hearing it made me submit.

"Kenyatta, we are not having sex so get it out your head."

He laughed.

"I get it, baby. As long as you're mine I'll do whatever. You look sexy as hell, by the way. You know I love these romper things on you, but if you wear this for anybody else but me I swear we gone have some big ass problems. Now, let's go to bed. I'm tired as fuck and haven't slept since this shit went down."

I smiled big as hell because I had missed the fuck out of him.

I hadn't slept myself, but I wasn't telling him that. We took our clothes off and showered together. Surprisingly, he didn't try anything besides kiss and wash me up. I was very pleased with his restraint. He stayed hard as fuck, but he still didn't try anything. He gave me a good rub down and I put on some pajama shorts and a sports bra.

Kenyatta gave no fucks. He slept naked. I didn't mind because he had a nice ass body. Now I was laying on his chest with the TV on but on mute. His hands were in my hair and I was playing with his ears.

"Erin," he called my name.

"Hm?"

"Why is it that you can draw good as hell, but you don't draw people?"

When he asked me that, I was taken aback a bit. I'd been ask that before, but the only person who knew the answer to that was my daddy. For some reason, I just wanted to share it with Kenyatta.

"Because art is beyond just seeing a beautiful thing. You have to look at your muse with your heart and soul. If I draw or paint an abandoned house I see on Fenkell, people turn their noses up. They see an old run-down house. But I see past that, I see what the house could look like if given some love and attention. I draw the house as if it was beautiful and had a family living in it. If I draw a person's true beauty from my eyes, I risk hurting someone's feelings or making them believe I think they're not good looking. A person will want me to either draw a picture of them that they picked out or they are going to want to model for me and have me draw a make-believe version of themselves. That's not real art. That's not beauty. So, I never draw or paint people."

I knew I had given him an earful, but it was the truth.

"That's some deep shit, baby. I never even looked at it that way. I got respect for your art and your passion for it. You see the world in a beautiful way considered how much fucked up shit is in it. That's wild as hell."

He hugged me tighter and kissed the top of my head.

Looking up at him I took notice of his lips I loved so much. Lightly tracing them with my index finger, I wanted to tell him that I started drawing him. I only had his chain and lips drawn, but it was what stood out to me the most whenever I thought of him. He would be the first and probably only person I would ever draw. A certain moment kept popping in my head and I just had to put it on paper. I couldn't even began to draw or paint anything else until I drew him in the way I saw him. I just wasn't ready to let him know that yet.

"I have never told anybody that before. Not even Dreka or Cassidy and those my main bitches."

We both lightly laughed.

"Have you ever painted or drew any pictures of anybody?"

I shook my head no.

"Never. But if I did, I must be very inspired," I looked at him and smiled.

"Yo corny ass," he started laughing and so did I after I hit him on his arm.

I laid back on his chest.

"Kenyatta."

"Hm?"

"What did your uncle do to get arrested?"

He still played in my hair, but I swore I could hear his heartbeat change.

"He didn't do shit, but I did."

I looked up at him. His eyes met mine and I asked my next question.

"What is it that you did? Better yet, why did you do it?"

He looked off for a minute and then back at me.

"Me, my uncle, Z, and Alaric steal for a living. We steal all kinds of exclusive shit that's worth some serious money. A nigga tried to test my uncle and threaten his freedom so I killed his ass with no remorse."

I looked at him for a minute trying to see if this was real or not. For my entire life my dad had raised me to know right from wrong. I'd heard stories from him of crimes people would do. Hurting innocent people, taking a life and stealing from people who worked hard for what they had made me sick. I had a strong dislike for criminals. They were the ones who fucked this world up in my opinion. Now the person who I was with and had been wanting to be with was telling me he did all those things.

"Erin, stop looking at me like that, man. I see a bunch of doubt and regret. I swear we don't be snatching bitches purses or breaking into hood houses. It may not sound right but we steal shit from muthafuckas that won't miss that shit. I'm not a fucked-up person that just hurts people or steals anything I see that I want. But, I will always make sure I eat, and if anybody fucks with anybody I love then I would kill they ass just as quick as I blink. Like how I feel about you ain't no joke. You will get that nigga Hayden killed if you don't fall the fuck back from him."

I sat up when he said that.

"You said you if anybody fucks with anybody you love then you would kill them," I looked at him and said.

He nodded his head.

"Right," he responded.

"So, you love me?"

He smirked.

"Very much."

I probably shouldn't have, but I smiled big as hell and I know I was blushing. Oh, my God, Kenyatta Niemman Bailey loved me! He was against everything I thought I would run from. Everything that I used to see and knew that person would amount to nothing. In a way, I thought like my neglectful mother. Her judgmental thinking and ways was something that I didn't want to inherit from her. Here I was doing the same thing to Kenyatta. I didn't want to be held back from how I felt or who I wanted to be with.

Looking at his gorgeous ass face I knew how I felt.

"I love you too, Kenyatta. Thank you for trusting me with what you told me. I promise it stays between me and you."

He pulled me back on his chest as we both laid back down.

"I know, baby."

We talked some more about everything under the sun. We were just laughing and talking until we both fell asleep around three in the morning. I was very much in love and I just hoped we didn't get any more salt thrown on us.

Dreka

"I swear when I catch this bitch I'm beating the baby right outta her!" I hit my steering wheel.

I was so heated as I sat outside of Tia's auntie's house. I was minding my business while going to pick up Cassidy. Alaric texted me and told me to come get her ass out the house, so she could get some air. Her ass was treating him like a baby and he was loving it, but he wanted her to be outside today. I swore if I could I would kill Alaric's daddy my damn self.

Anyway, I was at her house waiting on her to get Alaric straight. My phone chimed with notifications from Instagram and Facebook. This bitch Tia tagged me in so many ultra-sound pictures, a positive pregnancy test, and a doctor's appointment. She was making statuses saying her and Zamir are happy and he was taking her to her appointments. He was spending the night and talking to her stomach. I felt like I was having an out of body experience. This shit was ridiculous! She was purposely rubbing my nose in the shit, but it's all good because I was about to rub her face all in her dead fetus when I kicked that baby out of her.

"Calm down, best friend. We beating that bitch's ass, and if Zamir wants to do some shit I got my belt for his big ass. Brother and all," Cassidy was sitting in my passenger seat, looking ready for whatever.

All I wanted to do was take my best friend to the spa. Once we were done we were going to Fairlane Mall to mess with Erin at her job.

Cassidy was the store manager of Forever 21 and she gave Erin a job as the assistant manager when she came back from New York. We always looked out for each other like that.

Once Tia tagged me in all that shit I was going to handle Tia alone, but Cassidy wasn't having that shit. Alaric told me to let it go and ignore Tia. He was telling me she was lying. But, fuck all of that! Who the fuck makes up ultrasound pictures and shit?

"This is why I broke up with Zamir. I'm not dealing with this drama with her as his baby mama. I will fucking have that child motherless."

Cassidy and I got quiet for a minute. I had the radio off because I needed to think.

"Do you want to be with Zamir? Do you love him?" Cassidy had a serious expression and tone in her voice when she asked me those questions.

"I do, Cass. Like I love Zamir a lot even before we became a couple. I loved him as a good person and as a friend," I answered honestly.

"Now I love him as being my man and I can feel me loving him hard and from my soul. I just don't want to deal with Tia and her drama because---" my voice started cracking when I started finishing my sentence.

"Because I feel like she did have him first and I just came and took him. Even though me and Zamir have been friends longer. The two of them were fucking and who knows what he was telling her. What if I came along and fucked their shit up? Wouldn't she rightfully have the right to be pissed and ready to fight him for me? Am I making myself look like a fool?"

I was crying now and hadn't even meant to.

"Dreka, I know my brother like the back of my hand. You didn't steal him from Tia because he was never hers to begin with. They fucked boo and that's all. I'm not saying this because he's my brother. I'm telling you facts, you have had my brother's heart for a while even though I didn't know about y'all secret hangouts," she chuckled and rolled her eyes.

"We all could see how he would act when you came around. He would smile and joke. You would have his scary looking ass actually looking friendly. He let you call him Zamir and we both know how him and Yatta are about their names. He loves you Dreka, and if I know my brother like I do, he will not give up easily."

I wiped my face as Cassidy was talking. I heard her loud and clear. I wanted to fight for Zamir, but I just wanted to make sure I had clout to do so. I felt like maybe I was in the wrong.

"Oh shit!"

When Cassidy said that I looked up and saw Zamir's white 2018 Ford Expedition pull up across the street from my 2018 Honda Sonata.

When he got out I didn't know if I wanted to run from him or run to him and jump on his dick.

He was looking so good with his 6'5 300lbs solid ass. He had on some black faded Pierre Balmain jean shorts and a black basic t-shirt with Pierre Balmain on it. His dreads were on top of his head and I could tell he just came from the barbershop. That fucking beard was full and hanging, making his face look delicious. God, that big ass bottom lip was full and looking all moist. Of course, his all-black high-top Fila sneakers were crispy as hell. His same diamond stud earrings were shining in his ear with that nice ass Rolex watch. His expression was looking like he wanted to fuck some shit up in the D.

I locked my doors when he came to my side and tried to open it.

"Open the fucking door Dreka."

He was calm as hell but that voice was deep and heavy.

I shook my head no.

"I'm kicking Ric's ass. I know he called him, bitch don't open that door. My brother is bat shit crazy!"

This bitch was laughing while on the phone with Alaric.

I was annoyed as hell at her.

"Bitch, this is not funny!"

Turning to Zamir I said, "Zamir, go away! Don't come over here trying to check me about your baby mama. I'm fucking that bitch up on sight."

He started laughing which was normal to me because we laughed all the time together.

Cassidy's mouth dropped and Alaric's stupid ass told her to Facetime him so he could see. This bitch did it, too.

"Yo, are you fucking stupid? That bitch don't got shit of me swimming in her. She got my kids sittin' in the back of her throat, but that's it. Babygirl, open the door so I can talk to you. I ain't seen or talked to your ass in days. Shit fuckin' up my mental not being able to be with you."

My heart broke when he said that. Then, I heard some laughing. Alaric was on Facetime cracking up, teasing Zamir.

"Ric, shut cho ass up laughing at my brother. You cried when we had our reunited sex."

He started cussing and going off on her, making her laugh.

"CASSIDY, stop fucking playing and get yo girl to open the fucking door!" Zamir yelled, making both of us jump and Cassidy dropped her phone.

"AYE BIG NIGGA YOU BETTER STOP YELLIN' AT MY GIRL!" Alaric's stupid ass yelled from the phone.

"ZAMIR, JUST LEAVE! You must really care about your family if you ready to beat my ass over her," I yelled at his ass.

I could hear him cussing and getting madder. I didn't give a fuck though. He started pulling on my door handle aggressively as hell, making my car shake.

"OPEN THIS FUCKING DOOR!"

"NO!" I yelled.

"That bitch got ultra-sound pictures and all types of shit! You wanna sit here and lie about her not being pregnant?! Even though it was before we became official I'm still beating her ass. Your baby mama needs to learn some respect. Get the fuck on, Zamir. I'm done with you!"

I was yelling like crazy.

I had to calm my ass down because I needed all my energy for Tia's rat ass.

"I'm done being nice."

I looked out my window at him and this fool pulled out his gun.

POW!

"AH!"

POW!

"AHH ZAMIR STOP!" Cassidy and I yelled at him but that didn't stop him.

POW!

POW!

Me and Cassidy were screaming as Zamir shot all four of my tires up. I was breathing hard as fuck and scared shitless. I didn't think he would actually use his gun.

"That nigga's a straight nut. Dreka, you must got some fire pussy," Alaric said right before Cassidy hung up on him.

"Your windows are next, baby girl. Now, open the fucking door."

He had the nerve to sound calm and had a mellow tone. Before I could, Cassidy opened her door. She jumped out, swinging her belt at Zamir.

"Are you crazy?! You better hope nobody is calling the police on you!" I laughed when he snatched the belt from her and broke it in half.

Cassidy stood there mad and Zamir walked back over to me and snatched my ass out the car.

"Why the fuck you doing this shit to me, Dreka? I don't know how the fuck that bitch got ultra-sound pictures, but I'm telling you she ain't pregnant by me. It ain't even a possibility and the shit hurt that my own woman doesn't even believe me."

I was looking everywhere but at him. I just couldn't right now.

"Look at me when I'm fucking talking to you!"

That nigga sounded worse then my own father. I looked at him and he was snarling at me.

"Show me some fucking respect Dreka as your man and the nigga that loves yo' ass. I will get that bitch for you but you gotta chill and stop looking for her. As long as you making the shit known, her ass will continue to hide."

He pressed his gun on the side of my hip making my heart speed up.

"I told yo' ass don't fucking play with me or my feelings. I want you Dreka, and only you, but I swear if you tell me you're done with me again I will shoot you in ya fucking hip. You'll be rolling around this thing called life forever. Get'cho chunky sexy ass in my truck. I'm taking my sister home and we are going back to my house."

Looking at him I knew better not to protest especially because his gun was still pressed in my hip.

Lord, what did I get myself into?

Zamir pulled out his phone and called to have my car towed.

"Told yo' ass my brother was crazy. You got your hands full," Cassidy laughed and joked as we both got in Zamir's truck.

I smacked my lips and told her to shut up.

⏰

***

"Stop fucking running Dreka, I ain't even stuck my dick in you, baby girl," Zamir yanked my ass back down towards the end of his bed.

His face was so deep in my pussy I thought he was going to snatch my soul through that muthafucka. I had already came three times and I hadn't even had the dick yet! Oh my God, he was trying to kill me. My clit was so sensitive and numb, part of me couldn't take it and the other part of me never wanted him to stop.

"Zamirrr oh my God, you are killing me bae."

I had my back arched to the max and my hand was trying to pry his head up. His big head ass just wasn't budging. For the fourth time I came all in his mouth.

"Jesusssss take the fucking wheel!"

My goodness, I hoped I didn't go to hell for using God name in vain at a time like this. I just didn't know who else to call on. This man was doing some soul searching between my legs.

He was slurping loud as fuck as he finally pulled his head away. That beard was soaked and so were them lips. I thought he was going to let me get my life in order, but hell no he didn't. He pulled my legs back and looked at me like he needed a straight jacket.

"Hold them fucking legs back and you bet not let'em go."

I nodded my head yes fast as fuck.

"You dodged me for days Dreka," he said as he pulled his shirt over his head.

That solid ass body looked so good. He didn't have a six-pack or anything but because he worked out his body was hard and solid. Zamir was thick like I liked my guys to be. He had both his sleeves done on his arms and hands.

"I missed you so much that I started thinking all this shit."

He walked over to his drawer which was on the end of his bed. When he pulled this jet-black bag out, my breathing changed. I didn't know what he was about to do. All I knew was he had my ass naked and both my legs were back. As crazy as it was, I trusted Zamir with my life, so I knew I was good. At least I hoped.

"I started thinking crazy shit. Like you with someone else. Or you trying your best to get me out of your life. That shit made me sick to my stomach," he spoke calmly as he pulled two small boxes out the bag.

I still couldn't see what was in them because the writing was small.

"I told you before that you were my baby girl forever. I even told you that I love you. That's something that I have only said to my sister."

When he opened one of the small boxes he pulled out a long red satin sash. It was so long and there was no way in hell was he about to tie me up!

"Zamir you are not----"

He stopped and looked at me with a stern expression.

"Shut the fuck up Dreka."

For some reason I did, and he walked to me and started tying my left wrist to my left ankle. Then this crazy nigga started finishing what he was saying. My damn breathing was rapid as hell.

"Like I was saying, I told you I love you and I also told you not to fuck with my feelings. You think I'd tell you some deep shit like that only to turn around and play you? Naw, that ain't even me and you know that. But still, aside from my warning, you tried to leave me."

He opened the other box and pulled the sash out of that one. He did the same thing and tied my right wrist to my right ankle. After being satisfied with his work he looked at me and gave me a sexy ass smirk that made my pussy wet. I couldn't believe I was turned on by this crazy ass nigga.

"After today I gotta make sure my baby girl never tries to leave me again. This shit is forever Dreka and its time you got with the shits."

He dropped his boxers and his thick chocolate ten-inch dick sprung out. He stroked it as he walked over to me, biting his lip and looking me in my eyes. I was fucking speechless and so ready for him to fuck me so good. He climbed between my legs with his knees on the bed and his feet hanging off. He kneeled down to me and kissed me so deep I almost became a part of his king size mattress. I was Zamir's first kiss and he mastered it in no time. After our nasty kiss, he finally pulled away and looked at me.

"Don't you ever fucking leave me again, baby girl."

My heart broke when he said that because he looked sad but still pissed at the same time.

"I promise I won't—Ahh!" I yelled a little because while I was answering he slid his dick in my tight pussy.

It hurt like a bitch because he was so damn thick and long. With his left hand flat on the bed, he started slow stroking the fuck out of me. My legs couldn't go down, so my pussy lips were wide open. I felt his dick massage my walls as my clit swelled up to another size. Zamir was doing lightly moaning all in my ear turning me the fuck on. Every time his lips and tongue touched my ear and neck, I swear an electric wave went through my body.

"Fuck Zamir, I'm cummin' bae!"

As soon as I said that he pulled out and attacked the shit out my pussy. He had my entire clit in his mouth sucking on it hard and pressing his tongue on it. I died! Like straight fucking died!

"SHIT!" I yelled at the top of my lungs and I was never that loud during sex. I didn't know what the fuck Zamir was trying to prove but he had accomplished his point.

He pulled his head slowly from between my legs. His mouth was soaked and that big ass bottom lip had a trail of my juices hanging from it. My nasty ass was so turned on by looking at him. With it still hanging there he jammed his dick back in me. The slow fucking was over, now he was fucking the shit out of me.

"Yea baby girl, take all this dick that'cho ass tried to leave. I'm cracking yo' soul in half tonight. Fuck, Dreka."

He tilted his head back and those sexy dreads were down all over his face.

I was moaning like crazy which made the sash feel tighter. I was fucking loving it, but what really did it was when Zamir put that big ass hand around my neck. I never knew how much I liked rough sex until I started fucking him.

"Oh my God, Zamir. Squeeze harder, fuck me harder!"

My wish was his command because that dick slammed in me harder. He was choking me so hard that with his hand still around my neck my entire body came off the bed. All I could do was take it, and boy oh boy, did my ass take it. The shit was pleasure and pain that I had never fucking had. This was mind boggling and I felt like I would never stop cumming.

"Arghhh, I love you Zamir!"

He slammed me back on the bed, pulled out and attacked my poor sore pussy again. I came once again all in his mouth. My body started shaking and trembling like a wet person left outside in the cold. He started kissing, licking my stomach and biting my rolls which made me giggle a little. Then he got to my D-cup titties and handled them like I liked. That was one of the things that made Zamir that nigga. I never had to tell him how to do my body. Zaddy just knew and I loved him even more for that.

He put my nipple between his teeth and pulled so hard I swear I came again. I told y'all he turned my ass out with the rough shit. When he got to my face he was looking so good, all hot and sticky. As he kissed me he slid his hard ass steel back in my pussy. My eyes were closed as he started fucking me.

"Eyes on me, baby girl."

His sexy ass voice was low and heavy sounding so good. I did what he said and looked in his eyes.

"I will do anything for you, Dreka. You hear me? Any fucking thing you ask me to do, I'll do it. All you gotta do is point me in the direction. Just stay with me always, a'ight."

When he said that my crybaby ass cried. Looking at him, I knew I wanted Zamir forever. I also knew that me and him would do some dark shit for each other because our love was so strong.

"Ok bae. I love you Zamir, I'll stay with you always."

"I love you more, baby girl. Now brace ya self because I ain't near cummin' yet."

Lord be a shield because this nigga was going to fuck me into another time zone.

Zamir

"What the fuck Dreka?" I mushed her pretty ass in the head as I rolled out my huge bed.

Here I was having a good ass sleep and I opened my eyes to see her staring dead at me.

"Um excuse me!"

Her ass came barging in the bathroom while I took a piss.

"Some people would be happy to have someone gazing at them with love."

She stood in the doorway with her hands on her juicy ass hips. I flushed the toilet and walked over to my sink so I could wash my face and brush my teeth.

"That ain't no damn gazing, that shit mad fucking creepy. You'll fuck around and catch a bullet fucking with me."

I was just joking, ain't no way in hell I would ever hurt baby girl.

"Fine, I'll gaze at somebody else!"

She said that shit and I hurried up and put my toothbrush up. I was on her like white on rice while she tried to walk away, squealing.

"You gone do what? Huh? Repeat that again," I had my arms around her waist, squeezing the front of her stomach.

Dreka was a sexy ass BBW with a shape to her. She had this mocha skin tone and these wide hips. My baby girl was an hourglass with some extra minutes in her. I loved every roll, stretch mark and I loved mostly her confidence. Like right now she was ass naked and didn't give a fuck. Dreka loved her body, but it was nowhere near like I did.

"I'm not going to do nothing, Zamir! Would you stop? That tickles!" she laughed as we both got back in my bed.

Her skin felt so good next to mine and her wild ass hair was all over, making her look sexy as fuck in my book.

Dreka and her cousin Erin had long pretty hair that was big as fuck and curly. Erin embraced that shit, but my baby girl was always putting weave in her shit. Lately, she had been wearing her natural shit like Daddy told her to.

"How long you been up? Your hair smells like that bubble gum shit."

Thanks to her girly ass my bathroom looks like a damn beauty supply store. It wasn't sloppy just hair shit, gay ass shower gel and whatever those hair tools girls used to make their hair straight or curly. I didn't mind though.

"I been up for about an hour now. That bright ass sun was in my face waking me up. I took a shower and washed my hair. Then I came back to gaze at my Mir-Mir."

I rolled my eyes at the ugly ass nickname she gave me. She started laughing.

"Oh, you don't like the name I gave you, Mir-Mir? I love that name."

Her freaky ass started grabbing my dick and kissing on my neck while she talked.

Fuck, now my nigga was at full attention. He knew Dreka was about to take care of him too because he started bouncing in her small ass hand.

When she reached on my nightstand and grabbed a rubber band my big ass got geeked as fuck. Anytime a bitch put her hair in a ponytail it was on! Oh, you can believe she about to suck ya spirit through a nigga's balls.

Dreka got on her knees between my legs and got on all fours. She arched that back and left that big ass booty in the air. Her ass was shaped nice as fuck, not like other plus size bitches I saw walking in the D. She had form and bounce to hers and that muthafucka looked so good in the air.

"Shit girl," I bit my bottom lip, watching Dreka take her thick ass tongue and lick my dick like a lollipop.

Her mouth must have been wet because she was coating my shit. Her full lips put kisses around it and on the tip. When she put my dick in her warm mouth I started to propose to her ass. My dick was too thick to disappear, but she still let the tip hit her throat.

"Ssss. Suck that dick Dreka, just like that. Daddy likes that shit."

Her jaws tightened up and she went buck on my dick.

A nigga almost clutched some imaginary pearls. Her head was bobbing up and down and she had so much spit coming out of her mouth. She popped my dick out and trailed spit down to my balls. I don't know how she did it, but she gave both some love at the same time. Making love to my balls was my shit and that alone made me realize I was deep in love with this girl. She put her pretty hand back around my dick and started sucking it for dear life. She was jacking me off while sucking and made me lose my fucking mind.

"Fuck, I'm about to put some dependents in ya throat. SHIT!" I came so hard that it felt like buckets of cum.

My baby girl swallowed the whole fucking menu, every drop, and she cleaned my dick off with her tongue.

"Damn, you my nasty bitch. Get'cho ass up here," I pulled her on my lap straddle style and tongued her down. Fuck it, it's my dick.

"I want you with me all day today. I gotta swing by my pops crib and my mama shit or I'll hear Cassidy's mouth."

Cassidy texted me and asked if I could drop off that crazy ass lady something to eat. She blew all her money on some nigga so now she didn't have anything to eat until her check came tomorrow. I swear my sister had better be lucky I love her.

"I'll be with you today. I don't have any heads to do so I can't think of a better way to spend my day. I'll cook us something to eat and I just have to stop at my house so I can put on some clean clothes."

I looked at her pretty ass face while she talked. Dreka was so fine and had me stuck like a lame anytime I was around her. This girl had me doing shit like laughing, playing and being all caked up. Even before she became my girl she always had me on some soft shit.

"Get a few outfits and leave them over here or we can go to the mall and get you some new shit. It's up to you. I just want you to leave some stuff here."

She smiled all big, making her cute chunky cheeks rise.

"Ok, I can do that. We don't need to hit the mall, bae. I just want to run around with you and come back here. I'll cook tonight and we can watch some movies."

Her ass was like a big kid all giddy. That made me smile and I told her cool.

"Look Dreka, I'm dead ass for real about this Tia shit. I ain't stuck my dick in her since Yatta knocked Cleo up. I just didn't want to take any chances. I don't know who the fuck she pregnant by. All I know is it isn't by me and there is no way it's by me. I need you to believe that and know that bitch will not get away for trying to fuck me and you up."

I put my finger under her chin, so she could look in my eyes and see that I was serious.

"I almost lost you because of her. She gotta pay for that shit. To what extent will she pay is on you. I told you, just point in the direction and it's done."

Looking at her, I wanted to make sure she understood me. I also didn't want her to be scared but the truth of the matter was that Dreka owned more than my heart. She owned me, and I'd do anything for her. That was a dangerous combination but only if she let it get to that level.

"I believe you bae, and I'm sorry for jumping to conclusions. I just hate that damn girl and knew she was going to make my life hell if she was carrying your baby."

I grabbed the side of her face and pulled her in for a kiss.

Ever since Dreka gave me my first kiss I always wanted to do the shit with her. Even her spit was sweet. We kissed for a while naked as fuck and then Dreka got up and made us some breakfast. She whipped up some pancakes, eggs, Pillsbury cinnamon rolls and some bacon. We fucked up that good ass food. Baby girl can throw down in the kitchen.

After I made her ass shower again with me, we got dressed. I kept shit simple in some black hooping shorts, a white beater, some Nike socks and some black Nike slides. It was nearing the end of June in Detroit. It was 86 degrees and it wasn't even noon yet. Dreka re-twisted my dreads and put some of them up. My baby girl kept me right.

***

"Why the hell all them holes in yo' shorts? You tryna have me in the county jail?" I asked Dreka's juicy ass while she came out her room.

She smacked her lips and looked at her outfit.

"Zamir, I dress like this all the time and you never complained. You know I look good."

She wasn't lying though.

Dreka had on these jean shorts with holes and rips by her thighs and on the back of her thighs. I wanted to make her ass change, but she looked damn good. Her shirt was an all-white tank top that hugged her titties nice as fuck. She topped that shit off with this long ass see through thing that looked like it could have been a robe. Women's girly asses be wearing some difficult shit. Anyway, her feet were in some black wedges. She was showing them pretty ass toes I loved to suck on when I was drilling her pussy. Let me calm my ass down, her grandma was in the kitchen cooking.

"The first nigga that looks at you is getting fucked up."

She laughed and waved me off. I wasn't bullshitting with her. Dreka was gone learn fast that I didn't play about her.

"Zamir, cut it out bae. I'm yours, nobody else's."

She gave me a juicy kiss and grabbed my hand so we could leave.

"Grandma, I'm gone, okay? Tell my daddy I am so mad at him for not calling me back!"

I already knew why her pops didn't call back. Him and Emmanuel were handling some shit dealing with Lonell getting locked up but they asked us not to tell Dreka and Erin, so we kept quiet.

"I'm mad at both of them niggas. Before you go Dreka, give Grandma something for her diabetes."

I looked at her grandma and then at Dreka who was now laughing.

"Grandma, you don't have no damn diabetes and even if you did, weed don't help that. Daddy and Uncle E said Erin and I have to stop giving you weed. Last time you ate a whole tube of icing and three jars of pig feet."

I fell out laughing when she said that. Grams was wild as hell.

"How the hell you gone listen to them niggas? I smoked reefa when I was pregnant with both of their asses. Look how smart and handsome they are. I'm an old woman who just need her weed."

Yo, I was dead when she said that. Me and Dreka laughed hard as hell.

"No, Grandma. My daddy ain't about to yell at me," Dreka said through laughs.

Her grandma got mad as hell.

"Didn't grandma have your back when this tall nigga used to come over every night? Nigga bigger then the whole damn house. I kept quiet and stayed in my room."

I felt bad as hell when she said that. I couldn't do Grams like that.

I reached in my pocket and gave her my bag I had on me.

Dreka smacked her lips and hit my arm.

"See this young man cares about my life. Thank you, young man. You have my permission to put some giant ass kids in my granddaughter."

She hugged me and stuck her tongue out at Dreka. We were cracking up. Her little ass grandma stopped right under my stomach.

"Your grams is fucking crazy, man. That's my girl," I laughed while helping Dreka's fine ass in my truck.

I placed her two duffle bags in the back seat.

"Oh Lord, don't let her hear you say that. She already loves you because you gave her all that weed. I will be sure to let my daddy know you are her supplier," she laughed as I started my truck up.

"I'll tell him myself. You know I ain't scared," I winked at her as I pulled off.

My first stop was my pops' crib. Even though I was already on the westside and my mama lived on the westside, I still wanted to drive to Troy to see my pops first. Anytime and I do mean any fucking time I see that fucked up ass woman I didn't want to do shit else but go home and smoke.

I hadn't seen my pops in a few weeks and didn't want her ass fucking up my mood.

"Ok so look, before we go in there let me ask you something," I looked at Dreka and said to her.

We drove the twenty-five minutes to my pops' crib. I just wanted to make sure she knew what was up before she walked in this twilight zone.

"Ok," her sweet voice said.

"Has Cassidy ever told you about me and her pops?"

She shook her head no. I figured she didn't because Cassidy was always embarrassed by the shit.

"A'ight, so here is the deal. My pops and Cassidy's pops are brothers."

I wish I could pull y'all asses in this book so you could see my baby girl face. She had her mouth open and her eyes were bucked looking left and right.

When she pulled her phone out I thought she was about to call someone.

"I'm sorry, I just need to write out what the hell you said so I can get some clarity."

I grabbed her phone and laughed.

"Look, our mama had sex with my dad and his son."

She finally opened her mouth.

"So, your father is Cassidy's grandfather and her dad is your brother?"

I just looked at her and nodded my head.

"So, what the hell are you and Cassidy? Brother and sister/niece and nephew?"

I laughed at her silly ass and she did too.

"Listen baby girl, all you need to know is my pops and brother are cool as hell. They are not disrespectful or have any beef with me or Cassidy. I just wanted you to know what was up if you hear my brother call Cassidy his daughter."

She smiled and shook her head while opening the door.

"This some hillbilly, down south, Jerry Springer type of shit bae, but I still love you so much."

She grabbed my hand and kissed it like I was a flame nigga.

"Don't be doing that gay shit girl," I furrowed my eyebrows at her, making her laugh.

That shit wasn't funny.

"Pops! Pops, where you at, nigga?!" my loud voice boomed through his living room.

When I looked in the corner and saw Clare, the cat's little house. I hurried so I could grab her before Dreka saw her and hauled ass.

"Baby girl, stay here I'll be back."

Fuck! I was kicking my own ass. I forgot my pops had a fat ass grey cat.

Dreka was terrified of cats, I'm talking about crying and shaking type of scared.

I looked in the dining room, kitchen and then went in the hallway looking for her. Getting to my pops den, him and my brother were sitting in there watching TV and smoking.

My pops had a nice ass four-bedroom house. He was a fifty-four-year-old man who was taller than me and just as solid. We had the same brown skin and dark ass eyes. Shit him, me and Cassidy's Daddy, Neal, all looked like triplets. When I walked into the den, Clare was sitting on top of the pool table.

"What up, son? I told Neal I heard some shit in the front."

I walked past him and picked Clare up so I could lock her ass in the cage. Then, I went and hugged my pops and brother. I told y'all there was no bad blood between us. My mama was the nasty ass that fucked a father and son.

"What'chu put Clare up for?" he asked me.

I held my finger up as I went to get Dreka.

"I'm sorry baby girl. I had to put my pops cat in the cage."

Dreka squeezed my hand tight and she looked scared.

"Hey, look at me," I told her as her eyes got watery. "Dreka, nothing will ever happen to you when I'm around. I got you and I personally locked up the cat myself. I promise he will not come out while we are here. If that fucker so much as hisses at you I swear I'll blow his fucking head off."

I squeezed her hand and kissed it. She agreed, and we walked to my pops den.

"Pops, Neal, this is my girl Dreka."

Her beautiful ass smiled and hugged them both.

"My baby brother taking after me. Them BBW's be sexy as fuck, don't they?"

Neal gave me some play and joked.

I looked at my sexy ass baby girl and bit my lip before saying.

"Hell yea they are. She been mine since high school, she just didn't know it," I laughed and said.

Dreka smacked her lips and laughed. Neal had a bad ass BBW wife who he was marrying.

My stupid ass mama was bothered by the shit. For someone who claimed she was raped by him, she sure did give a fuck that he was getting married. Yea, my mama claimed my pop's son raped her twenty-two years ago. Fuck out of here. My mama was a nasty thot who fucked Neal when he was thirteen and she was seventeen. Now my pops ain't innocent in the shit. He let his son fuck his girl because he was a virgin. I guess he just never expected my mama to keep fucking him and get pregnant. I didn't know and didn't care. All I knew was all of them were nasty as hell. My mama was so fucking stuck on my pops that the shit is sad. He doesn't even talk to her ass, but she swears he still loved her. Bitch was delusional.

"She is beautiful, son. So, that's why Clare got put up, you scared of cats, little lady?" my pops looked at Dreka and asked.

"Terrified," she answered while looking at the cage.

Her grip on my hand wasn't loosening, but it wasn't hurting me.

"Well, let me take her cage out of here. I know my son is short temper and I don't want him killing Clare because she made a noise and scared you," him and Neal laughed.

I looked at Dreka and winked at her. She sat down and relaxed a bit.

Neal gave me a beer and her a wine cooler. When my pops came back in the room I started talking to them about the real reason I came over.

"You spoke to your daughter?" I asked Neal.

"Not in a week. Brittney has had me so busy with this wedding. She's good, right?"

Dreka took another sip of her wine cooler.

I looked at him and said, "She is now, but some shit went down and she was in the middle."

Neal and my pops looked shocked.

I started telling them what went down between Alaric and his dick of a father. That nigga was a walking corpse and didn't even know it.

When we were kids Yatta and I couldn't stand his ass. He always acted like he knew every fucking thing. That nigga had no pull in the city nor did he have any street credit. All that nigga had was money and bitches. Yea, he sold drugs but he wasn't that nigga. He wasn't even the connect. He sold drugs for this nigga in Traverse City.

Ric found that shit out yesterday and told me and Yatta. I gotta admit that nigga ain't letting the fact that German was his pops stop us from killing his ass. We just had to be smart about the shit.

"So this shit happens to my damn daughter and no fucking body thinks to tell me!" Neal stood up, yelling at the top of his lungs.

That nigga was a inch taller than me with a heavier voice. When I saw Dreka jump I stood up and got in his face.

"First of all, lower yo' damn voice in front of my girl. You scaring her, nigga, and I don't take kindly to that. Second, Cassidy was violated and didn't want to talk to any damn body. We already got a plan in motion on how we are going to move. I wanted to know if you want in or not. Alaric is in on killing his dad. He loves Cassidy and y'all know me. I don't fucking play about my sister. I already told Alaric if he hesitates even a little that I would personally handle his ass. I'm telling you Neal, that nigga wants German dead."

I looked him in his eyes so he could see I was on some hunnid G-shit.

"Ok, I apologize Dreka for scaring you. Cassidy is my only child and I just love her. Shit makes my stomach turn that this happened to my baby. I want that nigga to suffer in the worst way," he looked at me and said.

I nodded my head.

"I do too, Neal. Alaric will be all the way healed soon. I will call you when all of us are meeting together. The shit Alaric has cooked up so far is good, Neal. I promise German will die," he gave me some love and said.

"Man, don't no father want to hear this shit about their daughter. I gotta get my baby tomorrow. Maybe let her burn a hole in my credit card."

When he said that Dreka and I laughed because that was right up Cassidy's alley.

We chilled with my pops and Neal for another hour. My pops and Neal took to Dreka well. I was happy about that shit.

Once we left my pops' house, we stopped at Penn Station sub shop on twelve mile before we got back to the city. My big ass got a footlong pizza sub with a large order of fries and a Mountain Dew. Dreka tried to be like big daddy and get a footlong steak and cheese and fries. Her ass didn't even eat half because she filled up on their good ass fries.

We ate in the shop just talking and laughing like we always did. Baby girl turned up when she thought the bitch who made the subs liked me.

"She did like you, Zamir. Nobody is about to risk their job just to give a nigga some free food. Talking about their about to close and there is a lot of extra food," Dreka was pissed off ranting and shit while I drove in the direction of my mama's house.

I was cracking up because Dreka was mad as fuck. I had to pull her out the sub shop because she wanted to fight the girl.

"You wild, Dreka. You got my mama's food? I'm tryna be in and out," I said to Dreka while we got out my truck.

I stopped at China House and grabbed her some Chinese food and some pop. That should hold her ass over until tomorrow morning when her check came.

"I got her food, bae. In and out, remember that before you let her get under your skin."

I nodded my head as I put Cassidy's key in our mama's door. As soon as we stepped in, I got pissed off. I didn't know why the fuck I kept letting my sister guilt me into helping this bitch.

"Don't even focus on that, bae. Let's just drop the food off and we can go," Dreka's voice calmed my ass down.

There was a pair of jeans and KD's on my mama's living room floor. That meant she had a nigga here with her. A nigga that could have fed her ass and probably the same nigga who she gave all her money to. I was sure he knew she got paid tomorrow so dicking her down would ensure he got her check. Just dumb as hell, that was why I made sure Cassidy never ended up like our pathetic vessel of a mother.

"You right baby girl," I said as she sat the food on the table.

Dreka said the same thing Cassidy told me. Not to focus on what the hell my mama was doing. Just drop shit off and keep it moving. For once, I was going to do just that until I heard a voice.

"Hmph. I see you came to see me this time. Last time Cassidy came with these little----," my mama came from her bedroom, talking shit.

She stopped when she saw Dreka.

"I already know what went down last time. Look, here is your food and a few dollars. You need to thank Cassidy for this."

I grabbed Dreka's hand so we could leave.

"Boy, don't come in here acting like you doing me any favors," she smirked and looked at Dreka.

"You're in deep competition if you want this one to yourself. Cassidy got him pussy whipped."

When she started laughing and going through the food that I fucking brought I wanted to kill her ass. Dreka knew it too because she started pulling my hand hard towards the door.

I had to bite my bottom lip hard as fuck to keep from knocking her head off.

"You a piece of shit, you know that? Your daughter is so much better than you. And even though you tried, you couldn't break me," I looked her dead in her drunk ass eyes when I said that.

I must have hit a nerve because she started tweaking out.

"NIGGA, FUCK YOU! Don't come in my fucking house and disrespect me! What the fuck would you know about being with a good woman?! You use and abuse women just like your fucking no good daddy does! He had a good woman in me, but he chose to let me go over his rapist of a son! SO, FUCK YOU WIT'CHO RETARDED ASS! You and this fat bitch-----

SLAP!

"ZAMIR!" I heard Dreka scream my name because I had slapped my mama so hard across her face.

She went flying into this tall cedar chest she had in her dining room. Her bedroom door opened and a nigga came out. I looked at him ready for whatever the fuck he thought he was about to do.

"Don't mind me big homie, I just smelled the Chinese food from the back," he held his hands up in a surrendered way.

"Nigga, you touch this food and I swear I'll break ya fucking arm."

He thought I was playing because he smacked his lips and waved me off.

In one swift move, I grabbed his arm and broke that bitch with my elbow.

"AHH SHIT! NIGGA BROKE MY ARM!" he screamed at the top of his lungs like the pussy I knew he was.

My mama stood up with a bleeding nose and lip.

"Don't ever come back here. You and that fucking daughter I have are dead to me. You have never loved me since you were eight-years-old! All you care about is Cassidy and that FUCKING father who left me! GET OUT!"

I stared at my so-called mother with a look that would have made God himself question me. I hated this bitch and knew from here on out that I was done.

"Come on bae. Let's just go," Dreka snapped me out of my stare.

She stood in front of me and put her hand on the side of my face. Still looking at this fucked up woman I pointed at her, turned and left. I could hear her yelling and throwing shit.

On the drive home, Dreka held my right hand the entire drive to Canton. We had the radio on, but I knew neither of us were listening to it. The one thing I loved that Dreka did was never press me. We used to talk about everything under the sun and if I ever got to some shit that I didn't want to get into she never pressed me on the subject. Her pretty ass always fell back and waited for me to either change the subject or just drop it all together. I loved the respect and boundaries she gave me.

Before we got to my condo we stopped at Walmart to get some food for Dreka to cook. Her silly ass kept cracking jokes and shit all while we were in the store. I knew she was just trying to make me feel good. I appreciated that about her. I especially loved how she decided to make pepper steak and rice with some steamed broccoli. Then she went to the baking aisle and got some shit to make a devil's food chocolate cake. All my favorite shit, that was love right there.

Finally at my crib, I put all the food up for her and she started cooking. I, of course, played my game while baby girl cooked. Having her here with me made me not want to go smoke my brain cells up after dealing with my mama.

I didn't feel like I was alone in dealing with this shit. Even though Cassidy was my sister I had to be strong for her. I would never let her see me break or look defeated, but with Dreka here with me making all kind of loud noises in my kitchen made my heart smile. Plus, my entire condo smelled good as fuck.

After I played Madden for a few I decided to take a shower. I stripped out of my clothes and took my dreads down so I could wash them. Having the hot water hit my body felt good as hell. I thought about the shit that went down today. Dealing with Neal and my pops went better than I thought.

I was glad he didn't go too far with being mad about Cassidy. I wanted him to trust that we had it.

My stupid ass mama came to my mind. Tomorrow, I was having a real fucking talk with my sister. Cassidy was grown so I couldn't stop her from fucking with our mama, but I was 100% done with that bitch. I'd fuck around and be in jail dealing with her.

Stepping out the shower, I dried my hair and body off. Wrapping the towel around my waist, I walked out the bathroom and into my room. Dreka was standing in her robe and hair in a bun looking good as fuck. She was taking off her watch and necklace.

"Let me hop in the shower and we can eat," she said smiling at me as she stood on her tiptoes trying to kiss me.

I still had to lean down so I could meet her short ass half way.

Giving her a juicy kiss, I hit her on that soft big ass booty she had as she walked away. I had to squeeze my hard dick after we kissed just to calm him down. I put some lotion on and deodorant before I put on my Fruit of the Loom boxer briefs and a black beater. I grabbed me a pair of Nike footies and put them on my feet.

Just as I was about to put my dreads in a ponytail, Dreka came out the steamy bathroom. She was busy drying off and putting that gay lotion shit on. She didn't even notice me watching her. That mocha skin was flawless and soft as fuck. Her face was what made my hard ass mush in her hands.

I watched her put on some PINK panties and a matching tank top. When she put her pretty ass feet in these green furry house shoes I laughed to myself. Her, my sister and Erin were so fucking girly. Her big ass hair was a little wet from the shower. I was happy when she took it down and let it hang. Sounds crazy, but I loved having that wild shit all in my face while we were sleep.

"Ready?" she looked at me smiling and asked.

I nodded my head yea and we walked downstairs so we could eat.

While Dreka made our plates, I put the Firestick on and went to the movie Detroit. Neither of us has seen it yet so that was good.

Dreka came in the living room and sat both of our plates on my cocktail table. She went back in the kitchen and came out with a beer for me and some orange pop for her. Sitting down, I started the movie and we began eating. We were both hungry because we didn't do much talking. The movie was good as hell so that played a factor in it, too. We cleaned our plates. She cut both of us a slice of chocolate cake and we ate it while we finished the movie.

Dreka was really making me feel good as fuck like a king.

Now we were in my bed laying down. We were tired of being on the couch, so we came upstairs to get in the bed. I wanted to watch that other Detroit movie everybody was making a big deal about. It was called Plug Love. Dreka saw it but said she loved it and didn't mind watching it again.

While I was in the shower baby girl rolled me up a nice ass blunt. Man, this bitch was golden. Excuse my language, but y'all know what I mean.

We both were under the covers with our backs against the headboard. Dreka was smoking on her little ass cherry flavored hookah. Shit was cute as hell.

"Bae, I have to ask you something."

"What's good, baby girl?" I looked at her and asked.

"What did your mama mean when she said you stopped being there for her when you were eight-years-old?"

My fucking heart dropped when she asked that. Not only was I thrown off guard, I tried every day to block that bullshit out my head.

"She always talking stupid."

That was all I had in me. I didn't even look at Dreka when I said that stupid shit. She must have picked that shit up because she put her hookah down and straddled my lap. With both hands on my face, she made me look at her.

"You know I never pressure you to open up. I let you tell me what you're ready for me to know. But bae, I saw your face when you looked at your mama. That was hate mixed with some other shit. If you decide to tell me, I swear it stays between me and you. I would never use it against you in any kind of way."

I finally looked her in the eyes. I saw pure love, trust and a real care for me. A care that besides my day one's and my sister I didn't think anyone truly had for me. I figured why not.

"My mama was in love with my pops. She tricked for him and did a year in jail for him before I was born. He never had intentions on making her his wife. She was always just a ride or die bitch to him but nothing more. My mama has promiscuous ways and my pops wasn't the only woman he was messing with heavy. That's why when I was born he took a DNA test. A little after, my pops wanted to get some pussy for his son on his thirteenth birthday. The chosen pussy was my mom's. My mama always being the fool decided to do it. She claimed after that one-time Neal was hooked. He came in her room one night and raped her, which is what Cassidy is a product of. But my pops knew the deal, he knew Neal was still fucking her. He just didn't care until she got pregnant. He was madder about his then fourteen-year-old son having a baby," I paused for a minute but then continued.

"My mama wanted my pops back bad as hell. She used to use me to get under his skin. We'd stay days and days over whatever nigga's house she was fucking. Just to hide out from my pops. Neal was always in Cassidy's life from the start. My mama didn't give a fuck about that. It was my pops whose attention she wanted. From day one, I loved Cassidy and was happy as hell to have her around. We are only a year apart, but I had her back from jump. My mama hated that shit. One night, she came in my room and woke me up. She told me to come out my bed and go in the living room. I did what she said before I looked in Cassidy's room and saw her still asleep."

When I stopped, Dreka grabbed my hand and kissed it.

I took a deep breath and continued.

"My mama came out with my pops' old jeans and shirt in her hand. My pops is a big ass nigga. Even though I was eight-years old, I was tall as hell and solid because my pops had me in the boxing ring since I was five. Anyway, she looked at me and said she wanted me to put the clothes on. I could smell the heavy liquor on her breath and she wasn't standing straight. I looked at the clothes and then back at her shaking my head no. She slapped the dog shit out of me. Told me she was tired of me and my pops telling her no. She told me if I didn't do what she said then I would never see Cassidy again. At eight years old, I got scared and started crying. I looked up and my mama was taking her clothes off. She wanted me to touch her with my pops' clothes on. I was scared as hell. I just wanted the shit to be a nightmare that I had the opportunity to wake up from. She started yelling and telling me to shut the fuck up."

I couldn't stop the tears from falling from my face. I had never told anybody this shit before. I just kept talking.

"I picked up the shirt and was about to put it on. That's when I snapped and pushed my mama hard as fuck. She fell back and hit her head on the wall. I ran in Cassidy's room and closed the door. I moved her dresser in front of the door and grabbed the cell phone Neal gave Cassidy. I called him and told him what happened. I never told him about the nasty shit, I just said Mama was drunk and fell out. Him and my pops came over and got me and Cassidy the next day. We stayed with them for about two months. My mama started tripping and saying she wanted us back. After that, she hated me. Always claimed I never loved her. She started calling me all kind of names and always said I was touching on Cassidy because of how I was always looking out for her," I looked at Dreka and said.

"I swear I have never touched my fucking sister. I just always wanted her with me to protect her and make sure my mama never split us up. From then on, I just thought women weren't shit. If my mama could fuck a father and son and do the shit she did to me then all women were fucked up. I started looking at women as just an object. Aside from my sister, I hated all women. If I wasn't fucking one or getting my dick sucked I felt there was no need to have one around. My mama broke my heart when she did that shit to me. That's why I don't deal with feelings and relationships. My shit fragile as hell and I don't have time for the games. Now you know..."

Looking at her, I saw that she had tears coming from her eyes. We looked at each other for a minute until she gave me the warmest hug I had ever received.

"I love you so much, Zamir. Thank you for trusting me with this, I'm sure it wasn't easy."

I hugged her back tight as fuck. She leaned forward and gave me a sweet kiss.

"I will always be here for you. I hate you had to go through that, no child should ever have to experience anything like that especially from their own mother."

I saw her tears start up again.

"You're welcome, I'm good, Dreka. I was fucked up for a while when the shit first happened. But now I'm all the way Gucci. I promise you that. All I want you to do is keep doing what you been doing. Stay real with me, keep shit a buck and most of all just stay mine. Don't pull that space shit you tried to do before. I swear Dreka, I don't wanna hurt'cho pretty ass."

She smirked and nodded her head but I was dead ass.

"I promise to never do that again. I was just mad as fuck, but I never want to be without you Zamir."

I kissed her deep when she said that. While we kissed, I pulled her shirt over her head. She didn't have a bra on so those big titties bounced out. Her shit sat up all big and round with nipples matching that mocha skin.

I started kissing and sucking on her neck while she threw her head back. I got to her ear and nibbled on it before whispering, "I love you Dreka. I would stop breathing for you if need be."

With her straddling me, I laid her on her back with me on top. I made love to Dreka all night. I stroked my dick in her and she rode me so good. I knew nobody else would have this dick but her.

Josey

"Oh fuck Josey honey, fuck me good!"

Thurgood was moaning more than I ever had in all my years of fucking. I had him in doggy style position fucking him with my strap on dick. He was into all submissive shit. He had on a long black negligee and a blonde wig. I told y'all he was into the humiliation type of sex. It didn't bother me because I enjoyed humiliating him. Plus, he gave me his black card today so once he went to work I was going shopping.

"UGHH! OH LORD!"

He came finally and fell forward on the bed.

I smiled and pulled the strap out of his hairy ass butt hole. Going to the bathroom, I took it off and put it in the sink. He was the one who cleaned that thing. I wouldn't dare touch it.

"Josey, when is our son going to get the job done?" he asked as his fat ass came in the bathroom.

I was happy that he taken the wig and negligee off because I couldn't take him serious with that shit on.

"He's meeting up with her today," I lied.

I didn't want Thurgood to lock Jamie in the basement again. Anytime Jamie was bad he would lock him in the basement. There was food and everything he needed down there. Our basement was like a one-bedroom apartment. He would just make Jamie stay down there. Nobody could go down and Jamie couldn't come up.

"Great, that thug Lonell has a bond set. The way his lawyer is fighting for him makes me know he has the money to post his bond. We need Jamie to put that chip in Erin's phone."

I rolled my eyes as I stepped in the shower.

"Ok, Thurgood. I already know what needs to happen, honey. Jamie is staying down in Detroit for a few days. Erin needs to believe he truly is trying to bond with her," I spoke from the shower.

I was so ready for his ass to leave. Truth was, Jamie was already in the city. He met some girl down there and was staying with her. I would have hit the roof knowing he was fucking with a Detroit girl. All those little bitches were good for only staying in the slums. I wanted better for my son but I decided to keep my mouth shut. At least until he planted that chip in Erin's phone.

I was pleased when Thurgood yelled that he was gone. I was ready to get dressed and do some damage with his card. I couldn't wait for the day when Thurgood decided to give me my own money. He still only gave me either his card or I always had to ask him for money. Shit, we were married and I was fulfilling his sick ass sex cravings.

Stepping out the shower, I reached for a towel. I almost died and came back just to die again when Emmanuel was standing in my bathroom. He was holding my white towel.

"Looking for this?" He was leaning against the entrance swinging the towel in his hand.

My God, he still was so fine. It burned me that now when I looked at him and Erin's face all I saw was two people who looked just alike.

Emmanuel had those chestnut colored eyes and light skin. He was tall as hell with a bald head and his beard was sandy brown. It was so long that you could braid it. He was perfection in human form.

"What are you doing here? Did my husband see you?" I asked that on purpose to see if he was going to have some jealousy in him.

Instead, he stood there and smirked at my naked body.

"You know you still look good. You'd give these young bitches a run for their money."

He threw the towel behind him and leaned off the wall.

"Get on ya knees and crawl to me. Just like you used to."

When he said that I wanted to pinch myself to make sure I wasn't dreaming. Keeping my eyes on his, I got down slowly on my knees and started crawling to him.

He stood there biting his bottom lip and stroking his long ass beard. I could feel my juices slide down my thighs. Only Emmanuel could get me this way and only he could satisfy my sexual needs.

I stopped in front of him and he arched his eyebrow.

"Stop acting like you forgot what to do. I know you are used to being the man when dealing with your husband, but this is Manny baby, do what the fuck you know."

I licked my lips as I pulled his Adidas sweatpants down along with his boxers. I hadn't seen his beautiful eleven inches in so many years. I hadn't ran across a man yet that could top Manny's dick.

"Get him hard," he said in a dominant tone.

I picked his gorgeous dick out and started sucking. I could smell the Clive Christian body wash on his skin. I was in heaven, absolute heaven when his dick started growing in my mouth.

"That's right, Josey. Do what the fuck you was put on this earth to do."

I went crazy when he said that. I sucked his dick for dear life. I didn't care if we were in the house I shared with my husband. I had been so hungry for Manny even after all these years.

"See, you not being nasty enough on the dick," he said, and then this crazy nigga shoved his entire dick down my throat. My God, I could feel his dick touch my toes. I wasn't lying!

I gagged and before I knew it I was throwing up so much that last night's dinner even came up. I gave Linda Blair a run for her money. After what seemed like a life time of puking, before I could regain myself, Manny had his hand on the back of my neck. He was pushing my head in my own vomit.

"Yea, bitch, get all in that vomit. That's what I see you as, some nasty ass shit that lives in the pit of my fucking stomach. You think you would fuck with my daughter and not have me on you! HUH!"

I couldn't even breathe, let alone talk. I was struggling to speak but vomit was in my mouth, along with a short air supply. Finally, he let me go. I fell to the side, coughing and struggling to breathe.

"H-H-He will c-c-come looking for me if you k-k-ill me," I struggled to say.

He started laughing.

"You are an opportunist, so that works in my favor. Get the fuck up!"

He grabbed me by my now bruised neck.

I had throw up all on my face, in my hair and on my chest. With him carrying me by the back of my neck, we walked out of the master bedroom. Manny walked through my home like he lived here and paid rent. That meant he had been in here before.

When this man walked through my kitchen and picked up the garage opener that I kept on top of the windowsill, that confirmed my thoughts. He had been in here before. He learned my house and where things were so I already knew he took care of the surveillance cameras we had put up.

He opened the garage door and there sat a black van with no windows, except in the front. They were bagged in. It stopped in front of us as Manny closed the garage door. The door to the van opened.

"Josey, so good to see yo' hoe ass under these circumstances," Delon, Manny's annoying ass brother was in the driver's seat. He was smiling.

Manny slid the door on the side open. There was a woman duct taped sitting in the corner. Her eyes got big when she saw me and Manny. She had mascara running all down her face and there was tape over her mouth. I had no fucking clue who she was.

I looked down at the end of the van and Thurgood was laying on the floor with a hole in his head.

"No!" I yelled and cried when I saw him.

I didn't care if I didn't really love him. He still didn't deserve to die. He was a good man and spoiled me endless. Now I had to start completely over and find me a new one.

"Manny, you didn't have to kill my husband. He wouldn't have came for you," I said, crying.

"I'll take the blame for that. I was an Urkel fan, not Will Smith," Delon's old ugly ass laughed and said, referring to Thurgood looking like Uncle Phil from The Fresh-Prince of Bel-Air sitcom.

I looked at him with the evil eyes through my tears.

"Bro, why is she naked and what the fuck is that smell?" Delon turned his nose up and asked Manny.

"Long story, I'll tell you once we on the road," Manny answered as he got the tape out.

"Manny, you can't kill me. Please, I never wanted to do this shit. It was that fat nigga's idea to have Erin set those guys up. Lonell killed his friend and Thurgood wanted revenge, him and Jamie cooked all this up. I never wanted Erin involved."

He finished taping my legs and hands together. Delon was in the front seat laughing like he was watching a fucking stand-up.

"Weren't you just doing the ugly cry for this nigga? Now you're throwing him and your own son under the bus just so you won't die?" Manny laughed and asked me.

I shrugged my shoulders.

"Rather them then me. I'm just looking out for myself. I will always look after myself."

He looked at me for a minute. Then, he shook his head and said, "Yea, death is exactly what the fuck you need."

When he said that, I snapped.

"Fuck you! You fucked us up when you wouldn't let me kill that mistake!" I yelled that and Manny's whole face and posture changed.

"Aw shit," I heard Delon say before Manny's closed fist met my face.

Everything went black and I knew that I was going to die. It was all because of my daughter.

I swear I hate that bitch.

Yatta

All I wanna do is lay up with you
All day (all day)
All day (all day)
Nothing else, nothing else (nothing else)
Than spend time with you all day
But I gotta get to the money, baby
We both love these hunnids, yeah
Once I'm finished with my job, baby girl
Yeah, I'm on my way

I was sitting up on my bed with my back against the headboard. My 60-inch TV was off and the only thing on was my Bluetooth speaker playing Partynextdoor's "Peace of Mind" song.

I was high as fuck and looking at the most beautiful sight I had ever fucking seen. Erin had my blinds wide open in my bedroom overlooking the night lights of Detroit downtown.

I was on the top floor of my 22-story apartment building. I had always wanted to see her paint or draw in front of me. I took her to the art store and let her get everything she needed. That shit was expensive too because Erin used quality art supplies. I didn't give a fuck though, Cutie Pie could get whatever she wanted from me, especially after the way I did her. Even though I had Erin back, I still felt like a piece of shit for the way I did her.

Even though money never made Erin pussy wet I still wanted to show her that I would do anything for her to trust me again. I wanted for her to know that I wouldn't jeopardize me and her ever again. That girl was riding for me and I shouldn't have questioned her loyalty. Her ass still hadn't given me any pussy though. Women knew when they had a way of forgiving you but still punished yo' ass at the same time. I was going crazy by not being able to be inside of Erin, but I understood why. A nigga fucked up and that was my punishment but looking at her fine ass sit in front of me painting was testing my restraint.

Erin brought a black wooden stool at the art supply store. She had this stand that held her drawing pad up. She had all her paint, brushes and all this other shit on the foldout table next to her. Her sexy ass was in nothing but a black thong. Did ya hear what the fuck I said?!

Erin's sexy ass had her big curly hair on top of her head. Her back was facing me, and she was in her own zone painting the scenery in front of her. I wasn't tripping about her being topless in front of my open window because of how high up we were. Not only was she looking so fucking sexy painting for me but her shit was so damn good. It looked like she took the scenery and just put it on the big ass paper she was painting on.

It was just fucking sexy how good she was at her craft. Like, I was good at what I did, but Erin was born to do this. As long as I was in her life I would always encourage her to follow her dreams of art.

I didn't give a fuck how much it cost or if we had to live out of suitcases. As long as she was doing what she loved, then I was all for it. My eyes were low as fuck and red, but they stayed glued on her sexy ass. That light skin was smooth as fuck and the way she set up on that stool. Mm! She had a sexy ass arch in her back which made that ass poke out, even though she was sitting down.

When it feels this good you better keep it
When it feels this good you better keep her around
When it feels this good she get the key to the house
I'ma treat her like my spouse

Because in exchange you give me peace of mind
Baby, you could take all my time (you could take all my
time, yeah)
All I needed was a piece (all I needed was a piece)
All I needed was peace (all I needed was peace)
Someone that gon' listen to me (someone that gon' listen to
me)
Real niggas need real relief

"Stop stretching like that, Erin," I said to her while biting my bottom lip.

She held both of her arms up over her head and stretched her body. That back went in some more and she let out this light moan that had my dick breaking out of my boxers like a nigga breaking out of jail.

"I can't stretch, Kenyatta?" she looked back at me and smirked.

She knew what the fuck she was doing by teasing me and shit. I shook my head no while I took a pull of my weed. She smacked her lips and laughed.

"You're supposed to be quiet so I can concentrate. Shhh," she said while picking up her brush again.

"Stop fucking with me and I'll be as quiet as a church mouse."

She looked at my hard dick and licked her lips. Erin stared at my dick like she wanted that muthafucka.

I put my blunt in the corner of my mouth and grabbed my dick, squeezing it. Our eyes met and she was biting her lip.

"It's yo' dick, baby. All you gotta do is come get it."

I swore when I said that to her I could smell her sweet pussy call out to me from where I was sitting.

"Naw I'm good," she smirked and turned back around to paint.

Naw, scratch that shit I was talking earlier. I needed some of her and I needed that shit now. That was why even though I did get my dick sucked a few times when me and Erin were apart I just couldn't fuck anybody else. It was as if my shit only wanted her pussy and even the thought of fucking someone else didn't do it for me.

I put my blunt down in the ashtray on my nightstand. Erin was so busy painting that she didn't hear or see me get off the bed. Once I got to her, I stood behind her and grabbed the back of her neck. Before she could say anything, I stuck my tongue down her throat. Kissing Erin was different from kissing any bitch. Not because I haven't kissed many bitches but more because the way we kissed. The shit always took my breath away. I had a baby with Cleo and had never kissed her on the mouth.

I never thought twice about kissing Erin. Hell, I knew when I first saw her freshman year that I wanted to kiss her.

While we made out, I slipped my right hand in her thong. All I did was touch the top of her pussy and my hand was drenched.

Pulling my hand out I pulled away from her kiss and said, "Look at this shit, Erin. You want it just as bad as I do, baby. Stop playing."

While I looked her in her eyes I slid my hand back in her thong. This time, my hands went between her thick ass pussy lips. Still looking in her eyes, I rubbed her wet pussy. Her shit was so warm, wet and felt good as fuck against my fingers.

"You don't want it?" I asked her while I put one finger in her tight ass hole.

Her back arched and she let out a sexy ass low moan.

"I do, but I'm not ready. I may be new to this sex thing, but I know that what's between my legs is special. I know whoever I decide can get between them needs to know it's an honor. They need to know that they can't treat me any type of way. The next guy will understand that."

When she looked at me and said that shit I got mad as fuck. Even though her voice was sweet and low what she said still blew my shit.

"Ain't gone be no next guy. It's either me or yo' ass is never having sex again. Stop trying to see how crazy I am over you, Erin. I swear you will get a nigga killed."

"I---- ssss mm Kenyatta stop before you make me cum," she moaned her entire sentence out.

I was about to bus all on the back of her ass. Damn, this fucking girl was fucking me all up.

"Gone and cum, baby. You don't want this dick cutie pie, huh?"

I swear if she said yes, I would be the happiest nigga on earth. I'd be happier then I was when she said she was with me again.

"I do, but I'm just not ready baby."

I couldn't even get mad at her. Hell, at this point it would be down right wrong to. I had hurt Erin bad as fuck.

"Look, I know I was on some fuck boy shit Erin and I can't apologize to you enough. But I will do the shit every day and show you that I'm dead ass for real about me and you. No fucking body could ever have me tweak out on you again. I fucking swear to God on that."

I was face to face with her when I told her how I felt. My hand was still working that sweet pussy. Erin came hard in my hand and I fucking loved that shit.

"Mmmmm, baby. Damn."

Her sexy ass had her head back against my chest. She came hard as fuck, turning me on to the max in the process.

"Can you just do two things for me, cutie pie?" I whispered in her ear.

Her breathing was coming back to normal.

"Yes?"

"Can I eat that pussy while you say my name? I promise I won't stick no dick to you. I just miss tasting you. I need that shit!"

She bit her lip and nodded her head. Shit, she didn't even get to completely nod before I picked her up and laid her on my bed.

I got on top of her and kissed those tasty ass lips again.

While we kissed, her hands were all over my chest. Then they went all over my back, lower waist and then to my dreads. Erin's touch did some shit to a thug. Like my entire fucking body lit up and made me feel some type of way. I liked the shit but then I didn't because I felt like she was turning me on some soft shit.

Her hand pulled the rubber band I had around my dreads.

I slowly broke our kiss and just looked down at her pretty ass for a minute. She gave me a light smile and rubbed the side of my face. I kissed her palm when it went past my lips.

"Damn," I said low, but I knew she heard me.

Still just taking her in I just thought about how long I had been wanting this. I was about to lose it from my hot head temper. I thought how rare Erin was and the fact that she could have any man she wanted. I didn't even think she knew how fucking rare her breed was. Erin had it all, from looks to intelligence and her gift that she was blessed with. Sex appeal poured from her even without her trying. In sweats, a messy hairdo and house shoes on her feet. Erin just had it all on top of being sweet, fun to be around and she was easy as fuck to be around. She was all of that wrapped in one and she was all fucking mine. I wasn't fucking this shit up ever again.

"What?" her pretty ass asked me with a curious look on her face.

"You be having me on some corny soft shit. I hate it, but I love it all the same," I chuckled.

"It's wild as fuck. I sound like a bi----"

"Like a damn man who is telling me how he feels. Kenyatta, its ok to be vulnerable with me. It's only me and you, baby."

I didn't even say shit. I just went back to kissing her deep and long. I went to her neck and put my prints all over it.

"I love you, cutie pie," I said to her between my kisses down to her titties as I started sucking and showing so much love to them sexy things.

"I loved you first, Kenyatta," I looked up at her when she said that to me.

Shit threw me off guard.

"Since freshman year."

Given me a light smile she hunched her shoulders.

I smiled and bit my lip at her. Diving my head between her legs, I buried my face in her pussy. She was so wet that besides shuffle music playing on the Bluetooth, I could hear her wetness between her legs. Erin had a taste that was indescribable, but at the same time, sweet. I didn't even know the right words for it. All I knew was that I craved that taste. I was going crazy on her pretty ass pussy. She kept her shit bald and there was not a hair bump in sight. Erin had the kind of pussy I just wanted to look at first before I did anything to it. I could admire the sight later, now I wanted to just fuck her world up with this head.

"Ugh, Kenyatta, I swear you're so good at this, babyyyy. Oh my God!" Erin came all in my mouth and I didn't miss a drop of her sweet juices.

Still not done eating her up I sat up between her legs. Looking at Erin, I saw that she had her head thrown back with them eyes closed. My face was soaking wet and that shit was turning me on. I ain't never been this into eating a bitch's pussy. Like this shit was straight satisfying me to satisfy her. Maybe it was the Pisces in me that enjoyed making her feel good. Looking down at her sexy ass, I wanted to capture this moment.

I grabbed my iPhone X and went to the camera option.

"Umm, what are you doing?" Erin asked me, looking at me with a crazy expression.

"I want you to record me eating this pretty ass pussy," I licked my lips because her juices were still on them.

Damn, she had me on some other shit. Erin started trying to move, but I grabbed her thigh with my left hand.

"Hell no, Kenyatta. You are not about to record me for you and your friends to look at later."

Now, it was my turn to look at her crazy as fuck.

"Are you fucking tweaking on some shit? Why the hell would I show any fucking body your damn body?!"

I put my phone down next to her and grabbed her neck, bringing her close to my face. Not hard, but just enough so she could know I wasn't bullshitting.

"You know I'll go fucking crazy if a nigga saw you like this, for real. I wish I could poke every nigga's eyes out that even looks at you but since that ain't possible my job is to make sure only I see you like this. You're recording it because the shit turns me on when I'm eating your pussy," I looked at her and said while still holding her neck.

Erin was looking at a nigga like I was a meal and the same look was given from me as well.

She finally agreed and I gave her my phone.

Once she started the video, I looked in the camera and smiled which made her smile, too. I grabbed both of her knees and put them by her ears. Her pussy was on full display now and I dived right back in. I took that pink ass clit in my mouth and made slow love to it with my tongue. This was some 'forgive me I fucked up' head. That 'never leave me' head and that 'I love you so much' head.

I finally let her clit breath as I stuck my tongue deep as hell in her hole. I moved it in circles while my thumb massaged her clit.

"Sssss, mmm. Damn," Erin moaned while I kept her legs pushed back by her ears.

I was having a feast on her.

"Say my name, baby," I told her and went back to work.

I loved whenever Erin said my name. Whether it be her just talking normal or in pleasure. My name just sounds so good rolling off her tongue.

"I'm cummin', Kenyatta. God, I'm cummin so hard! I can't hold the fucking camera! Ugh!"

She came so hard her juices slid down her ass crack. My tongue followed the trail and licked it right up. Yea, I must really love the fuck out of this girl for me to do that nasty shit. I loved it though!

"Damn baby, you dropped the camera right at the best part," I laughed at her as I used my hand to rub her juices in my goatee and lips.

Her shit was so good and smelled even better.

"I'm sorry but I got weak," she laughed as I let her legs down and got between them to kiss her.

"It's cool, baby. I knew I was fucking you up when your body started shaking. I thought you were having a seizure on me," I joked and she mushed my head while laughing.

"Thanks for letting me see you paint. I hope that will be the first of many times I get to see greatness being created," I told her while flipping her on top of me.

She still had that sexy ass thong on. I kept it on while I ate the fuck outta that pussy.

She put her chin in my chest and looked up at me.

"I love that you take interests in my passion. I didn't think anyone besides my dad would bond with me on that."

Her soft ass hand was in my dreads and her other hand was under her chin.

"I love anything you love, baby. If your mine forever that's how it has to be. We are supposed to love each other's passions. Invest in each other's dreams and I don't mean financially. Ain't nothing wrong with that, but you can invest in my passion by just listening to me talk about it. Giving me ideas on it and suggestions and shit. That's how it should be in relationships. I got all the financial shit covered," I told her as I pulled her rubber band out her hair.

I wanted to see her big ass curly hair down. She smirked at me as I ran my fingers through her hair.

"I'll have a great art gallery and you will have a high-end tattoo and piercing shop. Celebrities will come from everywhere to get inked up by you. Except the girl celebrities, they gotta go somewhere else," she slid that last part in there making me and her laugh.

"I don't give fuck if Keyshia Cole herself came to get some work done by me. I wouldn't even blink at her twice. And that's the finest bitch in the world after you."

She smacked her lips and rolled her eyes.

"Damn, look at you being possessive over yo' nigga! I like that shit. It lets me know I ain't the only one on tip."

"Hell no you're not! I have never been this way with any guy I have talked to. I mean I never wanted to get played, but I didn't care what they did. It's different with you though. I'll fight over you," she said that shit and shrugged her shoulders.

I looked at her and said, "I'll kill over you, dead ass."

She stared at me for a minute and I knew she was searching my eyes to see if I was lying, but she wasn't about to find deception on my eyes. I was so fucking serious.

"Don't leave me again, Kenyatta."

Man, she fucked my gangsta all up talking like that. Her voice was so sweet and low. The shit broke my heart but at the same time it also made my heart smile knowing she really wanted me.

"Erin, I swear to God I will never pull that fuck boy shit on you again. You have nothing to worry about. As far as me leaving you, naw, never that. Ain't no me without you and my son and that's hunnid shit. I love you so much, Erin."

Those chestnut eyes got watery.

"I loved you first, Kenyatta," she put her hand on the side of my face and brought her lips to mine.

I had my hands around her waist and then her round ass. Her tongue was so sweet and wet. I was hard again and knew what I wanted to do.

I reached for my phone on the bed and gave it to her.

"Sit on my face and record it. This time yo' ass bet not drop the phone," I told her while biting my lips while looking at her.

She blushed and nodded her head. I fucked Erin's life up three more times just off head alone. And as hard as it was, she didn't dropped the phone this time.

***

"Yatta, listen to me. Yo' hot headed ass needs to keep chilling and staying out of trouble. Our lawyer did his job and I'm getting out this muthafucka in three days," my uncle told me.

Me and his wife, Juziel, went to go visit him. I was happy as fuck when our lawyer called us yesterday telling us the good news. The judge dismissed the charges due to circumstantial evidence. That was why our lawyer was so expensive, sometimes he played dirty as hell to get us off. He was well worth the pay.

"Unc, I'm cool. As long as you getting out of here then I'm on chill mode. Emmanuel and Delon wants to meet with us when you get out. They came back from out of town this morning," I told him while he kissed and loved on my auntie.

I chuckled at them because my auntie was my uncle's everything. He did his dirt in the past, but it had always been her. He didn't have any kids outside of her, but he still was a dog back in the day. Or at least that's what he told me. But I dare somebody try and separate the two of them. They are going to lose ya life trying.

"I knew they were making moves as soon as I got locked up. That's why I told yo' hot tamale head ass not to tweak out on Erin like I know you fucking did. I love you nephew, but you lucky as hell Emmanuel wasn't around to see the shit I heard you did. He would have killed you and then I would have had to kill him and Delon. Before you knew it me and yo' auntie would have been dead because believe me Emmanuel would have a hit on us from his grave. All because you thinking some shit the wrong way. You gotta get that overreacting shit out ya behavior, nephew. Shit gone fuck you up in the long run."

"I know man, I was just heated and thought all kinds of shit ran through my mind. It all pointed to Erin and I just hit the roof. I know that shit was gay as fuck, Unc. But I did fix it, or at least I'm still fixing it."

I tried not to smile while thinking about Erin forgiving me but the shit came on my face by force. It made my auntie and uncle look at me while smiling hard as hell.

"Oh shit, look at my nephew all in love and shit! That's what the fuck I'm talking about, my nigga," he slapped my hand and started laughing, making me laugh as well.

"It doesn't get no better than Erin for yo' young ass. She got it all to be so young and a dumb nigga would let her fall through his fingers. You just keep her happy and be real with her."

I nodded my head at him speaking some true shit.

"So, what's up with Alaric and his daddy drama? That shit his bitch ass pops pulled makes that nigga the true fuck boy. I know Z ready for war."

I shook my head at what he said because every time I thought about that shit my stomach turned. How the fuck could you do that to your own son and his girl? That nigga was a life size bitch for real.

"Z and Alaric is on tip. I looked at Alaric in his eyes, he wants his pops dead," I looked around the visiting room to make sure nobody heard me.

"Y'all don't do shit until I come home. German is me, Emmanuel and Delon's generation and y'all gone need our help."

"Alaric said he got a plan but he knows we waiting on y'all. He wants to handle yo' shit first, then this D.C. shit. You heard from Havoc?"

When I asked my uncle that he gave me a look.

"Yea I have, he been up to see me. Some is shit off, I had our lawyer follow him and ain't shit been up with Havoc. I still got a feeling and you know I told yo' ass to always listen to that feeling. We doing D.C. without him. For all he knows it's still going down next Saturday. Keep it that way. I'm moving shit to next Sunday. No more talking to Havoc about shit, a'ight? Tell Z and Alaric as well. I don't give a fuck if Havoc call y'all on the phone trying to talk business. Act like you don't know what's up or just don't answer. Don't meet up with that nigga, don't text that nigga or nothing. If he say some shit like I want y'all to talk to him he's fucking lying."

My uncle was dead ass serious and I took all his words in. I swear I hoped he was just being paranoid and Havoc wasn't up to shit. They had been friends for years and I knew that would be a straight curve for my uncle.

"I got it, Unc. As soon as we leave here I'll let Z and Alaric know. So, your right-hand man who you have been friends with for years is up to no good? Or so you think. Now you see how I was conflicted about Erin."

I had to throw that in there because he was basically doing the same thing I did.

"Nigga, get the fuck outta here. You see how I'm handling my speculations calm and like a fucking man. I ain't popping off on no fucking body without having all my fucking facts first. Don't come for me, lil nigga," he laughed and my auntie joined in.

I sat back in my chair and waved him off. We had a nice visit with my uncle until it was time for me and my auntie to leave.

"Yatta, do me a favor and go pay the deposit for the hall. Make sure you get the receipt and drop it off to me later," my auntie told me while we got in her Lexus.

We were on the way to her house so I could get my truck.

My uncle was coming home in two days which just so happened to be his 42nd birthday. The nigga looked like he was still in his twenties with his big yellow ass. A lot of people swore he was my pops because we looked so much alike. He was just taller and had more muscle. We even had matching dreads but his were down his fucking back.

Anyway, me and my auntie were throwing him a party at Luna in Royal Oak. We rented the entire building out and was giving him a birthday/welcome home party. We had the shit catered and a decorator to make the shit slap. My uncle's favorite color was black and white, so she wanted all of the guests to be in black and she and Lonell be in white.

"I'm on it, Auntie. I just gotta pick up my girl and I'll go make that run for you."

When I said that, she did that goofy ass smile.

I smacked my lips and said, "Why the hell everybody gotta look like a cornball every time I say Erin's name?!"

She laughed harder.

"Because it's cute how you look when you say her name or talk about her. You can't see your face but we can. I feel like a proud mama right now."

I laughed and turned the radio up on my annoying ass auntie. All of them were so extra with the smiles and shit when it came to me and Erin. Speaking of my cutie pie, I needed to text her and see how her day was going.

As I pulled my phone out I could feel my entire face change. My heart started beating fast and I could feel that same goofy ass smile on my face. Erin had me on some other type of shit.

I looked over at my auntie and she was still smiling and laughing. I turned the radio up louder on her ass.

Alaric

"Cass love, I'm good boo I swear I got it," I was picking up our plates and taking it to the kitchen.

After three weeks, I was ok to walk without help or without being in a lot of pain but my girl was still babying my grown ass. I appreciated her though and all she did. For her to go through that horrible shit with German's pussy ass and still play 24-hour nurse to me made me love her to death.

Cassidy still worked, did her nails on the side and took care of me all in one day.

My own damn mama felt some type of way about not being able to take care of me. She liked Cassidy and always thanked her, but I knew my mama.

"Ok Ric, but the minute you feel some pain then just sit down."

I smiled and shook my head as I headed to the kitchen.

Lonell's birthday party was tomorrow and I was excited as hell. Cassidy and I were going to Twelve Oaks Mall to get something to wear. I told her to get whatever the fuck she wanted. Anything that caught her eye, she could get it. It was the least I could do for her still wanting to be with me.

Coming out the kitchen, I stood in her bedroom door watching her put her clothes out for today. She looked so good in my black beater. It hugged her booty right and was waking my dick up. We still hadn't had sex but I would never press her. We kissed and felt on each other, but we didn't fuck. It was all good though because I knew once I did get in them guts I was showing out.

"Um, do you need a moment?" she looked at me laughing and pointed down.

I looked down and saw my dick completely out the slit of my boxers. I didn't even realize I was that solid because I was so caught up looking at her.

I laughed and squeezed my dick hard as fuck to calm his ass down.

"Fuck boo, I'm sorry. You just look good as fuck and he got a mind of his own. I'm sorry."

She walked up on me and grabbed my face.

"Ric its ok, I'm not turned off or scared of a man. I just want to be mentally ready when we have sex again. But, I know you're a man first and getting hard when your turned on is natural. You don't have to apologize, babe."

I looked down at her gorgeous self and nodded my head. She pressed her lips against mine and we kissed.

Cassidy was right. Anytime I solid up on her I was apologizing. I guess I didn't want her to think I only thought about sex after she had been violated in that way. I just wanted her to feel like a woman and nothing less.

As we kissed deep, I walked her backwards and pressed her back against the door. The inside if Cassidy's mouth was so fucking sweet. It was as if she just naturally had strawberries infused in her body.

Once I knew I was getting really into it, I stopped.

"My bad boo, I just love kissing you," I said to her, making her blush.

She pecked my lips a few times and went to finish getting her outfit ready.

I did the same and laid out some tan Polo shorts with a green Polo three-button shirt to match. I decided to wear my tan Yeezy 350's. I kept my jewelry simple with just my diamond studs.

"Damn, your dreads are getting so long. Dreka got her work cut out for her," Cassidy said while she ran her small hand through my dreads.

They were growing like fucking weeds. They were already touching the middle of my back.

Dreka was twisting them tonight at Z's crib and I was going to have her take some inches off. I decided to keep them down and throw on my army Detroit Lions fitted hat.

I came out the bathroom and looked at Cassidy's fine ass again who was fully dressed. Her slim thick ass had on some jeans that stopped at her knees but were ripped all up. She had her pretty ass feet in some Gucci studded sandals. Her fucking top was fitted and it wrapped around her stomach. It was sexy as fuck but see through and I could see her hard ass nipples.

"Where the fuck is your bra?" I asked her with anger in my tone.

She had the nerve to look down at her top in shock.

"There's a bra made in the shirt, Ric."

"Hell naw Cassidy, stop fucking with me and put a damn bra on. I can see how hard ya nipples are from here."

She smacked her lips and turned around to open her drawer. I knew she had an attitude but ask me if I gave a fuck. She was putting a bra on or we were not leaving her apartment.

"Better?" she turned around and asked me.

"Much better."

She had put on a nude strapless bra that covered her fucking nipples. I pulled her to me and kissed her again.

"Why you tryna have nigga seeing what the fuck is mine. Huh?" I asked her with my hands in her back pockets.

I swear it never took much to get Cassidy to blush.

"You're not even the jealous type, Ric," her voice was all soft and low.

She was right. I had never been a jealous nigga over any bitch but that shit was dead and gone now.

"Over you I am, Cassidy. I'm all that shit that bitches should run from. Jealous, possessive, aggressive as hell and needy. Not to mention spoiled for attention only from you," I licked my lips while looking at her sexy ass.

"Aw hell no, let me get the fuck on then," she laughed and tried to walk away but my hands were in her back pocket.

I pulled her closer to my once again hard dick. I could feel the heat from her pussy through her jeans.

"Where the fuck you think you going? It's too late to back out now, Cass love. Your heart belongs to me and always will."

She gave me that 'nigga please' look and I squinted my eyes at her.

"I'm just joking, Ric. You know what's up."

She tried to walk away again but I still didn't let her go.

She better stop fucking with me.

"You on some goofy shit, Cassidy. Your heart mine or not?" I gave her an option like she had one.

If she said something other then what I wanted to hear I didn't know what I would do.

"My heart is all yours, Ric," she blushed and smiled at me.

I couldn't hide my smile even if I tried.

"For how long?"

"Forever babe," she said and I kissed her beautiful ass lips.

Finally letting her go, we finished getting ready and walked out her apartment.

I ain't had nothin' that had me like this
She look me right in my eyes when we kiss
Listening to Biggie, just me and my bitch
I'm 'bout to get busy, I'm back on my shit
I ain't had nothing that had me like this
Bend it over, have her runnin' and shit
Listening to Biggie just me and my bitch
I'm bout to get busy, I'm back on my shit

[Chorus]
We never argue
I be in motion, soon as I'm free, I'ma call you
When I was broke I couldn't get next to you
Now it's a dub for the walk through
That's twenty thousand
She say I'm childish
I got the Rov' with no mileage
They think I got me a stylist
We walk up in Gucci we wildin'

"I told you yo' ass was going to like Dave East. Erin told us about him when she first got to New York. He's fire."

Cassidy rapped to the lyrics to "We Never Argue" from Dave East's mixtape Karma. She played his ass a lot at her crib so I gave the nigga a try and he was pretty cool.

"Yea, he got some tight joints I can fuck with," I said to her while driving my 2018 Yukon to the mall.

"Not to mention he's fine as shit."

I looked at her ass like I was ready to fight her.

"Keep talking Cassidy and watch I kill both of us in this truck."

Her mouth fell open and she started laughing. She thought I was bullshitting so I started adding speed. I was almost at 70,

"Ok! Ok! Ric stop playing."

Her ass wasn't laughing then. She sat up and looked around eyes all bucked out in a panic.

It was my turn to start laughing as I still didn't slow down.

"Naw Cassidy, its funny to play with me, right? Talking about other niggas look good, acting like your heart ain't mine. The shit's funny, right?"

This girl was scared shitless. Her chest was going up and down and I swear she changed complexions. We were going fast as fuck down 275 freeway.

"RIC STOP!"

"Say your mine forever and will never ever leave me," I said looking from her and then the road.

"I'm yours forever and I'll never leave you. SLOW DOWN!" she yelled as she was freaking out.

"I said say you'll never EVER leave me, Cassidy," I was talking calm as hell while doing 75.

"OH, MY GOD! I will never ever leave you and my heart is yours, now stop playing!" she screamed loud as fuck.

I slowed down and was cracking up. God was on my side because I didn't get pulled over or get a ticket. I came up on our exit, still cracking up.

Looking over at Cassidy, I saw that she was crying. Shit.

"Boo you crying? I was just playing, Cass love."

I turned into the Starbucks parking lot so I could check on my boo. I swear I didn't want her to cry.

I got out and walked around to her side and opened the door.

"Cassidy, stop crying boo, I'm sorry. I would never scare you like that again."

I took her seat belt off and turned her to me. I stood between her legs and hugged her. She wiped her face while sniffling and shit.

I used my hand and wiped her face all the way clean.

"You play too much, Alaric. That really scared the fuck out of me. I swear you better get me anything I want today," she poked her lip out and I kissed it.

"Anything you want boo, just stop crying."

I kissed her a few times and went back to my side so I could drive us to the mall.

***

"Cassidy, what the fuck girl? We been in this damn store for an hour. I done left and found me a whole damn outfit for Lonell's party. Some shoes, a hat and I stopped in Game Stop. You still in the same damn spot. I swear I'm about to leave yo' ass."

I sat down next to Cassidy and put my bags on the side of me.

She had her feet in yet another pair of heels. As I was about to make another complaint my phone rang. Looking down at it, I saw it was my pussy ass sperm donor again. He had been calling me now for the past two days. Texts, voicemails and phone calls. I didn't answer none of them. I also didn't tell Cassidy either because I didn't want to scare her.

My boo still woke up every morning, squeezing me tight. One morning, I woke up and wasn't in bed with her. I went to take a shower and I heard her screaming my name. She was so fucking scared that German had me. I hugged her and calmed her down. That shit fucked with me heavy and I couldn't wait to get my plan going on getting his ass.

"You ok?" Cassidy asked me, breaking me from my thoughts.

"I will be when my girl comes the hell on."

She laughed and finished trying on shoes.

We walked out of Lord and Taylors after an hour and thirty minutes. I was good and ready to go but Cassidy's ass wanted to go to Michael Kors and some store called Windsor. Surprisingly, she was quicker in Michael Kors and didn't break my pockets. She found a cute purse and matching wallet for three hundred. I was willing to spend whatever on Cassidy because she deserved it. Thanks to Lonell, we knew how to save and invest our money, so we could splurge like this. Walking into Windsor which I discovered was a girly ass clothing store, I grabbed a seat and started scrolling Instagram while Cassidy shopped.

"Well damn, I guess you don't fuck with me no more, huh?"

I looked up and saw Neshia standing in front of me with an attitude and her hand on her hip. Neshia was the bitch I brought to Cassidy's store she worked at. I was on some childish shit and trying to get under Cassidy's skin. The bullshit didn't work and Cassidy dropped my ass like a bad habit.

"Tha fuck you doing here?" I turned my nose up and asked her.

This trick had the nerve to roll her eyes.

"I work here, duh. And considering you sitting here looking lost I know you here with a bitch."

That made me mad as fuck.

"Naw, you got it wrong. I'm here with my girl. The only bitch I see is standing in front of me and she better walk away if she knows what's best."

She was about to say some smart shit but then Cassidy walked up.

"Excuse me, get out my nigga's face and go get this in a medium for me."

She shoved some shirts into Neshia's chest.

When Neshia looked up and saw Cassidy I could feel her attitude rising.

"You hooked up with that bitch from Fairlane?! I should have known his bald-headed ass would have fucked you. She was being extra nice and shit."

Cassidy was about to jump stupid when I grabbed her ass up just in time. Two of Neshia's co-workers walked up, talking shit with her.

"Bitch, you got the right one today. Come on and get'cho ass jumped!" one of the hoes yelled out to Cassidy.

I put Cassidy down and pulled my heat from my waist. I didn't give a fuck if we were in a mall or not. The mall was empty today anyway.

"I wish you bobble head billy goats would touch my fucking girl. Come on and try to be the first to lay hands on her. I swear I'm filling ya lace front up with hot lead," I was dead ass serious and the look on my face told them so.

Neshia had the nerve to cry and run in the back. The other two stood there with their hands in the air.

I looked at them as I put my heat back in my waist. Turning to a stunned Cassidy, I grabbed her hand.

"Leave this cheap ass shit right in this cheap ass store."

We walked out and she looked up at me.

"Ric, oh my God babe, I can't believe you just did that. I mean I have never been more turned on, but still. You could have been arrested."

Cassidy held my hand tight as we got outside to my truck.

I put our bags in the truck and helped her in.

"I could care less about that shit. Them bitches was frozen in their tracks and there were no cameras in the store."

When I said that Cassidy looked at me.

"How did you know that?"

Shit, I had fucked up. The work I did with my niggas and Lonell had me always looking to see if surveillance was around. I always used this security app on my phone to make sure my face was never scanned. It was amazing how many things were available when someone was good with computers and hacking.

"I could just tell because I didn't see any cameras," I played it off as we got on the freeway.

I changed the subject by asking her what she wanted to eat. Cassidy said she wanted to eat some Applebee's. I was cool with whatever she said as long as I could eat. Like always when we went out to eat, we ordered so much food.

Since I had some time before we had to go to Z's crib, we decided to swing by my mama's house to visit her and my baby brothers. My mama had four boys, including myself. I was the oldest, June was seven, Marcus was six and Lee was four years old. All of us had our own father. It could be said my mama was a little T.H.O.T in her day, but she was a bomb ass fucking mama and took care of all of us good as hell. I decided to get them some food from Applebee's as well. That way my mama didn't have to cook later tonight.

"I think your mama likes me, but I think she thinks I'm stepping on her toes."

I laughed when she said that because the shit was true.

"My mama loves all her boys. She raised us herself, so she is used to being the center of our worlds. Trust me boo, she knows how I feel about you. She just has to adjust to my heart belonging to someone else. That's always the homie though," I told Cassidy honestly.

I grabbed her hand and kissed it as we drove to Z's crib.

***

"My nigga, why you lookin' agitated?" I asked Yatta.

We were sitting on Z's couch, smoking. I passed Yatta the blunt and he looked annoyed.

"Nothing nigga, just pass the shit and hush," I looked at Z and then back at Yatta.

"Damn nigga. Erin forgave you but she ain't givin' up no pussy, huh?"

Z and I cracked up laughing at Yatta's face. A while back these two fools teased me for being all in my feelings about Cassidy not wanting to fuck with me. Now, this nigga was looking just like I was. It was my turn to laugh at him.

"Fuck y'all gay bitches, a'ight," Yatta gave us the finger as he passed Z the blunt.

The girls were upstairs in Z's second bedroom listening to music and I was sure they were talking about us.

"All jokes aside Yatta, what do you expect her to do? You straight played Ma over some shit you thought. Lonell been saying since we were little that you're too hot-headed. Hopefully, this drought will get ya ass in line," Z's big stupid ass said like he was a fucking God Father or some shit.

I couldn't help but laugh.

"Now all of a sudden since Dreka on ya team you just a man of many words? Fuck you Shaq Jr."

Yatta was pissed off which made my dumb ass laugh more.

"Y'all don't understand what I'm going through. She paints naked and shit, always smelling good. And I ain't even getting shit on the side. Cleo on my ass all the time to suck my dick and a slew of other hoes. But I only want Erin, she put some shit on me, for real. I ain't never craved a bitch so bad before. I'm talking about not just physical. I feel like a billboard for 'bitch whipped niggas'. The other night I went to sleep with my head on top of her pussy."

Z and I fell out laughing hard as hell when he said that.

"Look at ya face, my nigga! You look like a fiend on that shit!" I was on the floor holding my stomach laughing hard as fuck.

Z was laid back on his recliner with his fist on his mouth, laughing hard as hell too.

"Y'all supposed to be my day ones. Fuck you hoe ass niggas, Cassidy and Dreka got y'all gone too!"

He was heated as fuck.

"Yea nigga but not like that!" Z said through his laugh.

I agreed as the girls came downstairs.

Dreka was about to do my hair which was looking its worst. Cassidy wasn't about to let me go to the chick that usually did my dreads. I paid that bitch with dick so I knew that would never happen again. Dreka was bad as fuck though with the dread hook-up and she kept Z and Yatta looking straight, so why not? We chilled, ordered pizza, had liquor and weed going around. It was a good ass night.

I watched my nigga Yatta and I swear I wasn't being dramatic. That nigga might be on to some shit about Erin having put something on him. He was all up her asshole, rather he was kissing on her. Hugging on her or just touching on Ma.

At one point, I guess she was in the bathroom too long because that nigga got up and went in there with her. I wanna say the shit was funny but I truly felt for him.

He was gone as fuck over Erin, he had Z and I beat by a long shot. Erin seem to not mind his ass smothering her. Anyone could see she loved that nigga just as much. Dreka and Z were next up with the caking shit. She had his big ass wrapped around her finger. It was nice to see us happy and living life. In a few days, I had to tell Cassidy some serious shit about German's bitch ass. My niggas already knew the plan, but it was time for me to tell her what was up. I didn't want to keep secrets from her. I'll let her know the deal after Lonell's party. Shit was about to go down and just in case I don't make it back to her I just wanted her to know what was up.

**

"Today was eventful none the less," Cassidy sat next to me on her couch.

I was watching Sports Center waiting on her to get out the shower. I had been staying with Cassidy for a few weeks now while I healed. I was so used to climbing in her bed with her next to me. Even if she was working or just out I'd chill in the living room until she got back. I wanted to only be in her bed with her next to me. That was why I wanted to talk to her about some shit tonight. I just hope I didn't scare her off.

"Yea, I bet you do think that shit. I had to pull a gun on some stupid hoes who thought they were about to fuck with you. That shit turned you on, I could tell," I looked over at her and said.

She looked so good with her hair in that colorful silk scarf. Cassidy always wore this short black fluffy robe before she went to bed. I loved that fucking robe because it was so short and left little to the imagination.

She laughed and smacked her lips at my comment.

"Shut up Ric, I was more shocked then turned on. I have never seen your face look like that before. You were dead ass for real about shooting them if they tried to jump me. I'm starting to think Z ain't the only one crazy," she laughed and I looked her in her eyes.

I wasn't laughing.

"He's really not. I'd kill for you Cass love, in a heartbeat, and without a care. I'd flatline a nigga or a bitch in a minute over you."

She looked at my lips and then my eyes as I talked. I was so serious about what I had just said. I was gladly killing my fucking father for what he did to Cassidy. I'd hurt any fucking body that hurt her.

"I would never want you to harm anyone over me, Ric. I understand what has to happen regarding your father but if it is up to me, you'd never have to hurt anybody."

She looked down and then looked back in my eyes.

"I know your father has been calling you a lot lately. Ric, that man scares the hell out of me and if leaving me is the------"

I shook my head in disgust in her words.

"Cassidy, no way in fucks hell am I leaving you. Stop that crazy ass talking you doing boo, for real for real. Understand that the plan I have for German will fucking work. I was going to wait until after Lonell's party to tell you this but fuck it. I'm going to see him soon, Cassidy."

The look of fear she had on her face broke my heart. This nigga really had put fear in her over him.

"Boo listen, I promise as soon as I get all this shit together with Z, Yatta and the rest I swear I will get you all caught up on how this shit will go down. I don't want you stressing about me or any of this shit. Everything will work out and I will come back to you. When I do boo, I want me and you to live together. If you want, we can get a new place we both pick out or I'll move here. It's up to you Cassidy, but I want to continue living with you."

She smiled at me and said, "I swear if you would have told me I'd have you on some settle down shit before now I would have looked at you like you were crazy. You're different from before but I love it. I would love to move in with you Ric."

I showed her my happiness by kissing her deep. I knew we were doing shit backwards, but I didn't give a fuck. As long as we got to the road leading to all the long-term shit who gave a fuck how we got there, as long as we do. When Cassidy pulled her robe open, I broke our kiss.

"Boo, you don't have to have sex with me until you're ready. I promise I'm good with kissing and holding you," I told her while looking at her gorgeous face.

She took her robe completely off and went back to kissing me.

"You have been nothing but patient, Ric. I'm ready, I'm ok."

I nodded my head then went to kissing and licking on her neck.

She was naked under her robe which made me happy. She was sitting up on the couch with her hands running all over my dreads while I put hickeys on her neck. I got down to her pretty ass C-cup titties. Cassidy titties sat up perfectly and she had some caramel pretty ass nipples.

I took one in my mouth while my other hand massaged the other one. I hadn't touched her like this in a minute. I was kissing and licking every inch of her body. I lapped my tongue around her nipple and bit down on it a bit. Her hands felt good as fuck in my head which was making my dick grow. As I played with her nipples with my tongue and lips I could hear her pussy calling out to me.

"Oooo Ric babe, that feels so good," Cassidy's sexy ass voice was sweet as fuck to my ears.

I kept working on them nipples while I slid my hand between her legs. She was so wet that her juices were all on her inner thighs. I softly rubbed that clit while I licked and kissed up her neck back to her face. While still working my fingers I kissed her cheeks, her forehead and then them beautiful ass lips. We kissed slow and nasty while I finger fucked her nice and slow. I had my index and middle finger fucking her while my thumb slowly massaged that clit. Pulling away from our kiss, I bit my lip and looked at her sexy ass climax.

Her head was back and her eyes was closed. Cassidy looked fucking amazing naked on her couch with her legs open and letting me take her on a high.

"I'm cummin', Ric. Ohhhh my God ssssss," she soaked my hand and her leather couch.

I finished enjoying the show as I eased my fingers out of her.

"That shit was live, but I ain't done," I laid on her back and stood up.

Coming out my clothes I got down to my knees and ran my hand all down her naked body. Ain't a bitch walking this earth body better than my Cass love.

I kissed her deep for a minute then licked and kissed my way down to her belly button. My tongue and lips left no spot untouched. I skipped over her pussy and showed love to them slim thick thighs. I bit a little on them and kissed where I bit. Cassidy's moans were sexy as fuck. I kissed down her left leg and got to her feet. I was a feet nigga but not to all bitches.

My bitch, however, kept her feet so fucking right. They were always clean, done up and had no smell. I kissed her tiny ass feet and put her toes in my mouth. I swear, Cassidy came off me sucking her toes. That shit had my dick on strong solid. By the time I showed love to both of her feet and toes, Cassidy came twice. Now I was between her legs and kissing her inner thighs. I smelled that sweet pussy and couldn't wait to taste it. I used my thick tongue to part her pussy lips and lick and all around her wetness. I was in fucking bliss eating her pussy.

"Yes Ric, eat my pussy babe. It's all yours."

I showed my ass when she said that shit.

I ate Cassidy's pussy so good. Right when she was squirting I slid my dick in. It had been so long since I felt her insides. I had to pause because I wanted to soak that shit up. Looking down at her, our eyes met.

"I swear no fucking body will ever hurt you again. I'll kill whoever boo."

She licked her lips and nodded her head.

I leaned down and kissed her while stroking the fuck outta her pussy with my dick. Shit was fucking sensational.

"I'm about to cum Ric," she moaned so sexy out to me.

"Gon' head and cum, I'm bout ta get loose boo," I fucked Cassidy crazy on her couch, bed and on the bedroom floor.

I couldn't get enough and she was hanging in there with me. My boo never got tired while we out fucked each other.

Erin

"I'm sorry I've been MIA, my muse. I just had a lot of work shit going on. Everything is under control now, so I wanted to take my daughter out to lunch," my dad smiled and said to me as he sliced into our deep-dish pizza.

We woke up early and went to paint downtown on the riverwalk. We caught a wonderful sight of these two St. Bernard dogs being walked. Their fur was beautiful and sparkling under the sun. The water from the river made it look even more breathtaking.

My dad drew the people walking them as well. I, however, chose not to and just focus on the animals and the nature side of the moment. Now we were at Pizza Papalis by Greektown Casino. We ordered a meat lovers deep dish pizza with extra cheese.

"I'm glad everything is ok with work, Daddy. Uncle D had Dreka worried as well, but I understand how work can be for the both of y'all. You didn't miss much here anyway."

I opted out of telling him about me and Kenyatta fall out. First of all, my dad probably would want me to stay away from him if he knew he was in anything illegal. I loved Kenyatta and didn't want to choose between him and my dad.

"Erin, have you talked to your mother or her son?"

My stomach did a flip because I wanted to tell him about Lonell getting locked up and about Jamie's father being behind it. I just didn't want to involve my dad. I knew him, my uncle D and Lonell were cool now and were cool back in the day.

"Um, I haven't talked to Mama but Jamie texted me yesterday. He wants to meet up-----"

"No. Do not meet up with him Erin, under no circumstances. You hear me?"

I looked at my dad's face and he was dead ass serious. He had an expression that I never seen on his face before. It was almost like he was about to fuck some shit up.

"Dad, what is going on? Why did you snap like that, is something going on with him?" I asked him and I could look at his face and tell he was holding something back.

"No muse, it's nothing. I just don't want you talking to him until I talk to your mama about some shit."

What?! Now I was confused and had more questions.

"Daddy, I know you are a cop. You have access to what happens and who gets locked up. Does Lonell getting locked up have anything to do with you not wanting me to talk to Jamie? Please tell me," I really wanted to know what he knew.

He looked at me for a minute before he said, "I know about Lonell getting locked up but because it's not my case I have no access to it. I do know your with Kenyatta who is Lonell's nephew and I want you safe. That's all I know and need to know. I have no involvement in Lonell's affairs but like I said, you're with his nephew. My job is to make sure you're good."

My words were as stuck as I knew I looked.

"Daddy, you didn't answer my question. I'm not a little girl anymore and I can handle more than you think. Tell me the truth, does Jamie's father having Lonell locked up have anything to do with you wanting me to stay away from him?"

I looked in my dad's eyes hoping he could see how serious I was.

"Erin, some shit is just on a need to know basis. Now like I said, stay the hell away from Jamie."

And with that, he went back to eating and talking as I gave a fuck about anything he was saying at this point.

⁇

***

I went home and packed a bag so I could go over Dreka's house. I wanted to be away from my dad and near my grandma. I not only wanted to get some of her good ass food I knew she would be cooking, I also just needed her wisdom at the moment.

On the way over, Kenyatta sent me a selfie of him at work. He looked so good in a simple ass beater and basketball shorts. He had that damn 'Yatta' chain on that I loved. His dreads were on top of his head and he had his hot ass bottom lip in his mouth.

I could feel my pussy getting moist as hell. I wanted some of him so bad, but I just felt like he wasn't done getting punished for how he treated me.

Yea we were together, but I hadn't gave him any since we fucked in his kitchen the day after he took my virginity. He had given me so much head though and I was loving it. Every time I looked up, Kenyatta's head was between my legs.

I knew I wasn't shit for thinking this, but every time he ate my pussy on the inside, I would be screaming, 'Yea nigga eat this pussy that got you all fucked up.'

I kind of felt good riding his face and coming on his tongue and leaving him with a hard dick. I knew I couldn't keep this up, but I was still enjoying it.

"Now honey, you know Grandma loves you. Anytime you or Dreka are upset with my sons y'all know I'm ready to get my shotgun out. But on this matter, I have to agree with Emmanuel. Just do like he says and stay away from that no good mother and brother of yours. If what your telling me is true about Lonell being locked up, then maybe you should just listen to your daddy on this, honey. We will kill all of Michigan if something happens to you," my grandma said while giving me the spoon, so I could lick the filling from the banana pudding she was making.

Dreka and I always helped her cook and we always sneak a taste in also. Dreka had some hair to do at the shop though, so it was just me.

"I agree Grandma, and I know he is trying to protect me. It just feels like he's hiding something. I'm grown as hell now and I can handle whatever is going on."

My grandma hit me on my thigh with her oven mitten when I cursed.

I laughed and apologized.

"You're always a baby in your parent's eyes, chile. Emmanuel and Delon are some full-grown niggas but they're still my big head ass babies running around in diapers."

I laughed at her and we talked and cooked some more.

Now I was in Dreka's room about to do some drawing. I finished the painting for the side hustle I had with my dad's friend. He had an art shop that sold imitations of famous paintings. I had a Henri Rousseau and Claude Monet that I had to do. A couple was buying both for three-thousand apiece. That was a thousand apiece for my pockets and I was loving it.

Not to mention, I was still working at Forever 21 with Cassidy. Now, I was doing a drawing that meant the world to me. I was drawing Kenyatta in the image I saw him in every time I thought of him.

I never ever drew people or painted people. I didn't care who you are or what you wanted to pay. I did not do humans. We have become so stuck on looks and all this filter bullshit that we hide our true beauty. I had fun with filters and even sometimes wore makeup but I would just as quick post a selfie with no filter or no makeup. I didn't care if I had a pimple or bags under my eyes. My beauty was within and I wished most people saw that.

I wasn't sure if I would ever show Kenyatta my drawing of him. All I knew was that it was on my mind and heart. Every time I added more to it, I fell in love with him more and more.

Like right now I was drawing his manly hands. I loved how big his knuckles were, but at the same time I loved how neat and clean his nails were. I always cleaned them but still, it was sexy. He had a scar on his left hand that happened when he was seven and fell off his bike. In my eyes, it made his hands more flawless. I could feel him touching me with these sexy hands. Rubbing my face, my lips, all in my hair. And I could feel them touch my body and make me feel sexy, secure and safe.

I had my headphones on playing our song 112's "Cupid."

Girl if I told you I love you
That doesn't mean that I don't care, oooh
And when I tell you I need you
Don't you think that I'll never be there, ooooh
Baby, I'm so tired of the way you turn my words into
Deception and lies
Don't misunderstand me when I try to speak my mind
I'm only saying what's in my heart

I got to his strong arms and enjoyed sculpting them as they were on his body. He had a few veins in his arms, but it was so hot. They were athletically built and felt so good wrapped around my waist. They held me tight all night while we slept. If I even got up to use the bathroom, they would tighten around me. I loved the love they gave when he hugged me. Damn Kenyatta. As I finished his arms, my clit was jumping. 112's voice going through my ears and drawing Kenyatta body parts was really doing it for me. My breathing was changing and my heart was beating fast. I was beginning to get hot all over and I felt like I wasn't in Dreka's room anymore. Shit. I needed to calm down. That was enough drawing for me.

"My goodness Kenyatta, what the hell are you doing to me?" I said out loud to myself as I pulled my earphones out my ear.

My phone rang and I picked it up, seeing it was Jamie. Part of me wanted to answer but I remembered what my dad and grandma said. I was going to stay away from him for the time being. I wanted to call my mama and see what she had to say. Then, I replayed the moment when she told me that me being born was a problem for her. I decided to leave her alone for the time being too. I was just hoping all this shit would just go away.

***

"Aye lil homie, you trying to take daddy's girl?" Kenyatta asked his son while he laid on my chest.

This was my first time being around him overnight and I was in love. K.J was the cutest baby boy I had ever seen. I could survive off of his chubby cheeks. He had this curly fro that was so full and jet black. I knew he got his good hair from Kenyatta and Lonell because Cleo had some nappy shit. Not even hating but she did and K.J looked just like his sexy ass daddy.

"Leave him alone Kenyatta before you wake him up," I whispered as I mushed Kenyatta's head away.

K.J had been on me since I came from my grandma's house. Cleo knew Kenyatta and I were back together and been on some other shit lately. He had to go over there and almost kill her ass in order to get his son. Shit made no sense.

"Baby, just lay him down in his room. He's out for the night, I need time with you. You and him been booed up all damn day."

I cracked up because this full-grown man was dead serious jealous of a baby.

I shook my head at him laughing as I got up and walked K.J to his room. He was knocked out on my chest and I didn't want to move him but his daddy was being a blocker.

Laying him down, I kissed him on the cheek and so did Kenyatta. His night light was on and so was his baby monitor even though his room was next to ours.

"He is so precious, Kenyatta. You're truly blessed," I said as we both walked in the bedroom.

"Thanks, baby. That little boy is my heart," I smiled when he said that as I put my big hair in a ponytail.

Kenyatta walked up on me and pulled me to him.

"You're my heart too, Erin. You and my son mean everything to me."

The amount of butterflies in my stomach that came as Kenyatta spoke was crazy. I got nervous and had to look away.

"Stop playing and look at me, Erin," he demanded, and I did what he said.

His face was perfection and so handsome. That top lip with that dip in the center was calling me.

"I mean what the fuck I'm saying. You and K.J are my fucking world, on some real shit. I know I acted a whole bitch to you on that weak tip. I can't apologize to you enough baby, but I will do it every fucking chance I get," he pulled me closer and kissed me hard as hell.

This kiss was taking my damn soul. He pushed me against his tall dresser and was swallowing my face. I was loving every second of it and didn't want it to end. His tongue felt so good swirling with mine. Pretty soon, I was moaning with this kiss and my body was lighting up. I needed to chill out because I had not planned on giving Kenyatta some pussy.

"What's wrong?" he asked me as both of our breathing was rapid.

His sexy ass lips were wet from my tongue.

"Nothing, I just don't want to start anything we can't finish," I said as I tried to walk around him but those sexy arms were blocking me.

"I can finish whatever the fuck we start, Erin. I swear my balls turning red, fuck blue. You killing me, cutie pie. I need some of you so fucking bad. This shit is beyond words."

His hands were on my back and he was squeezing my ass. I swear I was about to break but I just couldn't.

"I'm still not going there with you Kenyatta so tame that hard dick," I laughed and pointed to his erection.

"Plus, K.J is here and that's not what's up."

I pecked his lips again.

He blew out a long breath, but he nodded his head and agreed. Shit, I wasn't lying. My pussy was crying out so loud. We showered together after I made all three of us some dinner. K.J was in his playpen watching Wonder Pets while me and Kenyatta showered.

"You can lay down with me and watch Netflix though," I smiled at him as I climbed in his big ass comfortable bed.

"Shut'cho ass up talking to me like I'm a kid. I want some of my pussy but I'm gone chill because my son in the next room. I want you hollering and waking the dead all the way from the twenty-second floor," he laughed as he passed me the remote.

I laughed at his silly ass as well.

My phone started chiming, alerting me that I had a text message.

"It's past ten o'clock, who is that?" Kenyatta asked me as soon as I picked it up.

He was all in my space.

"Tha fuck he hittin' you up this late talking about 'what up doe'?"

He got mad as hell as we looked at Hayden's text.

"Baby, I don't know. I haven't talked to him since our da— um movie we went to go see."

I was happy as fuck that I caught myself before I said date. I thought Kenyatta didn't catch it but I was wrong.

"Naw, gone and say that shit since that stupid ass date y'all went on. I swear to God I'm fucking that nigga up on sight."

I put my phone back on the nightstand and turned to face him. He was heated so I grabbed his face and made him look at me.

"I haven't talked to him baby, I promise. Hayden is harmless and just spoiled, but I don't want him. I'm yours, Kenyatta, ok?" I looked in his eyes and said.

He licked his lips at me.

God, why did you make him so fine?

"Tell me your mine again and say my name," his low sexy voice was deep and turning me on.

Hell, I stayed turned on being around him.

"I'm yours Kenyatta and no one else's."

He did that rough shit I loved and put his hand around my neck shoving his tongue in my mouth. I didn't know how the fuck I was able to hold out this long from having sex with him. Then, I replayed how he treated me and I got some strength. All was forgiven on my end. It was just a matter of when I was going to have sex with him again.

"Who you belong to, cutie pie?" he whispered in my ear while biting and licking on it.

I was shuttering because it felt so good.

"You, I belong to you," I was able to get out but just barely as his touch was setting me just right.

"Who the hell is 'you', Erin? Say my fuckin' name!"

Fuck, it felt like I squirted all on his walls when he said that. He had such force and almost a growl in his voice when he said it.

"Sssss Kenyatta," I was so wrapped up in how good he was making me feel.

I didn't even notice his crazy ass had my legs pushed back and was face down in my pussy. I had on a thong and one of his long beaters on. I loved when he held my legs back and ate me out on his knees.

The more I moaned and called his name, the more his nails dug deeper in my thighs. He went to work with the more I cried out and came.

"I love you so fucking much, Kenyatta. Ughhhh."

I came hard in his mouth.

I sat my head up and looked down at him. His nasty ass had his mouth open, letting my juices fall back on my pussy. He dived right back in and went for what he knew. I was going to thank God every chance I got for this man. Oh my goodness, no fucking body will ever make me feel this damn good. He licked my ass crack and back to my pussy, eating and licking my fucking spirit clean of all sins.

"Jeez Kenyatta, what the fuck? Mmmhmmm," I came again and my heart was about to pound out my chest.

I was trying to break free from his grip on my thighs, but he wasn't having it.

"Hell naw, I ain't done, cutie pie. Cum one more time for me."

Before I could protest, he dived back in my pussy. With the way he worked his tongue and his fingers, I was gushing juices in no time.

I soaked up his bed and we ended up back in the shower where he ate my pussy good as fuck in there, too. Kenyatta changed his sheets and now we were laying back down watching Bright on Netflix.

"Can I ask you something?" I was laying on Kenyatta's chest and a thought popped in my head.

"Anything, baby."

"Does my dad have anything to do with Lonell getting out of jail so soon?" I looked up at him and asked.

"No, he doesn't. My uncle didn't want him in the middle of his bullshit. Why do you ask?"

He then looked down at me.

"Because my dad was weird about me talking to Jamie. He kind of flipped out about me staying away from him."

I watched Kenyatta's jaw muscles tense up.

"Baby, I promise I am not telling him anything. I did, however, want to confront him on using me. He owes me an explanation."

Kenyatta turned his nose up at me.

"Erin, that bitch nigga doesn't owe you shit. He was raised to fucking hate you and all this shit will unravel itself. Meanwhile, I do think you should stay the fuck away from Norbit."

I couldn't help but laugh at his annoying ass.

"What the hell is wrong with you calling him Norbit?!"

I rolled over laughing and he had to laugh too.

"That nigga is Norbit wit' his big gums havin' ass! Get back over here baby," he pulled me back on him.

"I'm for real though, Erin. Leave that nigga alone for a while, cutie pie. If something happens to you, I swear on God I'm losing it. Kiss me."

I did what he said and kissed his sexy ass lips.

"You know you giving me more kids, right?"

I almost snapped my neck as I looked at him so fast.

"Girl, you better fix that pretty ass face. Act like you know what the fuck going on. I'm marrying you and you gone give me two beautiful little girls."

I started laughing and shaking my head.

"Kenyatta, you are moving fast as hell. How do you know they will be girls? But most importantly, how the hell do you know I'll marry you?" I arched my eyebrow and asked him.

I was fucking with him, but I still wanted to see what he was going to say.

"Do you wanna die?"

"WHAT?!"

I didn't even mean to yell and I was happy K.J didn't wake up. What the hell was wrong with his daddy?!

"I know them sexy ass ears ain't deaf."

He was calm as hell looking down at me.

I sat up on my knees next to him while holding my hand up.

"Wait a fucking minute, if I don't marry you I have to die?" I asked him smiling, but I was so serious.

"Yup, on God you will be meeting him and all the glory he has to give. You're fucking mine, Erin Khila Hudges. Forever and beyond death, you will always be mine. Nobody else will carry my last name or give me kids but you."

I sat there and looked at him in his crazy ass eyes.

Kenyatta was really nuts and if I never believed it then I believe it now.

"Come back and lay on me before I start missing you and get mad."

I swear I had so much to say but like a magnetic pull, I went to him. Who the fuck was I kidding? I loved his crazy ass.

"So, like I said you know you giving me more kids, right?" he asked, smirking down at me.

I looked at him and smirked back.

"That crazy shit doesn't scare me, baby. I'll think about giving you more kids just like I'll think about marrying you."

He laughed and said, "Ok, I'll marry somebody else then. Ain't no thang."

I got mad as hell when he said that. I used his move. I put my hands around his neck and climbed on top of him. My ass thought I was really doing something, but Kenyatta started biting his bottom lip and getting hard as hell under me.

"Mmhm now, look who's crazy. Stop talking all that bullshit actin' hard. Kiss yo' nigga."

I leaned forward and shoved my tongue in his mouth.

"Don't play with me like that, Kenyatta."

In the middle of my sentence, he flipped me over on my back with him on top.

"You don't fucking play with me like that either!"

We both looked at each other with a smirk and went back to making out.

⁂

***

"Girl, fuck Yatta. Don't be feeling bad because his dick begging for mercy!" Dreka's crazy ass said all loud as if we were not in the nail shop.

Me, her and Cassidy were getting our feet and eyebrows done. Cassidy usually always hooked us up on the nails and feet but sometimes we like to just go to the shop and be pampered.

"Bitch, would you lower your voice and act like we in public?" Cassidy nudged Dreka in her arm with her elbow.

"Ming know I'm speaking the truth. Yatta showed his entire ass including his asshole on my cousin. Now, his ass wanna hit her with the 'puss in boots' eyes and expect her to fall in line. Naw, keep that nigga waiting until you fucking done torturing his yellow ass. That's why I only do chocolate niggas. They behave themselves."

Me and Cassidy were cracking up at her goofy ass.

"Wait a minute, bitch! Pernell was as light skin as they come. Hell, his damn mama was white but yet and still he had yo' head in the clouds for nine months," I teased.

She had the nerve to catch an attitude.

"Damn Dreka, she got'cho ass with that one," Cassidy chimed in, laughing.

I was cracking up because my cousin was pissed.

"How long y'all sluts gone live in the past? We talking about current shit, bitches and currently who got my walls broken down is my big chocolate Mir-Mir," her high cheekbones were touching her eyes as she smiled big as hell.

"Ugh! Hell no, that's my cue to go pick my color out. I ain't trying to hear shit about my brother and breaking yo' walls down."

Cassidy got up and went to the wall where all the color acrylics were at.

"Naw, don't run hoe," Dreka started calling out to her while laughing.

I swear I loved these girls to death.

We were at our usual nail shop in Westland because Greenfield Village was too crowded today.

"Seriously though boo, don't feel bad about leaving Yatta thirsty. Like you said, you're not going to stay not fucking him. He did you wrong and at the end of the day, that's your damn pussy. You'll pop it for him again," she laughed and said just as Cassidy walked back over.

She was holding her color.

"I want to know how it was being on stepmama duties?" Cassidy asked as she got back in the pedicure chair.

"It was really good. I honestly enjoyed myself with K.J. He loved me and was all over me which annoyed Kenyatta. He is so sweet and so damn cute. When I left, I heard him crying. It took everything in me not to go back," I smiled and poked my lip out while thinking about baby K.J's cute self.

That little boy stole my heart right along with his daddy.

"That shit clutch, boo. I knew you would do good. What about you, boo? How had Alaric been with his bitch ass daddy and all?" Dreka turned to Cassidy and asked.

"He's ok, but he told me he was going to meet with German. I'm so worried about him and this bullshit with his dad. Ric told me not to worry but I can't help it. On a good note, he asked if we could live together," Cassidy's pretty face beamed when she said that.

Dreka and I smiled and told her we were happy for her. I loved Alaric and Cassidy together and was happy he got his shit together.

"What about your cousin? Has Tia fell the fuck back?" I rolled my eyes at the thought of that rat bitch.

"Girl, this hoe is doing the most from her hiding spot. She tagged me in more ultrasound pictures, baby names and baby shower decorations. All this gender reveal shit and labor videos. Zamir keeps telling me to block her, but I don't want to. I'm hoping she slips and reveals where she is, so I can fuck that hoe up. I don't think she is pregnant, but y'all these ultrasound pictures and doctors' appointments she keeps posting is fucking with me. What if she is carrying Zamir's baby? I can't handle dealing with her ass as his baby mama," Dreka shook her head as she talked.

"Cousin, she is not fucking pregnant by him. Even Kenyatta said her and Cleo were lying. She is just trying to get under your skin, boo. Don't let that bitch keep you from being happy with Z," I held her hand and smiled at her.

"Erin's right, boo. Plus, my brother will snap fucking legs in pieces if he can't be with you. Please spare us all Z's wrath," Cassidy said, making us laugh.

"Well listen, to take our minds off shit Wayne State is having a foam party at Elektricity in Pontiac next Saturday. We should go, have drinks and just have some good ass fun. Ladies night in full effect," I said as I pulled the flyer out my BEBE bookbag.

"Hell yea, I am so down!" Dreka and Cassidy both agreed and started getting geeked.

It had been a while since we partied and we were overdue. Tonight was Lowell's birthday party, but we were going to be too busy with our guys to really party. This foam party was just me and my boos; we were going to have a ball.

"Damn even in another city we still can't escape Detroit rats."

Cassidy, Dreka and I walked right into Cleo, her two sisters, and some gay nigga/bitch they were with.

"Cleo, you and your mutt crew need to get the fuck out the way. Bitter ass bitch," Dreka said, laughing.

"Well shit, let me make extra room for yo' fat ass," the ugly nigga/bitch said. The mutt crew started laughing.

"Is you mad or naw? You hangin' with these dusty bitches is the reason why you can't master the art of being a real woman. Ya adams apple poking out more than ya dick through that cheap ass Rainbow dress," Cassidy and I fell out when Dreka said that.

Even Cleo's sisters tried to hide their laughs.

"I know I personally feel like if you're an ugly nigga and an ugly bitch! Yo' ass should just stop and call ya'self a person. You just don't identify as shit!" I threw my two cents in there, making us laugh harder.

"Bitch, you need to shut the fuck up talkin' shit! You tryna steal my fucking man and baby, you want my life real bad, don't you?!"

When Cleo said that, I got all in her personal space.

"What life would that be, Cleo? I own Kenyatta, that nigga comes to me quicker than Jimmy Johns. Pretty soon, I'll own K.J too. I bet I'll be a better mother to him then you are."

As soon as I said that she tried to jump stupid, but I stood right there. I was ready.

The nigga/bitch grabbed her with his fat ass and pulled her back.

"Naw best friend, you are not about to fight and I just did your lace front. These bitches just trying to make you mad. Fuck they plain asses."

"Bitch, we got more flava than the ice cream truck. Fuck outta here! Just remember what the fuck I said, hoe!" I yelled as Cassidy and Dreka were pulling me to the car.

"Damn cousin, you read that bitch her rights and then some. I almost cried for her ass."

We were in my car getting on the freeway.

"I swear I cannot fucking stand that girl! All I need is five fucking minutes with that trick!"

I drove, heated as hell.

"I was hoping Tia was with her because I was ready. That hoe really is hiding out," Dreka said while finding some music to listen to.

"I was right there with you on that. Baby or not, she was going to get fucked up," Cassidy said from the back.

I agreed as we drove to get something to eat and then go home and chill before Lonell's party tonight.

Yatta

"Alright, let's get down to the shits. Alaric, you first nigga," Lonell pointed at Alaric and gave him the floor to talk.

My uncle had been home for about three hours now and we were all happy as hell. Being the nigga he was, it took him no time to get all of us together in his basement so we could talk.

"So, German's connect is in Traverse City and I know German's boys make a delivery to him every few months. That time is coming up soon. If I meet with him, I know for sure he will put me on. We can steal the money and drugs and keep that shit. Meanwhile, I want to hit that nigga deeper in his punk ass gut. Me and Emmanuel were able to come up with some shit."

He looked over at Emmanuel and gave him the floor.

"I take y'all three niggas on like family. The shit that nigga German did not only fucked with me as a man but as a father who has a daughter. If he was to do some shit like that to mine, I would have killed that nigga and everyone he knew."

My jaw tightened at the thought of someone doing some shit like that to Erin.

"When Alaric told me what he wanted to do I was down without question. My brother was, too," he looked over at Delon who nodded his head.

Hell, I was ready to know what the hell was going down.

"Everybody in here has shortened a life, am I right?" Emmanuel asked.

Z, Alaric, my uncle and Delon and I all answered yes.

"Good, this shit will end in bloodshed. Alaric came to me and asked me to get German's ex-wife. Me and Delon went to get her while I handled my baby mama. Speaking of that hoe, I got her too. Lonell, you ain't gotta worry about those charges. Shit is taken care of, but for some reason y'all are still being investigated. I have to move carefully because the streets know we boys. But I will get to the bottom of what's going on. It may be someone inside y'all operation helping the police out. Or it could be shit that my fat ass baby mama's husband cooked up. I will find out though," Emmanuel gave us a fucking ear full.

I looked at my uncle and he looked pissed.

"It's Havoc. I know it is, that nigga been on some other shit lately. I don't know why but it doesn't fucking matter. He's as good as dead. That's why I told him our meeting today was later then I told y'all. When he comes, we gone do small talk only to make him think shit still good."

We nodded our heads. I was so ready to make niggas bleed. You could be friends with a nigga for years, but a rat nigga was always going to reveal himself. Shit was sickening.

"Wait a minute, Lonell. If that nigga Havoc is working with the police, then trust me when I say he will have protection. Hold off on killing him or confronting his ass. I know the shit will be hard but y'all gone have to still treat that nigga the same. If he is the rat, then he probably snitched about me and Delon being down with y'all too," Emmanuel said and my nostrils flared.

Havoc was a true hoe.

"I did a sweep of all our cribs and cars for any hidden recorders or cameras. Everything came up clean," Alaric said and I was shocked.

I had no idea he was on his shit like that with all of this. I was happy my homie had our backs though.

"One more thing, my baby mama's son, Jamie. He doesn't know his mama is missing or that his bitch ass pops is dead. I gotta find that nigga, but he's hiding," Emmanuel looked at us and said.

"What if we ask Erin to meet up with him? We could follow her and set his ass up," Lonell suggested.

"HELL NO!" Emmanuel and I said in unison.

We looked at each other and he smirked at me and nodded his head at me.

"We are not involving Erin. My daughter is not being involved in this shit. It's bad enough her mama tried some sneaky shit with having her son set up Erin. Plus, she doesn't know this side of my life and I want to keep it like that."

I agreed with that shit.

"I agree. Find another fucking way that don't include her. Y'all keep saying I pop off easily. I will pop off like a corkscrew if some shit happens to Erin."

I meant that with everything in me. I swear I would kill everybody in this room and then serve my time after I kill everybody else who had something to do with this shit.

"That nigga ain't street smart at all so that tells us he will slip up and show his face," I added.

"So, when we doing this shit with German?" Z asked and we all knew he was just as eager to get that punk ass nigga just like all of us.

"I will let y'all know the day of the drop. I'm fixing the street cameras to keep y'all off the radar. Trust me, when German sees his shit stolen he will want me to hack all kinds of shit so he can see who did it. His connect will get his money and guns but not from German. He will get it from us. Me and Emmanuel already got that part on lock and it includes more money for us. When I call y'all and give the day we can meet back up and set everything up. It will only be German's same three guards that does the drop," Alaric told us.

"Z, Alaric, and Emmanuel will stay behind and handle German. Me, you and Lonell will steal the product and take it to Traverse City," Delon said.

The shit sounded good as hell from where I was standing.

"All right now we got about fifteen minutes until Havoc's bitch ass shows up. Remember, play nice and small talk. Make that nigga feel like shit smooth," my uncle said and everybody looked at my ass.

"Fuck y'all, man. I said I'm good," I waved them off and pulled my phone out.

I needed to text my girl to put me in a nice mood. I wasn't used to fake frontin' for no damn body but I knew our freedom was on the line, so just this once I was going to play nice.

"Let me holla at you real quick," Emmanuel stood over me and said.

I put my phone back in my pocket, stood up and followed him to my uncle's laundry room.

"Look, I know my daughter and trust me when I say she will try to meet up with that punk ass brother of hers. Help me keep eyes on her even if you have to follow her little ass. Erin's heart is good as hell and if Jamie makes her feel sorry for him she will want to hear his side and try to give him another chance. Looking at you, I can tell you love her, so I'm trusting you with this. Call me if some shit pops off no matter the time or day."

"I got you Pops," I laughed at his face when I said that.

"Don't call me that shit nigga," he said and I laughed harder.

Whether he was with it or not, I was marrying his daughter.

***

"Why the fuck you standing in the door lookin' like yo' pussy stank?" I turned my nose up at Cleo and her ugly ass facial expression.

I had K.J in my arms. I was dropping him off from being with me. My auntie had him while we were in the basement of my uncle's house having our meeting.

"Because you really playing house with yo' girl and our fucking baby."

I smacked my lips at her stupid ass as I walked in her apartment. K.J was asleep, but he had food all over him from eating some ice cream. I walked in his room so I could strip him and clean him up.

"Man, if you don't get the fuck out of my face with that bitter bullshit. This is my son, and Erin is my woman, so of course they would be together."

I didn't even know why I explained but since I had to play nice with Havoc I figured why not try to play nice with Cleo's ass, too.

"Yatta, we made K.J together, not you and her. You have never even given me a fair chance to be your woman. Don't you want him to have a two-parent home?"

I took a deep breath as she spoke because it was the same shit. I looked down at my chubby baby boy in just his diaper. My heart smiled. He was still knocked out as I went into his half bathroom and soaped up his rag. I came back out and wiped him down. I went back in the bathroom and rinsed his rag and hung it up.

"You don't hear me Yatta?"

Before I went back to attend to my son, I walked up on Cleo. She jumped, but I remained calm as I talked.

"That baby that we made together means everything to me. That's my mini-me down from his looks, his hair and his funny face expressions he gives when he is awake," I rubbed the side of her face as I kept talking.

"One of the best things I could do for him is to make someone so beautiful inside and out a permanent part of his life. That's where Erin comes in at," I smiled at her dumb ass.

She gave me an evil look and stomped away.

I laughed and went right back to putting my son's pajamas on. He stayed asleep the entire time. I kissed his chubby cheeks, told him I loved him and turned his light off in his room.

"Yatta," I dropped my head at Cleo calling my name.

I was almost out her fucking door, but she had to start some more bullshit.

"What, Cleo?" I turned around and she was in the middle of her living room with her robe on.

It was open. She was ass naked under it, showing me all her body. I was a nigga first and I would be lying if I said Cleo didn't have a nice body.

"Come on man, chill the fuck out girl. All I'm trying to do is co-parent with you, Cleo."

She licked her lips and walked up on me. I was standing in front of her front door and I should have just turned the knob and dipped out like I planned to. But shit, I haven't had any pussy in so damn long. I couldn't front like I wasn't enjoying having a naked girl on me ready for me to fuck her silly.

"Look how hard you are, Yatta. Please, just fuck me one good time and I swear I'll behave. It will be our secret. I'll even tell you where Tia is if you just give me the dick one good time."

Cleo was grabbing my dick through my sweatpants. As soon as she did that, my shit got soft.

"Why the fuck is you getting soft?" she looked down and then back up at me.

She was mad as hell.

"This ain't my dick no more, Ma. Erin owns this muthafucka," I started cracking up at her stupid ass.

"And you a desperate ass bitch to give your best friend up for some dick. Your body nice and all, but naw, I'll pass."

She smacked her lips and shook her head at me.

"I love you Yatta so fucking much! Why don't you see that?! I swear to God, you really fucking pushing me to do some off the wall shit."

I stopped laughing and got serious as hell. I walked up on her.

"I don't take lightly to threats, Cleo. You know that shit, so chill the fuck out. I do not want you and never will. Get the fuck over it with'cho stupid bitch ass. Be a mother to our son and that's all. For once in your empty ass life just do that right," I blew my breath in her face.

"You smell that sweet ass smell? That's Erin's pussy, that scent is infused in me, Ma. Find you another nigga because that fucking girl owns my ass. I'll hit you up in a few days to pick K.J up."

I turned around and walked out her house leaving her with tears rolling down her face.

Oh well.

**

Doing 80 in a 60 fuck a ticket

'Cause I ain't had that pussy in a minute (In a minute)
I told her when I get it I'mma hit it I'ma hit it
She told me that she want I'll be there when I'm finished
Ooh, girl, I'm on the way (Aye)
I just left the club and I'm bout to make a play, I'm on the
way (Way)
She told me that she cooking I said gon' and make a plate
I'm on the way aye ya ya ya
I'm on the way aye ya ya ya
I'm on the way aye ya ya ya
I'm on the way aye ya ya ya
Ooh, girl, I'm on the way

DJ Luke's "Nasty OTW" was playing through the club while everyone turned up. I had my arms around Erin's thick waist while I was rapping the lyrics in her ear.

Her pretty ass was laughing and blushing at me. This song fit us perfectly because I ain't had that pussy in a minute and the shit was fucking me up!

The club was decked out in white and black lighting. There were white and black balloons everywhere and a big ass banner with my uncle's face on it. It read Happy 42nd birthday Lonell and he had a six-tier red-velvet cake. I was happy all the black folks followed instructions and wore all black. My uncle and Auntie Juziel were the only people who had on all white. Erin and I looked bomb as fuck.

I had on black Gucci jeans with the matching shirt with the Gucci logo all over it. My chain was iced out along with my diamond studs and platinum custom Cartier watch. Dreka hooked my dreads up and I had them all down with my black fitted. My feet had on some crispy black and metallic gold LeBron's like I always rocked.

Erin looked so fucking good in this mini fitted dress that was ripped up all in the back. She had these tight ass thigh heel boots on and I swear I wanted to fuck her in front of her father. Her hair was big and curly all down her back. She was wearing her diamond Pandora bracelet and earrings that I got her. Erin was killing the game.

"Will you please behave and act like my daddy is in the same club with us?" she whispered in my ear.

Her sweet Bvlgari perfume was wrapped around my nose, making me kiss her neck.

"I'm your fucking daddy Erin, and plus he dipped out with one of the dancers."

Erin made a sour face and shook her head.

I looked around and my niggas were smoking and chilling with their girls, too. Even my uncle was caked up with his wife and one of the strippers she hired. Yea, sometimes they got down like that.

I took another sip of my Remy VSOP while my other hand was on Erin's ass. She turned and kissed my lips, teasing me more.

"You coming home with me tonight?" I looked at her and asked.

I was high and drunk but even still her beauty was speaking volumes even in low lights, loud music and a room full of people.

"Of course, baby," her sexy ass whispered in my ear. GoldLink Crew song came on and Erin started winding her hips to the beat. Her round ass booty was grinding all on my dick. Between her, the weed and liquor my ass was ready to nut all in my jeans.

"Aye, do y'all wanna break it up so we can sing happy birthday to my husband?" my auntie yelled over the music at us.

Shit, I couldn't let Erin move because my dick was hard as fuck and ready to celebrate with everybody. Erin knew, too, because she was cracking up as we walked to the center of the dance floor. We sung to my uncle and my auntie and I said some nice words to him over the microphone. He showed love to everyone for coming and then he cut his cake.

"Damn nigga, you can't feed yourself?" I teased Alaric as Cassidy fed him some cake.

"Fuck you, shit talking nigga! Erin rubbin' yo' head like you a damn puppy!"

We all cracked up and I looked over at Erin. My arm was around her waist and she was playing in my dreads and kissing my neck. I didn't give a fuck who was around. The shit felt good to be loved on. Shit, even Dreka was sitting on Z's lap loving on him.

"Let's go dance," Cassidy pulled Erin and Dreka up.

I watched Erin's ass move in the dress she had on. I tried not to look too hard because I knew she wasn't giving me any tonight. Shit was killing me not being able to feel her insides.

"Snap out of it, bitch!" Z's big ass snapped his extra-large fingers in my face.

"Why the fuck y'all always playing?" I turned my nose up and lit my blunt while theie ugly asses laughed.

"You told Erin about D.C.?" Alaric asked me.

"Naw, I'll let her know tonight though. I did tell her a few weeks back what we do though," I looked at Z and Alaric. I had no idea if they told Dreka or Cassidy yet.

"I want to tell Dreka what's up so that don't do shit but motivate me to quit being a bitch and just tell her," Z said and Alaric agreed.

I told them how I told her and what her reaction was. I also told them I didn't tell her about her father or uncle being down with us.

We partied some more and I looked on the dance floor to get eyes on my girl. I swear I was about to flip when I saw Hayden in her fucking face.

"Nephew!" I heard my uncle call me, but I ignored him and everyone around me.

I was sick of this bitch ass nigga.

"KENYATTA!" Erin yelled my name when I spun Hayden around and hit his ass with a closed fist in his jaw.

To be fair, he had had warning after warning about being on what was mine. He fell on the floor and I hit his ass again and then stomped on his left hand hard as fuck.

"AH!" he yelled in pain.

"Stay the fuck away from mine, nigga! I told yo' ass over and over!"

My uncle and Z pulled me back while Hayden was helped up by security. Lonell talked to them for a minute as Erin walked in my face.

"Kenyatta, are you out of your fucking mind?! You didn't have to do that to him. I was getting him out of my face on my own," she said in my ear.

I took a shot and shook my head.

"Well, I saved you the trouble of doing it myself. No fucking nigga is about to be all up in my bitch's face. You mine Erin, get that shit through ya head, cutie pie."

I pulled her on my lap and told her to dance on me.

Shit went back to normal and everybody went back to partying. Erin's soft ass booty felt so good grinding on me.

I let my head fall back as the weed and liquor mixed with the music and my girl made me feel good. I must have been in a trance because I swear I didn't see Cleo run up and push Erin to the ground.

"YOU STUPID BITCH!" Cleo, her two sisters, and Tia came out of nowhere too and tried to jump Erin.

Dreka and Cassidy were on them like a fly to dog shit. I swear Dreka was beating the breaks off Tia. What really got me was Cleo holding a fucking Remy bottle in her hand and she raised that muthafucka in the air.

I lost it and hit Cleo so hard in her face that I felt and heard her nose crack against my knuckles.

"HOE, IS YOU FUCKING CRAZY!" I yelled at Cleo as the Remy bottle hit the floor and broke.

I immediately went to Erin and helped her up. As soon as she was on her feet, her ass jumped from in front of me and tagged the hell out of Tia. She was beating her ass. Tia was screaming and had the nerve to call out to me.

I went and pulled my girl off that rat bitch.

"SCARY ASS BITCH! You gone try to sneak one in on me?!" Erin yelled while I had her in my arms.

I couldn't believe this shit was going down. black folks always had to start some shit.

"I GOT HIS FUCKING BABY BITCH, NOT YOU!" Cleo's stupid ass yelled.

I carried Erin over my shoulder and out the door. I would just text my uncle and niggas later to make sure shit was smooth.

"I swear to God, I'm fucking that bitch up the next time I see her! I tried to be cool because of K.J, but hell no! She fucking snuck me!"

I was on the freeway on the way to my apartment. Erin was pissed off and so was I.

"Baby, don't worry about me and K.J. I'll always see my son, no matter what. I'm pissed off because that bitch had a bottle ready to use it on you. She could have----" I got more heated as I thought about what the fuck would have happened to Erin had Cleo used that Remy bottle on her.

"Thank you, baby. I know she is your son's mother and I don't enjoy watching you do that to her. But still, thank you for having my back."

I pulled into my parking space and turned my truck off. I helped Erin out and grabbed her hand as we walked in my apartment complex. Getting on the elevator I hit the top floor. I grabbed Erin up and put her back against the wall.

"I will always have your back, baby. I don't give a fuck if it's a nigga or a bitch. Anybody who fucks with you I'm fucking up. Give me a kiss."

She put them pretty ass lips on me. I heard the elevator doors open but me nor Erin could stop kissing.

"Do you think you two can show some respect?" I pulled away and saw an old white couple step on the elevator.

Erin covered her face and I laughed.

"Lighten up, old homie. I know you used to fuck the shit outta the slaves you owned while she was asleep."

Erin hit my arm as the elevator door opened and she pulled me off.

I was cracking my drunk ass up as the old couple's mouths fell on the floor.

"You know you miss that black pussy!" I yelled before the elevator doors closed.

"My goodness, Yatta! You're a nut job, did you see those poor people's faces?!" Erin laughed as I unlocked my apartment door and we walked in.

"What the fuck did you just call me?" I locked the door and scooped her ass up.

"Stop playing Kenyatta before you drop me," Erin was laughing as I walked us to the bathroom.

We shared a hot shower and washed each other up. Erin's body was so fucking hot when soaked with water. Her hair was pressed on her back and her long ass eyelashes looked longer and brought her eyes out more.

After we showered, dried off and put pajamas on, we went to the kitchen to pig the fuck out. Erin smoked too so I know she had the munchies just like I did. We killed that chicken potpie she cooked last night. I opened some barbeque Lays potato chips and we drunk some A&W root beer.

Now, we were in my big ass bed laughing at Living Single that Erin recorded on my DVR.

"Which one did you used to have a crush on? I know you liked one of them," Erin looked at me when she asked.

She was smiling.

"Max's chocolate ass was my boo. I loved how hard she was because all she needed was some dick," Erin laughed and shook her head.

"I used to have a crush on DeWayne Wayne from A Different World."

I cracked up when she said that.

"That skinny ass nerd! Oh, I get why you had a thang for him. You were a little Whitley when we were in high school."

She smacked her lips and hit me.

"You know I was not stuck up. I was the same as I am now, ugly. You were too just busy chasing rats to notice me," she laughed and I got serious.

I wasn't mad or anything. I just wanted to be for real on my next statement.

"Erin, I always noticed you, baby. Even when you didn't think anyone was paying you any attention. I always was looking at you and that's real shit. Especially when you were drawing or painting. I used to watch you so hard Z and Alaric would talk shit about me."

She chuckled and looked away. Anytime she did that I knew she was getting butterflies and all nervous.

I grabbed her chin and made her look at me. I examined her beautiful face and all its features.

"Eyes on me, cutie pie."

When I said that, I could feel Erin's breathing change. Shit, we were only twenty-one. That wasn't shit as far as living and experiencing life, but this feeling right here was some shit I knew I would never feel with any other person on earth besides Erin. She felt the same because her eyes stayed on mine as she brought her lips to mine.

"Fuck me, Kenyatta, I want you to fuck me so good."

When she said that I fucking swear on the life of my child that my dick jumped hard as fuck. The words that left Cleo's mouth earlier made my dick run and hide. Now, hearing it from Erin had him locked and loaded.

Before we got back to it, I grabbed my Comcast remote and went to the Pandora app. I keyed in 112 radio and let it play. Usher and Lil Jon's "Lovers & Friends" came on which was funny, but I didn't give a damn. My baby was finally giving me some pussy. I was happy as fuck!

I went right to work and pulled my beater over Erin's head. Kissing her, I climbed between her legs while she was on her back. I attacked that neck and put my name all on it. I wanted everybody to know Erin was mine. That was even bitches who liked pussy, she was fucking mine.

Her nails and soft hands were all over my back. I got to them sexy ass C-cup titties and licked all on her nipples. They got hard as fuck as Erin's body was grinding under mine. I put hickeys all over them too. Cutie pie was going to look like a fucking leopard in the morning.

I shoved my tongue in her mouth while I pulled my boxers off. I was going to eat that pussy good later. Right now, I needed to be inside of her.

"Ugh baby, your so damn big," she moaned in my ear and I smirked in her neck.

"See what happens when you keep me away from my pussy. Now I got to train her all over again."

Erin's legs were wrapped tight around my waist. I kissed her deep and used my left hand and unwrapped them.

"You gotta open them legs baby and let me in. I promise it will stop hurting, Daddy got you. Shit Erin, yo' pussy is holding my dick tight," I leaned down and kissed her chin and then her lips again.

I could tell the pain stopped because she started moaning out in pleasure.

"God Kenyatta, mmm. Keep fucking me like this," she closed her eyes and leaned her head all the way back.

"Eyes on me, cutie pie. I need to see you look at me while you cum," I smirked because she tried her best to look at me while I fucked her, but she kept looking away.

"You own me, Erin. Ugh fuck. You know that baby, you won my ass," I looked at her and said.

Her pussy was so wet that it was talking out loud while I kept fucking her.

"Ahh. You own me too, baby. Arghhh, you own all of meee."

She came everywhere and I didn't ease up on my strokes. I was still hard as fuck and I wanted her to keep cummin'.

I kissed her as I eased out her pussy.

She moaned in my mouth when my thick ten-inch slid all the way out.

"Get'cho ass on top and ride yo' dick, baby. He misses you so fucking much," I said to her pretty ass.

She bit her lip and did what I said. Her warm wet thighs felt so good on my skin. I may have sounded like a bitch but I didn't give a fuck. This was the longest I had been without pussy and I did a year in jail. Then I couldn't even cheat if I wanted to. My dick only worked for her.

I watched Erin grab my dick and slide down slowly on it.

"Sssss," we both moaned out loud in unison.

Her pussy felt so fucking good. It was wet, warm and tight as hell. And it was all fucking mine.

Erin leaned forward and started bouncing slowly up and down. I felt like I was about to lose my mind because the shit felt that damn good.

"Shit Erin, work that pussy baby."

She was on my neck putting a hickey on my shit. I guess it was payback for me marking her up. I didn't give a fuck though, we would just be walking around all spotted out.

She started bouncing a little faster as she sat up and gave me a view of them sexy ass titties. When Erin put both her hands flat on my chest I felt like she was giving me CPR. Yes, save me bitch! Is what I wanted to yell out because she was riding me better than any bitch I ever fucked.

"Goodness Kenyatta. I'm about to cum baby."

"I'm wit'chu girl. UGH!" Shit, I felt like I was never going to stop nuttin' in Erin. This shit was so overdue I felt like I was about to meet Jesus himself. I grabbed her neck and pulled her sweaty ass to me tonguing her down.

"You ain't never rode my dick before. How the hell did you know what you were doing?" I asked her with my hand still around her neck. She better say the right shit or I was fucking her up.

"Pornos. I watched them and just remembered what the women did. From the way you were moaning, I must have did a good job," she smiled and licked her soft lips.

"Oh, you got jokes. A'ight baby. Get'cho ass on all fours and we will see who doing what right," she climbed off me and said.

"Whatever you say, daddy," I bit my lip and smacked both of her sexy ass cheeks. I was about to lay some good ass dick on Erin. Some shit that was going to put a new definition on sex altogether. Fuck the morning, I wanna fuck her good into the afternoon.

Cleo

"Sweet creator of all Pokémon. Gosh, this feels delightful!" I rolled my eyes while I sucked this lame nigga's dick. He was so lame and such a geek in street clothing. You know one of those niggas who want to be 'hood' so bad but will throw a rock and run?! Those types of niggas were only good for one thing. Money! This nigga Jamie I been messing with for a few months now and it was paying off. He was spoiled, weak and my two favorite things. A lot of money and a virgin. I played him like I played with my pussy while I sucked his big dick. Damn shame because his dick was a solid nine-inches, thick as hell and cute as fuck. But I wasn't about to be this nigga's first taste of pussy. Naw, I was already locked down and I didn't need Jamie's crying ass stalking me.

"Oooh I'm coming Cleo," when he said that I stopped sucking and let him come all on my titties. I fed his ego while he shot his babies all on me.

"Uhhh yea big daddy. Squirt that warm cum all over me baby," God damn, this nigga came for hours it felt like. When I looked at him and his eyes were closed with tears coming down his face and he started shaking. It took everything in me not to laugh my ass off. Damn, I was good as fuck at what I do.

"Come do what I like daddy," I said in my low seductive voice. Jamie dropped to his knees and started licking his own cum off my titties. He was licking my shit clean to. I don't know what was wrong with this fool. But he was into that humiliation kinky shit. I didn't give a fuck though as long as I wasn't being humiliated I was down. After he was done cleaning me off we both got up and walked to my bathroom. I peeped in K.J's room and he was still laying on his back sleep.

"Thank you booskie," I smiled and kissed his cheek as he gave me six-hundred dollars. I was about to spend all of this on my Miami trip I had coming up with my sisters and Tia. Now that the hat was out the bag that she wasn't pregnant she could use a vacation.

"You're welcome, Cleo. Are you going to tell me what happened to your face?" Jamie looked at me and asked. I had a nose cast on from my goofy ass baby daddy showing his ass over his bitch. His uncle threw me, Tia and my sisters out the club and an Uber took us to the hospital. My nose was fractured and Tia had a black eye and needed stitches.

"I got into a fight with some girl yesterday. It's nothing," I said as I hung my body rag up. Jamie followed behind me to my kitchen. I wish he would just leave because I was expecting someone soon.

"You need to take your baby and move out this city. Just visit like I do, I could take care of you and K.J," I had my back to him as I stood in my refrigerator drinking a Powerade. I rolled my eyes and turned around with a fake smile on my face.

"Jamie me and my baby will be fine. Listen, I have to get ready for work, so I will call you later," I made up a lie as his phone rung. I saw it said a name that caught my attention but I knew it couldn't be who I was thinking about.

"Who is Erin?" I asked like I was jealous but in no way shape or form was I.

"My half-ass ghetto sister. I have to act like I want us to have a relationship for our mother and father," he ignored the call and put the phone back in his pocket. I pressed the subject though.

"Why does your mama want you to do that?"

"Because Erin's people killed my dad best friend and it's a really long story. I actually been calling both my parents since I been down here and they haven't called me back. I know it's because they are mad because I haven't done my part with Erin yet. Now they keep sending me to voicemail when I call but I'll fix them later," now I was interested to see who the hell his sister was.

"The girl I got into a fight with name was Erin but I doubt it was your sister. The Erin I'm talking about has curly hair and light brown eyes," when I said that Jamie mouth hit the floor. He pulled his phone out and showed me a picture.

"Is this her?" he asked me, and I tried my best not to smile big as hell.

"Oh my goodness. Yes, that's her! You see, she wants K.J father to himself so when I let him get our son she hurt my baby. I found out and confronted her last night and she broke my nose," I worked up some tears.

"Why the hell would she do that to an innocent baby? What a fucked-up bitch!" Jamie yelled pissed off. I liked that.

"Erin went to high school with me and K.J's dad and she has always wanted him. I never had a thing for him. After we graduated and went our separate ways me and him were at a party. He drugged my drink, raped me and that's how I got pregnant. I decided to keep the baby and raise it on my own. Erin found out and was pissed off. Her and my child's father are together, and she hates that we have a child together. I saw some bruises on K.J that I just knew she did and we fought. K.J's dad was on Erin side which I should have known," I was crying hard as hell now as Jamie hugged me.

"I can get her for you, Cleo. I could set it up that we meet and you could kick her ass. Erin has always been trouble since she was born. She made our own mother's life hard. We don't have to kill her but we can make her pay for harming K.J," I smiled big as my head laid on his chest.

"I want nothing more than to break her damn nose like she did mine. I don't care if her and my baby daddy are together. I just want both of them to stay away from my child. You're who I want to be with Jamie," I fed him bullshit like I feed K.J baby food. Kissing him he told me he would call me with the place and time he was meeting up with Erin.

"I can't be with you Jamie because if she sees me she will get suspicious. Just bring her back to your hotel room and I'll be there," he agreed and gave me his hotel and room number.

He told me I would have a key at the front desk waiting for me. I smiled to myself when he left. All this shit was meant to happen. I told Kenyatta to stop playing with me or he was going to push me into doing some shit. Now he gets to see that I am not playing. He is mine and the three of us will be a family. Jamie left and I hopped in the shower and slipped on a maxi dress. K.J woke up and I fed him. Looking at me and Yatta son always made me smile. He was my ticket to Yatta's heart. There was no just K.J and Yatta. We came as a package and Yatta better get with it or I will really go to the extreme. I put my baby in his room to watch TV just as a knock came to my door.

"Damnnnn, Yatta put the business on yo ass."

"Fuck you nigga. He messed yo' ass up just as bad," I said to Hayden as he walked in my apartment. He always had some smart shit to say.

"That's the only reason I'm here is for you to fuck me. You about to fuck me good and then I'm out. And for your information, he didn't fuck me up to bad. I still can play ball with yo' smart mouth ass. Save that spit for my dick," he sat down on my couch and looked around. Me and Hayden been fucking since high school. Once I seen he liked Erin, I just had to have him. I needed to prove to myself that she wasn't better than me. I could have anything she had plus more.

"You ain't cook a nigga shit?" I shook my head no as I gave him a blunt and a beer. Hayden was the only guy next to Yatta that I would actually consider being with. But he had one fucking problem.

"I see you still stalking that bitch social media," I got so mad sitting down next to him. Hayden had it so bad for Erin. He was worse than Yatta for that boring hoe.

"My heart belongs to her. Always has. Which is why I'm going back to school. Her and Yatta shit locked tight and I need to move the fuck on. Shit last night could have been worst and I got a career to think about," I could have thrown up when he said that bullshit.

"Well she will never want you, Hayden. You have never been good enough for her but trust me I wish you were. Maybe than I could have my family and she would be out the way. But all of that is about to change," I said as I thought about me and Jamie plan.

"What the fuck does that mean Cleo? Huh, what the fuck you think you about to do to her?" he asked getting pissed off. I got mad and started yelling.

"What the fuck is so special about that bitch?! Answer me that! It's a million bitches in this city but every nigga keeps chasing after her plain looking ass! Get the fuck out! Me and you are done Hayden!" he stood up shaking his head and laughing.

"Man bitch you fucking crazy as hell. You a jealous bitter bitch but I swear you bet not do shit to Erin," when he said that I got madder.

"GET OUTTTT!" I yelled at the top of my lungs as Hayden left. K.J started screaming crying.

I put my hands over my ears and cried. I swear to God I have never hated someone as bad as I hate Erin. Picking my phone up off the floor I went to her Instagram, her Snapchat, and her Facebook. She was always smiling and showing how happy she was. Her perfect drawings, paintings, perfect smile, hair, and eyes. Yatta smiled big as fuck when he was with her. He kissed on her or looked at her like he would do any and everything she wanted. Her Snap videos were either of the two of them or her two bitch ass friends.

They all loved her which made me so fucking sick to my stomach. On Yatta's Instagram page were pictures of Erin with K.J. he captioned each picture 'my world in one flick'. Nothing of me or the fact that I gave him his first fucking child. Nothing of the history we had since high school. Nothing about how I was there when he was locked up still taking care of our fucking son. I am so sick of him not loving me and pushing me to the side. But its ok, all of this was about to change. Fuck fighting Erin when Jamie gets her. I was killing that hoe and Jamie could either fall in line or I would have to kill his ass as well. It was time for me to win!

Dreka

"How do you feel ma?" I looked at her smiling big and holding her hand. She wiped the tears that fell from my eyes.

I was so happy for her after the hearing she had. The judge let her speak along with myself. My dad, Erin, and my grandma. We let the judge know how much we needed her home. We would make sure she abided by her probation requirements. We would provide her with a good home life and help her gain employment. The best news ever was told to us after we spoke. The judge decided my mama would be granted release from jail in another month. I was so happy to have her come home. She had been locked up since I was four-years-old. My dad called himself moving on and my mama couldn't take it. She stabbed the girl multiple times killing the woman.

The only reason it's no excuse for her to have taken a life but she still was my mama. I wanted her home with me. She had no mental issues and my dad owned up to his part. He played games with both women. I learned her and my mama had gotten into some fights over my dad. Since my mama has been locked up me and her relationship was so tight. My dad not only made sure she didn't want for anything ever. But he also made sure I came to see her a few times each month since she has been locked up. They still flirted and shit when we would see her whch was gross.

My mama is fully aware that her and my dad were not together and the dates. Hell, all she talks about is getting out and doing her. Building a life for herself and to be a part of mine. It's funny because my dad flips when she talks like that. I told him to leave her alone and let her live. He claims she can live all she wants. Right next to him. I just wash my hands with them two as long as they both stay out of trouble.

"I feel really good cheeks. I get to come home to you and live life beyond these bars," I loved when she called me the nickname her and my dad gave me. I had high cheekbones that rose whenever I smiled big or laughed hard. It's what made me such a diva!

"Zamir gave me money to put on your books," I told her and she smiled for me.

"Aww tell him I said thank you and I appreciate it. I'm happy you were able to beat that bitch, Tia, up. I hope you tagged that hoe as if you were fighting in battle. I was so tired of her fucking with you," my mama looked just like me when she got mad. Her shape was the bomb and I swear she belonged in a rap video. That's why my shape was plus size but curvy in the same time. I had hips, an ass, and nice titties because my mama was built like a fucking stacked house. We had the same mocha complexion and long hair. We were in the visiting room of the women's prison in Ypsilanti. My family left and gave me and her some time to visit alone.

"Me to ma. It felt so good to fuck her up but even better to know she wasn't pregnant. I kicked the fake ass belly off her ass and she started screaming like it was real. I swear I wish you were there," I cracked up thinking about that night of Lonell party.

"I'm just happy you fucked her up. Ol' silly hoe."

"Me and Zamir got into it though because she popped up at his job at the boxing ring. I swear ma I am so sick of this bitch. Like I'm not about to break up with him but I just want the drama to stop. Of course, he sees it as I'm leaving him so he freaks the hell out. Not on me but he just gets scared," I told her. Thoughts of me and Zamir breaking up over Tia always made me mad. I loved my Mir-Mir to death and never wanted to break up. He just made me mad acting so nonchalant about Tia's bullshit. He always tells me to not worry about her and he would fix it. Like I just said, I just want the drama to stop.

"Let me tell you something. Jealousy is a worst disease than pride in my opinion. Never let someones jealousy keep you from being happy. As long as Zamir is not trying to have his cake and eat it to. Then stay with him through the storm. Now, you're not about to be fighting bitches y'all entire relationship. Hell no! But this one situation can be handled and the minute you think he is not trying to stop it. Then you can walk away Dreka," my mama kissed my hand and we finished our visit, ate and laughed until it was time to go.

I thought about what my mama said the drive back to Detroit. I did love Zamir very much and wasn't about to walk away from him. We were both stubborn and not about to bag down if we both feel we were right. I texted him and told him about my mama. He was so happy for me and said he couldn't wait to meet her. It's funny because when I'm mad at him I won't talk to him. I know its petty but he be pissing me off. When he is mad at me he calls me Dreka and is dry. Like if I called him right now he would be so dry. Like he knew I was thinking about him my phone rung. I couldn't even hide my big ass smile.

"Yes Mir-Mir," I answered my Bluetooth that was around my neck.

"I feel yo' pretty ass smiling through the phone baby girl. I need you to come to my crib so we can talk," I blushed and could feel my cheeks rising but I stopped when he said we need to talk.

"Is it bad because if so just save me a trip and tell me now. You wanna break up?" I asked and my eyes got watery that quick.

"Stop fucking playing with me Dreka with that crazy talk and just bring yo' ass. Park in my garage and come through the garage door," I told him ok and we hung up. My crybaby butt wiped my eyes and took the freeway to my babe crib.

I parked my car in Zamir's garage next to his truck. As soon as I turned my engine off he opened the door in his garage that led to his condo. He looked so damn good in some simple black Nike track pants. He had a black Nike t-shirt on that fitted his solid body so good. His dreads were half up and some down. That sexy ass big bottom lip looked so juicy I could just bite it off his face. He walked up to my car as I got out and surprised me by kissing me deep as hell.

"What was that for?" I asked him catching my breath.

"I missed you and for yo' ass thinking I wanted to break up. We for life Dreka and I need you to understand that shit. Stop letting this bullshit keep you from me or I swear I'm gone pop the fuck off. I gotta ask you something though," I looked at him and told him to ask me.

"Do you love me and do you trust me?" I looked him in his eyes and said yes to both. He smiled and grabbed my hand as we walked in his condo. Coming up the two steps in his kitchen I sat my purse on the counter. He pulled me to the living room and I stopped dead in my tracks at the sight in front of me. Tia was in the middle of Zamir's living room duct taped to a chair looking like she seen a ghost.

Zamir

"I told you to stop sweating the bullshit this bitch was throwing at you. I know it looked like I wasn't giving a fuck but I know how she moves. I needed her to get comfortable and start moving carelessly," I looked from Tia bitch ass to Dreka. She was stunned as hell and I just hope I don't scare my baby girl off. That was the last thing I wanted to do but this hoe Tia was doing too much.

"It's your call Dreka on how you want me to handle her. I told you before, all you gotta do is point in the direction and its gone," Dreka looked at me and then at Tia. Dreka walked to Tia and took the duct tape from around her mouth.

"All of this could have been avoided if you would have just stopped. He was never yours to begin with Tia. You lied about being pregnant, had ultra sound pictures and all. How did you even get all that shit?" Dreka asked and Tia looked off looking mean as fuck at me.

"Cleo sister is a nurse assistant at Sinai-Grace hospital. That shit was easy as fuck to get. Spare me the lecture Dreka. I wasn't about to lose my man to no fat bitch. Simple," Dreka laughed and put the tape back over her mouth.

With eyes still on Tia she pointed at her and looked at me. I nodded my head and walked behind Tia with a black trash bag and put it over her head. Tia started moving the best she could being that she was tied down. You could hear her muffling through the tape as she fought to breathe. The bitch had fight in her but I had patients. It was a joy to take this bitch last breath from her. Slowly but surely Tia became limp and then she stopped moving completely. Me not wanting to chance it, I snapped the bitch neck.

"What about her body?" Dreka asked me as I left the trash bag over Tia's head.

"Not your concern baby girl," Dreka looked at me and nodded her head. I walked over to her and rubbed the side of her pretty face.

"You mine Dreka?" she said yea and asked.

"You mine Zamir?"

"Forever," I said. I was shocked when Dreka pushed me against the wall and dropped to her knees. She pulled my track pants down along with my boxers. My dick was hard as fuck as she wrapped her pretty ass hand around it as much as she could. I bit my big ass lip as she took my dick in her warm wet mouth.

"Shit," I moaned while watching her suck the fuck out of my dick. Dreka had gave me head plenty of times before but this shit was different. First off her doing this after she seen me kill someone let me know she was my ride or die bitch. Having her not take off on me when she saw Tia tied to the chair let me know Dreka was truly mine. Then the fact that she wanted to suck my dick in front of Tia dead body let me know Dreka was just as twisted and cray as I was. I loved that shit.

"Fuck Dreka, get the balls to babygirl. Aw shit," she was so nasty with her head game. My dick and balls were soaked. Looked down at her wet mouth and full ass lips around my dick was all I could take. I picked her up and carried her juicy ass to my recliner. Taking off my shoes and pants she pulled her dress over her head. I snatched her strapless bra off with one hand as the D-cup titties popped out. On my knees, between her legs, I roughly sucked on her titties. Pulling and sucking on her nipples I could feel her scratching my back up as she pulled my shirt off. I pushed her sexy ass back in my chair and put both of her thick legs around my shoulders.

"Ugh Zamir," she moaned as I started eating her pussy like Sunday dinner. Dreka was grinding in my face smearing her juices all over my lips and beard. I was eating that shit up. I played with her clit good as hell with my tongue. My index finger was inside her massaging her tight walls. Swear if I couldn't eat her pussy on a regular then my life would never be right.

"I'm cummin' bae so fucking hard! Ahhh!" she soaked my face and recliner up. I slowed down and just made out with her clit for a minute. Dreka was breathing hard and trembling. Kissing and biting on her extra thick ass thighs I pulled her ass to the floor on all fours. My dick was hard as fuck and ready for the inside of her pussy.

SMACK!

SMACK!

"Throw that ass back bitch, yeaaaa just like that Dreka. Fuck daddy dick just like that," I dug my nails in her big ass booty as she arched her back and threw that ass in a circle. Her pussy was made just for me. That shit was taking me on a high that no weed and liquor has ever done.

"Oh God Zamir," she moaned out my name and my ego grew.

"Look back at me Dreka," I growled at her and that beautiful face looked at me and our eyes locked. I licked my bottom lip as I felt my nut building up

"Anytime you point its gone, you got that baby girl?" ,he nodded her head yea as I came all inside of her.

"UGH SHIT!" My nails were so deep in her soft ass booty. Dreka creamed all on my dick the same time I nutted in her. I was out of breath as I pulled out her sweet ass pussy and stood up. Helping her up I sat down on my recliner naked as hell with her naked ass on top of me. I reclined it all the way back and just listened to me and her hearts beat fast as fuck.

"You know you're sitting in my juices, right?" she looked up at me laughing and all sweaty.

"You think I give a fuck. My kids inside of you so were even," I laughed back and she smacked her lips.

"Shut up punk. Your only being careless because I'm on birth control."

"Shitttt. You mine Dreka and even if you weren't on birth control I still would cum in you if I wanted to. You having my baby doesn't scare me," she looked back up at me and kissed my lips.

"You'd be a good father to our child but not right now babe," I kissed the top of her head.

"Agreed baby girl. I got something to tell you," she waited for me to talk.

"I have to go to D.C. just for a day with Yatta and Alaric."

"Ok but why only for one day? What are y'all going for?" she asked and I told her the truth.

"For work," I said and she looked from side to side and then back at me. She still was laying on my chest while I played in her pretty ass hair.

"Um what do you mean work? What kind of----" she stopped and we looked at each other for a minute.

"I'm a thief Dreka, we're thieves. Me, Yatta, Alaric, and Lonell," her mouth was agape, and she squinted her eyes like she was trying to figure out what to say.

"Um, ok hold on. So y'all break in houses and just-----," I shook my head at her.

"Naw baby girl. Were the real fucking deal. Thousands sometimes millions worth of shit we steal that is split between us. Shit if we were ever caught we would do some serious time. We been doing it since we were fifteen. Lonell heads it and we all play apart. My smart ass knows the worth of all shit we take. Alaric computer smarts handles surveillance. Lonell gets us the hits and Yatta can pick any lock or safe you give him," I gave her a second to process what I said. I have never told anyone including Cassidy about what I do.

"Wow, Zamir I huh I don't know what to say. That's all a lot to swallow and honestly, I can't. I just can't," I grabbed her arm as she was about to get up.

"Wait, what the fuck," I went in a panic and her annoying ass looked at me and smiled big as hell and started laughing.

"Zamir you just killed someone in front of me. We fucked inches away from the dead body and laying with it inches from us. You think you telling me you're a thief would scare me off? Naw, forever remember," I yanked her chunky ass back on me.

"You play to much Dreka, I thought you was for real. I'm like hell naw she not about to bounce on me. You petty as fuck," she was on my chest laughing. I looked down at her beautiful face for a while.

"Dreka you have a classic ass beauty. One that I know will get better and better as you age. I want your face tatted on my back," she looked at me in shock.

"Really?"

"Real shit. You ain't gotta get tatted. I'm doing the shit for me and because I want to," she grabbed the side of my face and kissed me. Before you knew it she was riding my dick in my recliner. Right in front of Tia dead ass corpse. That shit was lit!

***

"I told Dreka about us and our operation we got going on," looking at Alaric and passing him the blunt. We were in my motel room in D.C. chilling before we hit the Hay-Adams hotel and do this job. Lonell planned every fucking thing with Emmanuel and Delon. Havoc stayed far away from this hit as possible. Until we knew for sure if Havoc was an opp then Lonell wanted him far as fuck from what he did. As far as he knew we were still scheduled to do this hit next month.

"How she take it? I still gotta talk to Cassidy about this shit. I told her we were going to help Lonell look at a building for a business he wants to start. I hated lying to her," I watched him as he talked and I saw some shit in him I never seen before.

Besides when we talk business, Alaric is a bullshitter. He bullshits about important shit and about shit he tells women. Everything was games and selling dreams to bitches. Me and Yatta were his niggas so we all would sit and laugh at the way Alaric played hoes. Seeing him be sincere about someone other than his family. In less words, the nigga was a true asshole.

"I'm about to be on some other shit for a minute. If the shit leaves this room I swear I will kick yo' ass," Alaric nodded his head to what I had just said.

"You and Yatta are like my brothers. Even though in Kindergarten y'all bitches befriended me because I was the biggest in the class," we both chuckled when I said that.

"You two still became my brothers and have had my back more than anyone after my sister. All the times my mama was out drunk, hoeing around or gone for weeks. Y'all were right there helping me and Cassidy. My point being is, you know what my sister means to me. I want nothing more than her to be happy and have a great life. If this was you and any other woman I wouldn't give a fuck about the relationship," I took a pull of the blunt Alaric passed to me.

"But this is my baby sister. My first real love I have had and that's including the bitch that birthed me and her. My goal was to not have Cassidy be like our mother or to find a low life nigga like the ones our mother fucks with," Alaric looked at me as I talked.

"You made me conflicted as hell when I found out about you and Cassidy. Me, you and Yatta don't care about these bitches. As fucked up as it is we took pride in driving these bitches crazy and not giving a fuck about their feelings. Shit so sad because the three of us each have reasons why we thought love and feelings made us weak," Alaric chuckled and shook his head.

"I'm giving you my sister to take care of better than I did. To make sure you add to her happiness and not stop it. If you destroy my sister then I gotta step in and I will lose a sister and a brother. I don't want that so please Alaric, the look I see you get when you talk about her. The sincerity in your voice needs to be as real as I feel it is," I passed him a shot alone with the one I had. We clicked our glasses together and knocked them back.

"My feelings and all that good shit I feel for Cassidy is real as fuck my nigga. Man to man I'm telling you, I got her for life. The same way you are on some real shit about Dreka. It's the same way with me and Cassidy. I'm willing to kill my fucking punk ass dad for her and for what he did. I never once question that. Him taking his last breath is something that I cannot way to see. You my brother nigga and I wouldn't play with that," he held his fist out and I hit with mine.

"A'ight we done being gay. Let's get to this money." I said and we both laughed and stood. Up. We were meeting in Lonell and Yatta room so we can get this shit in motion. The hit was scheduled to take place in an hour and we were more than ready.

***

"That shit was so fucking live! I'm ready tuh go home and fuck the shit out of Erin bro!" I could hear Yatta loud ass all hype and shit.

We just got done with our hit at the Hay-Man. I can't even front and say shit didn't go smooth as a baby hair because it really did. Emmanuel had that shit covered as far as the pigs on to us. He had some niggas on the police squad in the county he used to fuck with he was in the streets. Of course, they got they hands dirty and got some shit for themselves, but we didn't give a fuck. Protection on all areas cost when you were in the crime field. This shit right here is the biggest hit we ever fucking hit. Havoc wasn't with us so we had to do extra work to cover what he usually did.

Now, four niggas walking in a five-star hotel where an expensive auction took place was way to fucking suspicious. So, we got the fake identities as hotel staff. Emmanuel got us some palm stickers that fitted the inside of your hand perfectly. It gave us fake fingerprints and of course, Alaric covered the security cameras. Not only in the hotel but the street cameras, the cameras at the airport and when we land back in the city. We had all our shit covered because of Alaric tech smart ass. Yatta did what he did best and was able to open both of the safes we stole. Me and Lonell were the housekeeping employees. They get keys to every room in the hotel so it was perfect.

Yatta parked cars for the valet so he had our van ready as we loaded it up. The whole job was done in fifteen minutes. Before anyone would notice it would be far too late. They would be looking for guys who doesn't exist and describing different people to the police. Me Lonell and Yatta wore fake facial hair, contacts and Yatta stupid ass wore a fat suit. That shit was funny as fuck and looked real as shit. He even had the fucking head and neck part to match. This crazy fool found it on eBay for three-grand. The seller told him it was used for a Hollywood movie and looking at his ass with it on. I believed that shit.

Now it was my turn as I sat with the buyers from Canada. We sold to them before and thanks to Dreka's pops Delon we had untraceable cars waiting for us at the airport. Emmanuel once again had security taking care of. Now we were in a hotel suite downtown meeting with our buyer. Lonell, Alaric and Yatta crazy asses were in the other part of the suite while me and the buyer discussed prices. He had three specialists who knew the value and worth for everything. If they picked a price I didn't agree with then the whole thing was cancelled. Like I said earlier, this was the biggest hit we ever did. Sitting with our buyer for three hours as we discussed and went through all the merchandise. We came reached an agreement and I had to keep my sexy when we shook hands.

"A'ight big nigga, lay the shit on us," Yatta stood up and put his blunt out as I walked in the room. I kept my same mean serious expression as I cleared my throat.

"We reached a price. After I calculated the fees we have to pay to Emmanuel, Delon, everyone else who worked with us," these three fools looked like kids awaiting Christmas morning to come so they could open their presents. It took everything in me not no laugh.

"The four of us are taking home over two million apiece. We had over eleven million worth of merchandise," Lonell dabbed me up and we started laughing and celebrating. Alaric came with the shot glasses and the Hennessey. He poured us some shots and we toast to our success.

"I got something to say before we leave out of here," Lonell said. Me and my niggas already knew he was about to lecture us.

"First off let me say how proud I am of you lil niggas. Y'all listen to me and stayed out of trouble," He looked at Yatta and arched his eyebrow.

"Well, most of y'all," we all chuckled and Yatta smacked his lips and put his middle finger up.

"But for real y'all stayed out of trouble, don't be all flashy and shit and y'all don't run ya mouth to niggas or bitches about our business. I know all of y'all pussy whipped now like my ass been for years off of Juziel," when he said that we laughed but ain't none of us deny the shit.

"My point being, keep them ladies happy. I know it will come a time if it hasn't already. When you will want to tell them. Just make sure shit is all the way hunnid and that they know the basics. Not no details. Another thing, Emmanuel told me about Havoc and what the fuck he been up to," I saw Lonell's nostrils slowly flare and his tone change. This nigga was worse than me and Yatta put together as far as his anger and attitude.

"That nigga has been working with the feds. The niggas from Flint that he had us meet up with a few months back. Those niggas were cops. But Emmanuel did some digging and found out they are dirty cops. They were setting us up with Havoc help but then were going to kill him and take all the shit we stole today," all of us had a nasty look on our faces.

"Yo' unc let me kill that bitch and them musty water drinking Flint niggas," Yatta popped off and said first. For once I didn't think he was being hot-headed. I was ready to kill all they dirty asses as well.

"Naw nephew I need y'all to let me handle this myself. I got over twenty years of friendship with that bitch nigga. I want to kill his ass but I need y'all to continue doing what I said. Playing nice with Havoc and not talking to him about shit. No meeting up with him, phone convos or nothing. Me, Emmanuel and Delon got this. Y'all just enjoy this nice pay day alone with the money we already had. Shit gone be nice as fuck moving forward. Alaric, you focus on the task at hand. German is next on the list and just know you will walk out of this shit alive. I put my life on that," Lonell dabbed us up and gave us a hug. He always hugged us after a job and it was a hug like a father would give a son. Hell, he was like a father to us including Alaric.

"Now that I got that off my chest. Let's get the fuck outta here and go be with our women," Lonell said laughing as he opened the door.

"And nigga take that fucking fat suit off. I can't take yo' ass serious," I said looking at Yatta retarded ass as we walked out the suite.

I pulled my phone out and texted my baby girl. I was missing her like crazy and wanted to know where she was. Dreka didn't know it yet but she was moving in with me. I wanted her in my shit turning my boring as condo upside down with all her girly things. I wanted to wake up to her wild sleeping ass every day. Go to sleep with my dick inside her pussy every night. Except when she on her cycle. Then we gotta just fuck in the shower. Don't none of y'all bitches reading this turn ya nose up at me or my girl Londyn for that shit either. Most of y'all either have done that shit before. Or thought about it!

Anyways, I was ready for Dreka to live with me and she better be ready to. After I linked up with Yatta and we got rid of Tia's body. I told him about Dreka still rocking with me after I killed Tia. He was happy for me and told me I wouldn't have gave Dreka a choice anyways. He was right though. Baby girl had no choice but to rock with me. I wasn't letting her go, ever so why not make shit easy on yourself.

"Your back in the city?" Dreka said on the other end of the phone.

"What I tell you about answering the phone like that. Start that shit over," I hung up the phone and dialed her ass right back.

"Hey, my Mir-Mir. You back in the city?" I knew her ass was cheesing which made me smile. I was in my truck on the freeway on my way to her.

"Yea I am and I need to see my girl. Where you at?"

"I'm at Fairlane with Erin and Cassidy. I know Yatta and Alaric are back to meaning these heffas about to leave me hanging," Dreka said and you could hear Erin and Cassidy talking shit in the background.

"Don't talk shit baby girl because you the first to leave them hanging. Ya man wants his woman with him right now so give kisses and hugs at get'cho ass to my crib. NOW!" I licked my bottom lip thinking how I was gonna have Dreka as soon as I saw her.

"Ok, zaddy Mir I'm leaving now," I heard Cassidy and Erin yell and act like they were throwing up all in the background. I laughed at their silly asses. I told Dreka I loved her and hit the freeway to my crib and my baby girl.

Erin

"Cousin you look so freaking cuteeee! Oh my Goodness, we killin'em tonight!" Dreka crazy ass laughed and started twerking hyping Cassidy's ass up right along. Tonight was the foam party at Elektricity in Pontiac. I was happy to be getting out with my boos and have a girl's night out

"Thanks, boo. I'm happy we decided to get ready at Cassidy's crib. My uncle and daddy would not have let us leave the house like this," I smiled as I looked myself over in the mirror.

I was looking good as hell. Shit all three of us were looking hot as hell. I had on a two-piece thong bikini. I wasn't as bold though because I had some tiny ass shorts on. But they were fitted as hell and unbuttoned. I purposely made sure you could see my thong over them. my hair was in a high bun and I had some black BEBE chunky flip-flops the same color as my swimsuit. All three of us were dressed similar. Cassidy hooked our feet and nails up with this matte nude acrylic on our fingers and toes. Dreka straighten me and her hair out for the first time ever.

I was loving my cousin rockin' her pretty ass natural hair lately. Nothing was wrong with her and her gorgeous ass bundles she would wear. But our family was blessed with some long ass hair. Sure it's big, curly and hard as hell to keep up but it's still beautiful none the less. Anyways, Dreka trimmed Cassidy's side cut up and flat ironed her hair over her left eye. Cassidy had some pretty ass hair as well but she kept cutting it. Her roots were so curly and looked like baby hair all over.

"Yea it's no way they would have let us leave. Speaking of overprotective fathers and uncles," Dreka's eyes got big and she looked at me and Cassidy.

"Girl the guys are out having fun and they know we are having a lady's night. They just don't know what we are doing. They'll live," Cassidy came from out her kitchen chewing an apple. She had on a strapless two-piece swimsuit with some tiny shorts on as well and some yellow BEBE chunky flip-flops matching her swimsuit. Dreka stood up laughing and I admired how good she looked to.

"Dreka I don't know why you call yourself a BBW. Your shape is out of this world and to me you just don't seem like a plus size," I said as I hit her big booty she was twerking. It doesn't even have to be any music playing and this girl was always dancing.

"Well boo look at Cassidy's shape. She has a flat stomach and small-toned arms. But her ass is round, she has hips and some jiggle to her thighs. Cass bear would be what they call slim thick. You have wide hips, flat stomach, some jiggle to your thighs," she laughed and started slapping my thighs making me and her laugh.

"Your stomach is flat and your arms are not as toned but they're still nice. You're a thickums boo, video hoe thick," her and Cassidy laughed and I threw a Pringle at both of them that I was eating on.

"Me, however, I have wide hips, a nice big booty but I got major jiggle to my thighs and I have a little stomach. My arms are bigger than both of you but I don't have any hang time," Dreka held up her arm and shook it.

"I would be considered a BBW. The best of the best with some nice perky D titties that Zamir likes to------"

"Bitch shut up!" Cassidy covered her ears making me and Dreka start laughing. My pretty ass cousin went back to fixing her hair. Dreka had on a two-piece swimsuit but her top was a fitted crop top that stopped in the middle of her stomach. It was mint green and she had her tiny ass shorts unbuttoned on to. Her feet had some mint green and gold BEBE flip-flops. We finished getting ready acting silly. Twenty-minutes later we were getting in the Lyft we ordered and driving off.

I've never seen a diamond in the flesh
I cut my teeth on wedding rings in the movies
And I'm not proud of my address, in the torn up town
No post code envy
But every song's like gold teeth, Grey Goose, trippin' in the bathroom
Bloodstains, ball gowns, trashin' the hotel room
We don't care, we're driving Cadillacs in our dreams
But everybody's like Cristal, Maybach, diamonds on your timepiece
Jet planes, islands, tigers on a gold leash
We don't care, we aren't caught up in your love affair
And we'll never be royals
It don't run in our blood
That kind of lux just ain't for us
We crave a different kind of buzz
Let me be your ruler, you can call me Queen B
And baby I'll rule (I'll rule I'll rule I'll rule)
Let me live that fantasy

Lorde song Royals was so loud all over the club. This was our first foam party and the shit was on the lit side! There was foam all over the club and even the bar area. We were nervous about being to revealing but these white girls in here had us beat. The crowd was mixed with white, black and a few Mexican people. I can't even lie, the men in here were fine as hell. We didn't have to stand in line because the bouncer looked at the three of us and let us right in. The club had pink, purple and blue laser lights going all through it. The colors bouncing off the foam made the atmosphere the shit. Dreka walked back over to me and Cassidy as we danced. She had some tube drinks on a trey in her hand.

"The bartender said there the best-selling drink. I got us rounds all night so we are getting white girl wasted tonight!" Dreka yelled as she passed us a tube.

"Hell yeaaa! Whoo-whoo bitches!" I yelled making Drekas and Cassidy yell to as we clinked our tubes together and threw back the drink. It was different colors and had a sweetness to it with a kick at the end. Before you knew it, we knocked back four apiece.

"HELL YEA FUCKING PARTYYYYY!" A group of white boys yelled as we stood on top of tables taking shots and dancing.

Girl, I wanna see you, twerk
I'll throw a lil money if you twerk
Ion really think you could, twerk
(Twerk)
If you broke, go to, work
Make that big booty, twerk
Make that big booty, twerk
Can I touch that booty?
That booty, that big ol' booty
Shake that booty, can I lay on the booty?
Mike Tyson on the booty
Copyright that booty
Bounce that booty on the floor (shit)
Shake 'til you get a lil sore (shit)
Show 'em, yo mamma made a hoe (shit)

Go ahead and get a little low (shit)
Shake that booty in the car (shit)
Shake that booty in the store (shit)

We were twerking our asses off to Blac Youngsta Booty song. Me, Cassidy and Dreka were still on the tables dancing. By now we had a crowd of guys around us. I swear I was having the time of my life. I felt like this was what being young was all about. Having friends, good family, a passion that you can put your all into and a good relationship. After this night, I was ready to tackle any drama that came my way. I just needed one night with my boos and some good drinks. The foam was feeling good all around me and I just let the music take me away. Between the music, dancing, and alcohol that was in my body. I must have let the shit take me far away because the next thing I knew I was in the air being yanked off the table. When my feet touched the grown I was staring in Kenyatta's face.

"WHAT THE FUCK ARE YOU DOING!" he was pissed the hell off. He had my arm in his grip and even though he was mad I couldn't get pass how good he looked. So basic in a Cleveland Cavilers jersey and some jeans. I couldn't see his feet from the foam, but I knew he had on some Lebron's. His arms were out looking so damn good and that signature 'Yatta' chain was shining.

"Um, nothing I was just dancing," I was drunk as hell so the room was spinning and so was Kenyatta. I was trying not to laugh. I was one of those drunks, goofy as hell.

"Shaking yo' fat ass booty in these little ass shorts! I can see ya' fucking thong you got on! And what is this!?" He was yelling and ran his fingers through my hair.

"What happened to your curly hair I love?! This ya' thot hair-due?!" I couldn't help but crack up laughing. I mean I had to hold my side I was laughing so hard. Kenyatta's nostrils flared as he got closer to me and said.

"You think this shit is funny but it's not cutie pie. You in the club shaking what the fuck belongs to me. You drunk as hell and you got'cha hair all different and shit. Where the fuck my Erin at, huh?" his deep voice was all in my ear lighting my skin up. I looked at his still angry face, put my arms around his neck and said.

"She is right here. I just needed to let loose a little and have some fun. You know you like my swimsuit baby. I'll model it for you tonight," he was grabbing my ass for dear life as I kissed his neck.

"Aye nigga, you want me to rip ya'fuckin' eyes out'cha face! Stop looking at my bitch!" I turned around and saw some guy staring but he quickly looked away and walked off when Kenyatta said that. Giving me back his attention he was about to say something but we both heard Dreka yelling Zamir's name.

"Zamir stop!" This giant boy had some dude by his neck all in the foam. All you saw were the poor guy legs kicking struggling to get up and breathe. I was scared and Kenyatta and Alaric started laughing.

"Don't worry baby, he ain't gone kill the nigga. Just put his ass to sleep for a while," he turned his attention back to me and kissed my lips. I could taste liquor from both of us and Orbit gum he was chewing. We kissed so deep and with so much tongue that when he pulled away I had his gum in my mouth.

"I'm keeping this," I said sticking the gum out between my teeth. Kenyatta hunched his shoulders as he pressed his dick into me. He was hard as hell and that top lip with that dip in the middle called me. I ran my tongue lightly across it and kissed him again.

"Say bye to your girls. My dick hard as hell and I'm ready tuh teach yo' ass a lesson," I licked my lips and nodded my head. I hugged Dreka and Cassidy along with Z and Alaric.

"God damn Erin my fucking dick is about to fall off," Kenyatta squeezed his dick biting hard on his bottom lip. We were in the parking lot of the club inside his truck. The liquor took over me because I unbuckled my seat belt.

"I got'chu baby," I reached over and let his seat all the way back. I unbuckled his pants and before I could pull his dick out. That fat big thang was meeting me halfway.

"Shit," I heard Kenyatta whisper as I wrapped my hand around his dick the best way I could. His dick was long and so damn thick.

This was my first time sucking dick, so I hope I was doing it right. Again, I was just going to do what I saw in pornos. I licked the sides of his dick slowly leaving it wet all over. I got to the tip of his dick and tickled it with my tongue. When his dick jumped I smirked. I would have never done this in a public place with fear of someone seeing me. But in my Chris Brown voice, there's something in this liquor. Once I got his dick nice and wet I slid as much of it as I could down my throat. I could feel in hitting the back put I just relaxed my throat and that helped me not gag. I started doing what I remember seeing and moving my head slowly up and down. My hand was around his dick moving up and down matching the rhythm of my head.

"Mm," Kenyatta let out a moan so that must have meant I was doing it right. I wanted to make sure so I opened my eyes and looked up at him while I was still sucking.

"Ugh fuck Erin don't look at me, baby. You gone make me nut and I don't think you ready for that," saying that made me want to fuck his world up so I kept my eyes on him as I fucked him with my mouth.

A scene popped in my head from a porno I watched. The girl sucked and pulled a little on the guys balls. I didn't know if Kenyatta was into that but I still wanted to try. If he didn't like it I'm sure he would tell me. I popped his dick out my mouth and held it back with one hand while I sucked and licked on his balls. I could smell his Dove for men soap he used in the shower.

"Shit Erin," I swear this man thighs were shaking as I soaked up his balls and pulled them. I had never seen Kenyatta so aroused and at the mercy of being pleased before. When we have sex don't get me wrong he is so into it. But this was something different. Him loving me doing this to him was making me give my all. I got done with his balls and went back to sucking his dick. Now, I was nasty with it as my mouth got wetter. When Kenyatta wrapped my hair in his hand and started making my head go up and down. Oh, my God, I was so turned on.

"Move baby so I can cum," he said but I didn't want to stop. I was loving sucking his dick.

"Erin move—Ugh fuck!" I could feel his sperm slide all down my throat. I still didn't stop and surprisingly the taste wasn't as bad as it looked when Kenyatta nuts on my ass and takes a picture. Finally, I slowed down and eased his dick out my mouth. Looking at Kenyatta his eyes were closed, and his chest was going in and out fast as hell.

"Tha fuck Erin, I swear I'm getting yo' ass drunk more often," I laughed as I downed his half bottle of water he had in his cup holder.

"Come on baby I'm ready to go home and get the lesson you got for me,", I said licking my lips at his sexy ass.

"I'm coming cutie pie shit a nigga gotta get his shit together. You fucked my head up with that move," he let his seat up rubbing his hand across his sexy ass face. He started his car and we pulled off.

"Get'cho sexy ass over here," Kenyatta sat on his bed and called out to me. We got in his apartment, stripped, showered and he had me put my swimsuit back on.

I walked over looking in his eyes with so much fire and desire. He was ass naked sitting on the edge of his king size bed. I stood between his legs and pulled his band out his hair letting his dreads fall. I loved when we fucked with his dreads all over his head. Kenyatta ran his hand slowly up my thigh turning me around so my ass was in his face. He started tongue kissing, licking and biting my ass all over. I held my head back and closed my eyes. Kenyatta's touch was everything to me. It was so soft, gentle but at the same time rough like I love it. Only his touch could do this to me.

"You so fucking sexy Erin," I looked back at him as he continued kissing, licking and biting my ass. He pulled the strings on the side of my bikini bottoms making them fall on the floor. Kenyatta nasty ass opened my ass cheeks and licked between them. Oh, my God, I could have died. He kissed up my back and pulled the strings to my top making it fall on the floor too. When he stood up and turned my now naked body around so we were face to face I had to catch my breath.

"On God, you mine forever Erin. You will never be with another nigga as long as I'm walking this earth. I'm so fucking crazy about'cho ass you don't even know" before I could say anything he lifted me up and kissed me deep and hard. Pulling away he threw my ass on the bed and flipped me over. The shit was all in one move and I wanted to cuss his ass out but before I could he had me face down ass up literally.

"Now about yo' ass at a fucking club."

SLAP! Kenyatta slapped the fuck out of my ass making me grip the sheets. I don't know what it says about me because I was turned on so bad.

"Half fucking naked."

SLAP!

"Shaking what the fuck belongs to me. Having niggas look at'chu and want what the fuck is mine."

SLAP!

SLAP!

"Ugh," I moaned out as he slapped the hell out my ass. It was a pleasure-pain type if feel.

"I'm about to drive yo' ass wild just like you did to me when I saw yo' ass dancing tonight," I looked back at Kenyatta. I swear he had my ass tooted up so high as he dove his head in my pussy from the back.

"Ahhhh goodness Kenyatta," I gripped the sheets tight as hell as his thick ass tongue on my clit, He knew how to massage my clit, add pressure to my clit and suck on my clit just right. This man was a fucking beast at eating my pussy. When he added two fingers in my tight hold I went crazy. Kenyatta slapped my ass and made my ass cheeks shake. I reached my arm behind me and grabbed the back of his head. I started riding the fuck out his face.

"God Kenyatta I'm about to cum," when I said that he stopped and stood up holding his hard dick. He slid that big ass fucker in me and I felt like he was about to fuck my world up.

"This good ass pussy is all mine. You hear me, Erin, this pussy belongs to Kenyatta," he said as he fucked me so good. His nails were on the side of my hips while he pounded into me.

"Yes daddy, it's yours, baby," I moaned out loud meaning every word.

"Then why the fuck would you play with me then? Huh, you know yo' nigga crazy as fuck," I couldn't answer because my orgasm was building higher and higher.

"Answer me Erin, why the fuck would you play with me?"

"I-I don't know Kenyatta. Ugh fuck, I'm about to cum," I moaned that and this nigga slid out. I felt like a damn record scratched and stopped the music. I looked back at Kenyatta breathing hard with my mouth open and eyes bucked. He stood there breathing hard too and stroking his now wet dick.

"Naw, you can't cum until I say you can," I was about to go off but her jammed his dick back in my wet now sensitive pussy.

"Yea, I told yo' ass I was driving yo' ass wild. You not gone ever fuck with me like that again," I should have run then but the dick was too damn good. I'll fix his ass, I'm not gone say when I'm cumming. Kenyatta kept pounding into me fucking me like his life was on the line. I felt my shit build up but I refuse to say anything. My pussy muscles gripped his shit tight as fuck as I was about to cum so hard. And then guess what, a fucking record scratch. Kenyatta started cracking up stroking his dick.

"You thought because you weren't gone tell me you were cummin' I wouldn't know? Baby, I know your body better than you," he continued laughing and I couldn't say shit. I was breathing so hard and my pussy was beating like a damn rapid heartbeat.

"Kenyatta I swear to God if you don't fucking stop," I managed to get some strength to say that. He laughed and slid back in me.

"You love me, Erin? Tell me you love me," his crazy ass said while fucking me from the back good again. I was so ready to fight his ass but I really wanted to cum so I told him the truth.

"Yes Kenyatta, I love you, baby. Mmmm," I promise I hope this nutty ass nigga let me cum.

"I love you too cutie pie. You bet not ever act up on me like that again," he slapped my ass cheeks while fucking me like the star he was.

"Argh shit, I promise I won't. Just let me cum daddy, please let me cum," I felt his dick grow inside of me. This nigga liked me begging him. I felt my orgasm come again and this time my baby let me get mine and he came with me.

"Shit!" we both yelled and I collapsed flat on my stomach. My breathing was lost as I closed my eyes to collect myself.

"That's five-star pussy right there," Kenyatta pat my pussy and said. My eyes still closed I smirked and rolled on my side. I was fucking spawn fucking with Kenyatta's ass.

"Hell naw, I ain't done with'chu," he stood up, grabbed my ankles and pulled me to him. I was on my back and he was between my legs.

"Noooo baby I'm done fucking with you," I whined to him. He licked his lips and started softly massaging my clit with his fingers.

"Naw baby, I want you all night. I'm about to fuck you good as hell with you wearing my chain. I want another video to," his sexy butt smiled and there was no way I could say no to my fine ass baby. I laughed and told him to come here so I could kiss him. Kenyatta fucked the soul out my body all night.

***

"Jamie why do you keep calling me back to back," I was in Kenyatta's bathroom whispering. After me and Kenyatta's wild sex night we slept until noon. He was still sleeping and we both were off work today. I had been up for about thirty minutes and Jamie was blowing my phone up. I had to sneak in the bathroom and turn the water on in the sink so Kenyatta wouldn't hear me.

"Erin I really need to see you. Our mama and my dad are so mad at me for not wanting to help them anymore. They kicked me out and now I have no one or nowhere to go. I'm alone baby sister and I just need some help," I felt so bad for Jamie. To be put in the situation by our own mother and his father is awful. If Josey wasn't so rotten to me I swear I wouldn't even believe it myself. Even though my dad and Kenyatta want me to stay away from Jamie I just can't leave him hanging like this.

"Jamie calm down. I'll help you and you will never not have anywhere to go. We're family and I got your back. Tell me what you need me to do," I wanted to calm him down because it sounds like he was crying.

"I slept in the parking garage at Greektown Casino. I didn't want to call you last night so I just slept in my car. I'm to messed up to drive so can you just meet me here? I'm in a red Cadillac CTS."

"Ok Jamie, give me a few minutes. I'm already downtown so it will only take me about ten minutes to get to you. I'm about to slip on some clothes and I'll text you when I get to Greektown," I said as I grabbed my face rag. We said goodbye and I washed my face, body parts and brushed my teeth. When I walked out the bathroom Kenyatta was sitting up on his phone. I knew he was talking to Z because I could hear his deep ass voice on the other end. I smiled at my baby and went to put a sports bra and panties.

"Imma hit you back about that," Kenyatta said to Z as he hung up the phone. I knew he was about to trip on me leaving.

"Fuck you going cutie pie? You said you were off today," he walked up behind me and put his hands around my waist. I turned around and put my arms around his neck.

"I know but Cassidy needs me to open the store because one of the girls called off last minute. I'll be back over here though when I get off," I kissed his lips a few times. It took everything in me not to deepen our kiss. If I would have poor little Jamie would be all night waiting for me.

"We need to talk about this living thang we got going on," I furrowed my eyebrows because that threw me off guard. I walked in Kenyatta closet to grab something to wear.

"What do you mean living thang? We don't have a "living thang" going on," I smiled using air quotes.

"Exactly, we need to get one going on. I want you and me to live together baby," my heart dropped and the butterflies were twerking in my stomach. I never knew he was ready for such a big step.

"I'm glad you feel the same way baby. If yo' ass smiles any harder you gone split cha'damn lips," I smacked my lips laughing and threw a pair of socks at his head.

"Shut up I just didn't think you were ready for that big step. I would love to live with you," I said that as I put my shirt over my head.

"You wearing that to work?" He stood up off the bed pointing to my outfit. I didn't have on anything special. A PINK jogger set and some burgundy Puma's matching the set. My hair was now curly because I got in the shower last night.

"Yea why what's wrong?" I asked looking down at my outfit and back at him.

"Nothing it's just usually when you go to work your extra as hell. Girly, accessories and all that other girl shit you do. You look good as hell baby it's just dressed down from what I'm used to seeing."

"Well this is fine, I'm only going to paint so it's cool," when Kenyatta shot his head up at me I realized that I had fucked up. Fuck, Erin!

"Paint? You said Cassidy needed you to open the store," he arched his eyebrow and put his phone on the nightstand. I had to play it off and put on my best performance.

"Oh shit, I must be still hungover. I meant to say I'm only going to open the store so I can dress down now. Look, baby, I gotta go ok," I walked up to him and kissed his lips. I had to get going before I fuck up and slip again. After kissing his lips twice I grabbed my keys and purse. I was happy as hell I left my car here yesterday morning. I didn't want to ask Kenyatta for his truck. On my way out his bedroom, he said.

"Erin," I turned and looked at him.

"I love you cutie pie," I smiled and blushed.

"I love you to Kenyatta," I blew a kiss at him and left out.

On the drive, I rolled my eyes because leave it to downtown Detroit to always have construction going on. What would have taken me ten minutes is now taking twenty. As I sat and waited for the traffic to move I thought about my mama. I wanted to call her and give her a piece of my mind. But I decided against it because once I get Jamie and talk to my dad. I knew he would want to get at my mother. I just don't understand her all I have ever wanted my whole life was a relationship with her. I thought if I get good grades, stay out of trouble and fall in love with art that she would love me. But I'm starting to think that will never happen. It's sad but unfortunately, it's the truth. I got to Greektown parking garage and text Jamie.

The garage goes around and around and has twelve levels. He texted me back and told me he was on the second level and he would flash his lights when I got there. I drove to the second level and as soon as I got there he must have saw me first because he flashed his lights. Greektown was a casino so the parking garage was twenty-four hours. I was happy it was slow today and there was an empty space right next to Jamie's car. I put my phone on the passenger seat and got out my car the same time he did. I smiled when I saw him and went up to give him a hug.

"I'm really sorry you ever were put into the middle of this Jamie. Hopefully, my dad can talk some sense into our mother and get all this straightened out," I was talking as I walked back to my car. Jamie stood there shaking his head.

"You ok?" I asked him as I walked back up to him.

"Did you get in a fight last night with a girl named Cleo?" he looked at me and asked. I had a confused look on my face.

"How do you know Cleo?"

"Erin just answer the fucking question. Did you get into a fight with a girl named Cleo last night?" He walked a little closer to me and at that moment I knew my hard headed ass should have listened to my dad and stayed away from Jamie.

"Jamie, did our mama and your dad really put you out or was that a lie?" I asked and he started laughing while still looking at me.

"You really won't answer my question. Maybe this will make you talk," when he pulled a gun on me my eyes got big as hell. I wasn't ready to die but there was no way I was getting out of this.

"I am going to ask you again. Did you get into a fight with a girl named Cleo last night?" I felt my eyes water and the tears were trying to fall but I stopped them.

"Yes I did but she ran up on me first Jamie. How do you know her? Jamie, she is not a good person," I stood in the same spot not wanting to move and startle him.

"A good person!? Bitch you are the one who is not a good person. You purposely hurt her son just because of that thugger of a boyfriend you have. An innocent child who has nothing to do with anything," I shook my head as he talked.

"No Jamie, Cleo lied to you I would never do anything like that. True I am with her son's father but there is no reason for me to hurt K.J," he pressed the gun up to my head making my head go back.

"Stop fucking lying Erin! You're a spoiled selfish brat and our mother has warned me about you our whole life. You are not destroying another person's life the way you destroyed our mothers. Get the fuck in the car," when he said that I started crying.

"Jamie please, I swear I didn't-----"

"Get the fuck in the car and shut up before I kill you right here and now," before I could move he looked at me with the gun still in my face and said.

"You're such a stupid ghetto girl. You really came to meet with me thinking I needed you. I love my parents and after we put your boyfriend, his low life friends and uncle in jail. Me, Cleo and her son will be together and you will be alone. Now, get in the fucking car."

"Naw you bitch ass nigga, she ain't going no fucking where," Kenyatta came from the back and had his gun pressed against Jamie's head. I had never been so happy to see him. Jamie's eyes bucked, and he froze.

"Get your fucking gun out my girl's face or I will blow your brains all over this parking lot," Kenyatta said through his gritted teeth. Jamie looked at me and slowly lowered his gun. As soon as he got it down Kenyatta took it from him. By the time I blinked Kenyatta hit Jamie in the face with his gun. I was to stunned at what all was going on to even react. Before I knew it, Kenyatta was beating the fuck out of Jamie with his fist. He had put his gun on the hood of Jamie's car. I saw blood coming from Jamie's face and Kenyatta looked like a raged animal.

"Ok nigga that's enough!" Z came out of nowhere and grabbed Kenyatta off of Jamie. Before Kenyatta stopped fully he kicked Jamie so hard in his face I saw a tooth fly out his mouth. I was stuck crying and just still in disbelief.

"Come here, baby," Kenyatta walked up to me and hugged me. I broke down.

"W-W-Why would he do that? He was going to kill me. I swear Kenyatta I never touched K.J. I swear. Please believe I would never do that," I was crying hard as hell now.

"Erin baby calm down. I know you have never hurt my son and I know you were just trying to help this faggot ass nigga. Shh, stop crying cutie pie," he hugged me tight and rubbed my back. I saw Z pick Jamie up and put him in the trunk of his truck.

"How did you know I was here?" I looked up at Kenyatta and asked.

"I heard you're trying to whisper ass on the phone with him earlier. I had already hit Z up and put him on game. He was dropping Dreka off to work so he just met me here. Even if I didn't hear you on the phone you're a terrible liar so I would have still been on it," he lifted my wet face and kissed my lips. I felt so safe.

"Listen to me Erin, I need you to trust me and know that I am going to handle this. There is so many pieces to this shit and I will tell you the basics later. Right now I need you to get in your car and go back to my place. Wait there for me and as soon as I'm done dealing with some important shit I will be back to you. A'ight?" I nodded my head and he kissed me again.

"Ain't shit ever gone happen to you cutie pie. I put that on my last breath," Kenyatta hugged me and told me he loved me. I got in my car and drove back to his apartment. I had to thank God for being with me today because had Jamie had his way. I might be dead right now. Wow, my own fucking family.

Cleo

I don't believe this shit! I fucking waited in Jamie's room for an hour after he told me he was meeting up with Erin. I texted and called him but his phone kept going to voicemail. I know damn well this bitch ass nigga didn't pussy up on me. I knew once he saw Erin's sweet face she would talk his ass into being on her side. I shouldn't have even asked his weak ass to help me. I thought God was on my side with me in this.

"UGH!" I picked up my glass with the Chardonnay I was drinking and threw it against the wall. I just don't get why I can't get rid of this bitch Erin! She was ruining my fucking life on so many damn levels. I knew better than to stay in that hotel long waiting on Jamie. That soft ass bitch was useless. Feeling more and more frustrated I got up and went to my kitchen. I started smashing everything in there. All my glasses, plates, silverware and appliances. I was trashing that fucking room.

"AHHH!" I let out another hard scream and leaned against the wall. I just cried and cried loud and ugly.

All I ever wanted was Yatta to myself. I was fucking here first, I met him first and staked claim on him first. This boring basic ass bitch came and stole him! I have his one and only child and Erin still inserted herself in our lives. I love Yatta so much and could have been everything he ever needed. It pisses me off that he will never understand that. How the fuck could he with that bitch Erin clouding his way. Sitting here crying all the tears I had in my body a thought came to my head. I tried my best to push the thought up and not pay it no mind. But it kept coming to me louder and louder. Yatta would kill me if he even thought I was thinking this.

At this point, it doesn't even matter. He would never love me. He would never see that I would do any and everything for him. I was just as good as Erin if not better. That beautiful baby boy in the room came out of my pussy, not Erin's! I put my head between my knees and screamed so loud. I started pulling my hair so hard I heard the track and thread rip from my braid. All I wanted was Yatta. I wanted him, me and K.J. to be a family. Why won't he love me? Why won't he see me as he sees Erin? I thought and thought through my crying. Then I made my decision.

"If Jamie told Erin about me and his conversation then Yatta for sure knows. I am not about to sit here and have him barge in here on some bullshit. All he is going to do is put his hands on me and tell me how I'm nothing. How even if Erin wasn't around I still wouldn't have him. He'll call me all kinds of names. Try and take K.J away from me just because of that BITCH!" I yelled talking to myself out loud.

"Hell no, he is not about to keep breaking my heart in a million pieces. If he come here, he will find us long gone," I wiped my face and got up. I was not about to stay here and watch Yatta give Erin everything that belongs to me. They were not about to rub their happiness in my face. Play house with my fucking son. I think not! I went to my room and walked in my closet. I pulled out this pretty yellow and nude dress.

I grabbed my nude pumps and my nice jewelry. Laying my clothes on the bed I went to K.J's room. He was sleep as I went in his closet and took out his suit he wore this past Easter. It was a little big on him so I knew it would fit perfect now.

I went to the bathroom and grabbed my storage bin with all my hair stuff in it. I fixed my sew-in that I messed up and then put my scarf on. I needed a hot shower. My mind was so blank as I let the water hit me. I needed to clean all the drama off of me. I was going to have a happy life and I knew just how to get it. There was no happiness here if I couldn't have Yatta.

I couldn't get him to see it and I was tired of trying. But I said this shit earlier in the story. Me and K.J are a package deal. He can't have one without the other. Now, he will have neither of us. I know how smart Yatta is and how much he loves K.J. he won't stop until he finds us, so I just have to make sure he will never find us. I stepped out the shower and dried off. I put lotion all over my body and grabbed my makeup bag. I did a full face including my eyebrows and lips. I wanted to look good as hell. I took my scarf off and curled my bundles. Walking to my room I put some black panties and matching bra on.

Putting my dress over my head I looked in the mirror and spun around. The dress stopped at my knees and fitted me perfectly. I put my feet in my heels and walked out my room. Going to K.J's room I took his clothes off of him. He woke up while I was washing him up. I went back and forth from his bathroom to him washing his whole body up. I wasn't in the mood to give his wild ass a bath. I put some oil in his big curly fro and put Johnson & Johnson lotion all over him. Putting his diaper and dress socks on I grabbed his suit and put it on him. Just like I said, it fitted him just right. He looked so handsome. I picked him up and kissed his cheeks.

"Daddy does not love us anymore K.J. and mommy is heartbroken about it," my voice cracked as I looked at him and confessed.

"But mommy is about to take us far away. We are going to see grandma and she will make it all better. That's why we gotta dress in our best. Grandma loves us dressed up," I kissed his chubby cheeks a few times. Yatta was going to be so sorry that his sorry ass made me come to this. I hope him and that bitch enjoy life without us because we are out this bitch! Now, who gets the last laugh.

Alaric

"Look who came to their fucking senses!" German bitch ass stood up clapping when I walked in his living room.

I swear seeing him made me want to pull out my gun in my waist and kill his ass where he stood. He had his typical all black on with his white kufi hat and platinum chain on. His Cuban cigar smell was all through the room. I smiled to myself though when I saw his three men putting stacks in duffle bags. They had guns, drugs, money and I saw some diamonds that were being put in a suede black pouch. This was the day German takes all of this to his connect in Travers City. Lonell, Yatta, and Delon were at the spot waiting for German's men to arrive and then they were making their move.

I grew up with these three niggas who were my father's guards. I have had good times with them and they were like an extended family to me. But every fucking thing went out the window when Cassidy was fucked with. Z, Emmanuel were close by and waiting for my word to make their move. All this shit ended today and I was about to be free of this man who I thought for so long I wanted to be like.

"Ginger, fix ya son a plate and a drink, nigga looking all sad and shit," he yelled in the kitchen to his wife Ginger. She was my age and cool as hell. I used to joke with her and call her mama number two. It's funny that this nigga was married because he didn't believe in love. He just believes in a bitch having wife privileges. He still fucked around on Ginger all the time but she was the only one who got the perks. The money, cars, trips, shopping sprees and big ass house in Novi. He didn't love her and considering how he did me and Cassidy. This nigga was incapable of love. He needed to be dead.

"I'm cool dad, just tell me what I'm supposed to do," I almost threw up when I called that nigga my dad. This muthafucka was just a sperm donor to me now. I stood there and put my hands behind my back. German smirked at me and snapped his fingers at one of his boys. This fool got up and searched me. He pulled my gun from my waist and gave it to German.

"Really? Since when I get searched?" I turned my nose up and asked him.

"Since I know yo' ass really don't wanna be here. Since I watched my only fucking son shed tears over a bald-headed bitch. Since nigga, I see hate for me in ya' fucking eyes," he put his cigar out and walked in my face. He put his hands on my shoulders and said.

"When you realized how I'm savin' yo' ass from the games, heartbreak and money that all bitches make niggas waste. You'll thank me, meanwhile let's get to work," he turned and walked me over to where his three guards were.

"Today is shipment day lil nigga. Also known as payday so you picked a good day to come join the money team. The money you been making messing with Lonell and ya' little friends is a change compared to what you can make fucking with ya pops," he laughed and slapped my back. Ginger came and put my plate of spaghetti and fried chicken down on the table. She sat my drink down next to me and went to sit down on the couch.

"So again I ask, what do you want me to do?" I was tired of him smiling and shit in my face. I didn't want this nigga to keep touching me or to keep speaking on Cassidy. I felt like Yatta hot-headed ass and was ready to pop off.

"Ok ok, you ready to get to work. I got you. Follow me downstairs so I can show you the first thing on the list," he took a shot of his Crown Royal drink and walked towards his basement. I watched his three guards walk out the side door to the van and load it up.

"See I know you and know that you are only part of me. You got some of your mama in you too. Meaning, weakness. I watched your face when you looked at your bitch that day in your room. You love her and really don't want to be here. So, I went and got a little insurance to make sure you be a good son to the only father you will ever have," he spoke as we walked down his basement and into his storage room. He unlocked it and opened the door but told me to step in first. I had no idea what the fuck this nigga was up to until I walked inside the room.

"WHAT THE FUCK!" I rushed over to my little brother who was out cold on a twin-size mattress.

June! June!" I was shaking him but he wouldn't move. I swear I was about to break down but I just couldn't in front of this bitch nigga.

"Yo' what the fuck! You killed a seven-year-old?!" I stood up and was face to face with German.

"Nigga calm yo' ass down. That lil bitch is just drugged. His school needs to do better with watching the kids while they play outside," he started smiling making me mad as hell. I wanted to spit in this niggas face. I just kept remembering that I wanted to make it back to Cassidy.

"What the fuck was the point of doing this shit. I dumped my girl, walked away from Lonell and the operation we had going on. You fucking won!" I stood back and held my arms out looking in his snake ass eyes. He pointed at June.

"This is to make sure I really have my son. By now I'm sure your stupid ass mama and his school is looking for him. I don't give a fuck no one will ever find him. It's up to you if this little nigga gets to go home or not. Make me believe your still my fucking son. You ain't on no sneaky shit and he can go," I looked at June and then back at German.

"You ain't being my fucking father. All this shit is to fucking far. Do you have any fucking limit!" I yelled while nose to nose with him. He had a no fucks given on his face as he smirked.

"I do actually but unfortunately you will never know what that is. Now, behave or I have a friend on the east side who just loves the company of little boys," when he said that disgusting shit I wanted to fucking flip out. He winked at me and smiled.

I can honestly say that I do not know this man that I once called dad. I couldn't wait to kill him. We walked back upstairs, and his three guards were gone. I was happy as hell because that meant shit was flowing. I sat down at the dining table and tried my best to eat the food Ginger had for me. German went on his couch and picked his plate of food up to.

"So, next on the list is to take you to the house I got for you out here. Leave that city bullshit behind and come out here. You can send your mama money and shit since I know you like to play daddy to your brothers," he said to me from his couch. I nodded my head and just kept eating. My brother was on my mind and I just knew I had to get him out of this bullshit. I know by now my mama is going crazy as hell looking for him.

"Sounds cool. Ginger this food is slapping," I said to her just trying to pretend I was now calm. She said thank you and put a plate of food and some Kool-Aid on a trey.

"Damn love this ain't a hotel. You leaving room service by the lil niggas' bedside and shit," German laughed as Ginger walked downstairs smacking her lips. What the fuck. She knew June was downstairs?

"I know what you're thinking and the answer is yes. She the one who got his ass to come to the car so I could kidnap his ass," my stomach turned and I felt sick. These muthafuckas needed to be tortured. I can't believe Ginger stupid ass was in on this shit.

"I gotta take a piss," I stood up and walked to the bathroom. In there I had to splash some cold water on my face.

My body was hot and I was ready to just kill him and Ginger right fucking now. I pulled my phone out and went to my security app. I fixed the street cameras that German's men would be driving on. I sent Yatta, Lonell, and Delon a text telling them to be on the lookout for the van. I texted Z and Emmanuel and told them in fifteen minutes they can go. I also told them about June being here. Emmanuel told me he was on it with my mama and making sure she was ok. Walking back in the living room I saw Ginger on German lap kissing him. He had his hand up her dress. I set down and went back to eating.

"I'm about to fuck ya' mama pussy up. I'll be back," I just nodded my head. This would be his last nut so I hope he makes it last. I went to the kitchen and threw the rest of Ginger's food away. My stomach couldn't eat shit else. I heard a noise in the basement as I went to the living room and picked the remote control up. About a half an hour later I heard German yell and muffling in his bedroom. Seconds later he was walking downstairs looking pissed. He had his red robe on and house shoes that I bought him for Father's Day.

"What?" I asked as he stood over me. Next thing I knew he punched me in my jaw.

"WHAT THE FUCK DID YOU DO?!" he yelled at the top of his lungs. I wiped the side of my lip and stood up. I balled my first up and hit his has hard as fuck in his jaw. The shit felt good as hell. He stumbled backwards, and I went into my role of confusion.

"WHAT THE FUCK ARE YOU TALKING ABOUT!" I shouted back at him. His lip was now bleeding and he pulled his gun on me.

"Nigga why the fuck my guy calling me telling me they were robbed. This shit got your name all on it. You don't know who the fuck you fuckin' with or whose shit you fuckin' with. Where is it?!" he yelled and it was my turn to smile and laugh.

"Oh, you think this shit is funny? Ginger, bring that lil nappy head boy up here," he said and like a Nazi soldier she went and marched to German's order.

"I'm killing that lil nigga, your friends, that bald-headed bitch in front of you if you don't open your mouth and tell me where my shit is!" he looked at me with blood on the side of his lip and with so much anger.

"I ain't telling you shit! All you had to do was let me live my fucking life! This shit happened because of you. Fuck you German! Fuck you!" I yelled at him and he pressed the gun harder in my head. I kept my eyes on his and said.

"Pull it. Be the hoe ass coward I know you are," he was shaking and staring at me in my eyes with a menacing look. I didn't break my stare either. I wasn't fearful at all I just knew I was keeping my promise and coming home to Cassidy.

"UGHHHHHHH!" German moved his gun and yelled loud. He was breathing hard and then looked back at me.

"I got something better than death for you. GINGER HURRY THE FUCK UP!" We both heard her coming up the steps. Or what we thought was her. Z came from the basement with Ginger in his arms bridal style.

"Ya' bitch seem to have slipped and fell into a bullet," Z said as he dropped Ginger on the floor hard as hell with a hole in her head. I smirked and looked back at German. He was about to pull his on Z but Emmanuel came in at the right time holding my father's weakness by the arm. Some other nigga was with him to who I didn't know but Z seemed to.

"Drop it, nigga," Emmanuel said as he had a gun to German's ex-wife head. I looked at him and couldn't believe what I saw. He dropped his gun and was stuck.

"Beth?" he looked at her and said. She looked at him to with tear filled eyes.

"German, I always said you would be your own demise. I knew when I was taking from my home it had something to do with you," she said and then looked at me.

"So this must be your son. The one who you had on me while we were married. Nice to meet you," I nodded my head at her.

"Let her go. She ain't got shit to do with this," he had the nerve to look at me and say.

"Nigga shut the fuck up! June doesn't have shit to do with this! Cassidy didn't have shit to do with this but did you give a fuck?!" I yelled and Z walked past me and started fucking German up. So did the nigga who came in with Emmanuel and Beth. They were stumping and punching him all over.

"Where is June?" I looked at Emmanuel and asked.

"He in the truck still knocked out. I talked to your mama and had her tell the police she forgot he was with his father. They saw me and knew shit was good. Lonell called me and said shit went smooth. Another two-mill apiece," Emmanuel smiled at me and said. I nodded my head and looked back at German all bloody and fucked up.

"Who the hell are you?" I asked the nigga beating German ass with Z. He looked at me out of breath and extended his hand to me.

"I'm Neal, Cassidy's dad. Thanks for looking after my daughter. Z told me a lot about you and I apologize for you being put in this fucked up situation," he said to me as we shook hands.

"Nice to meet you and no need to apologize. I love your daughter to death so this shit was bound to end this way," I looked back down at German and kneeled down. He was fucked up but still conscious.

"I used to want to be you growing up and even being grown. There was never a problem with you and I's relationship until you did some shit to my girl. Hell, fuck her being my girl she's a woman first. You fucking violated her and for what? Because your wife left you after you cheated on her with my mama? You didn't even blink twice when Z killed Ginger. You are incapable of love," I said to him as I looked in his bloody eyes. He smiled and spit blood on his floor.

"Y-You think I gave a fuck about that bitch Ginger. She kept my bed warm and my balls drained. I don't have no love for these bitches," he laughed and spit some more blood on the floor. I stood up.

"Oh, you don't?" I walked up to Beth and shot her in the head. Her lifeless body hit the ground and Emmanuel, Z and Neal looked at me in shock.

"YOU MUTHAFUCKA!" German yelled as he ran towards me but I stopped him with a bullet in his head.

"God damn my nigga, I thought we were leaving Beth alive?" Z said as he looked at her body and then me.

"Shit changed when my little brother got involved," I said as I walked passed German's body.

"Let's get the fuck out of her. I got a crew coming to handle everything," Emmanuel said as we walked outside. I was happy as hell June was out cold from all this shit. When he wakes up he'll be at home and won't know what the fuck was going home. I pulled my phone out and texted Cassidy.

Me: It's over boo, we all good. I'm on my way to you.

Cass Love: Thank God. I love you, Ric.

I smiled at her response.

Me: I love you too Cass love. Always will.

Putting my phone back in my pocket I took a deep breath in and out happy this shit was over and that I came out on top. With a nice ass payday at the end of it to.

Yatta

Swear I am killing this bitch, Cleo! I tried over and over to get her to see that I didn't want her. Me and Cleo never have been together. I never even treated this bitch like we were a couple. I would go weeks and weeks without talking to her. We didn't do dates, phone conversations, text messages or any of that cute shit. I never even held the bitch-hand. In high school, I went to prom with my niggas and left with two bitches. The most intimate I ever have been with Cleo was the drunk and high unprotected sex we had the night we conceived our son. I have done more than make her understand that I never, ever, ever, ever want her. But this bitch just wouldn't get the picture.

Cleo just had to do some shit that she knew would make me kill her ass. Two fucking people in the entire world that I don't play about Two! Since we took a DNA test and K.J. was proved as my son he became one of those two. Since the first day in 9th grade, Erin Khila Hudges walked her gorgeous ass in my homeroom she quickly became the first person on that list. I love my uncle, auntie and my day ones but they all can handle themselves. Erin and K.J are fucking innocent and all fucking mine. I will kill anybody that messes with them. Norbit hoe ass could have killed Erin and I would have been no fucking good.

Being the nigga I am and knowing my girl the way I do. I knew to listen to her on the phone. I had Alaric bug her shit anyway to make sure she never met with her brother on the low. I knew she would feel sorry for him or want to reach out. That's just the type of heart my cutie pie has. She can't stand to see someone sad or feelings hurt. That's why I was still kicking my own ass for the way I treated her when my uncle got arrested. It ain't in Erin to do people foul. That's one of the things I loved about her. She wouldn't even fuck with me because she thought me and Cleo were a family. Y'all see how I nipped that shit in the bud.

I never in a million years thought Norbit was fucking around with Cleo. Did y'all hear that nigga say he was going to run off with Cleo and my son!? I swear if Z wouldn't have stopped me from kicking his ass I would have beat his ass to death. I called Emmanuel and filled him in. He was livid but I told him we had the nigga. He wanted us to bring him to the house that he held Erin's mama at. I was glad to drop that trash off to be handled. Now after shit with Alaric's bitch ass dad went smooth. It was time for me to get rid of the rest of the trash. I swear if this bitch didn't have my son I would have been killed her.

I was trying to spare Cleo's ass but fuck it. I'm killing this bitch and Erin will be K.J's mama. What the fuck. I said to myself as I pulled into Cleo apartment complex and saw police cars and EMS truck. I parked my car and opened my door. I couldn't see shit because of all the people who were out there crowding around the area. Swear black people nosey as hell.

"Yatta!" I turned around and saw Cassidy and Alaric walk up.

"Fuck y'all doing here?" I asked as I gave Cassidy a hug and Alaric a five.

"All this chaos is right next to my apartment complex remember and you know black folks nosey," Cassidy said laughing. I forgot her and Cleo were next door neighbors.

"Yea these muthafuckas about to let me through so I can make sure it ain't Cleo's unit that's having problems," I said as I moved through the thick ass crowd. It was getting late in the evening. I wanted to fuck Cleo up and take my son home with me. Pushing through the crowd, my heart dropped when I saw Cleo's door wide open.

"Aye yo' what the fuck!" I yelled as I pushed people out my way.

"Sir! Sir! You can't come in this area! Police only sir this is a crime scene!" A cop held me back from going into Cleo's apartment.

"What! Crime scene! Tha fuck you mean!? Man, my son lives here!" I yelled at the stupid white cop. His eyes got wide but he still held me back.

"Sir, is your child a baby boy about 11-months?" I was nodding my head yes before he even finished his sentence.

"Yes, it is now move and let me the fuck through!" I was yelling at the top of my lungs and I know I was looking crazy as hell but I didn't give a damn.

"Sir please calm down and I can tell you what is happening!" he was talking to me as two muthafuckas came out holding both ends of a black body bag all zipped up. I fucking lost it.

"YO' WHAT THE FUCK! IS THAT MY FUCKING SON!" I went wild and knocked the cop on his ass running to the body bag. I swear I felt like I was out my body at that very moment. I ran over to them scaring the two muthafuckas holding the bag. Rushing them I pushed one of them and unzipped the bag. I saw Cleo's lifeless body and I didn't even give a fuck. I dropped that shit like the garbage it was, head first on the ground.

"AYE WHERE THE FUCK IS MY SON!" I yelled barging into Cleo's apartment. Three officers grabbed me and K.J was being rolled out pass me on a gurney.

"SIR PLEASE CALM DOWN OR WE ARE GOING TO HAVE YOU ARRESTED!" This black cop stood in front of me and said. I was going wild as fuck with so many emotions going through me.

"Yatta please calm down so you can be with K.J" Cassidy came in crying hard as hell. I heard my son name and calmed down the best way I could.

"Listen to me carefully sir so I can let you be with your son. He is alive and being taken to children's hospital. You can ride with him and later I will come talk to you. Ok?" I didn't say shit. Tears just fell from my eyes as the cops let me go and I ran outside to be with my son. I don't know what the fuck was going on but I was about to bring this city to its knees over mine.

Emmanuel

"Wake the fuck up," I popped Josey in her forehead hard making her jump up.

I had this bitch chained up in one if the trap houses I ran on the west side. Ever since this bitch gave birth to my daughter she has been a pain in my existence. I tried to give Erin that two-family home. Hell, it was a point when I loved Josey with everything in me. She was my woman, maybe not the only bitch I was fucking but still. She was a wife and when she told me she was pregnant I was on top of the world. But then I seen a side of her that I didn't know she had. I tried to say it was because she was new to motherhood.

I blamed it on her hormones and even some post-partum depression. By the time Erin was one-year-old. I realized Josey issues were deeper than textbook shit. This hoe just flat out didn't like our daughter. What the fuck kind of woman dislikes their own child. My mama used to whoop me and Delon ass. We knew we got on her nerves but never once did we not feel love or feel our mama didn't want us around. Hell naw, I knew then that I had to take my daughter and quit fucking with Josey. When I found out she was cheating it was more on the lines of respect. Verse me being heartbroken.

I stopped loving Josey when I realized she had a problem with our own daughter. I was yet again hopeful for Erin's sake. I thought as the years went by Josey would eventually get a relationship with her daughter. Shit, I was wrong as fuck, all this bitch did was break my muse heart. I have checked Josey so many times. A few times I wanted to just snap this bitch neck but I thought of Erin. My daughter has a good pure heart. She believes in chances so I didn't want to mess that up for her. But now, oh you can best believe this bitch was as good as dead.

"Manny, please can I have some clothes? At least a blanket or a hot shower. You already have me exposed to your thugger friends who come down here and feed me," she started coughing and sitting up. I kept Josey fed but she was still naked and dirty as hell from when I grabbed her at her house.

"Bitch don't know fucking body care about your problems. Look I wanna ask you some shit before we get this party started. I want some honesty from you and I will let you out of here. You can collect the insurance money from his death. Knowing you, I'm sure you get all that fat farts money. As far as the police will know, dude committed suicide. Was it a homicide-suicide depends on you and how honest you can be now," I looked at her and said. Josey stood up all naked and dirty and nodded her head.

"When we were together, I gave you everything. I paid for your classes and books in college. You had the finest of clothes, cars, jewelry. We traveled together to some of the most beautiful countries. Saw all the art, culture, we went swimming in the ocean and met Kings. Knowing I did all of that for you. Knowing how eventually the way we fucked, you were going to give me children. Am I right?" I looked at her and asked.

"Yes," she said looking at her knotted fingers and then back at me.

"So why would you look at the child we made and have such a dislike for her?" I sat on the edge of an old desk I had in the basement waiting for Josey to answer.

"I have a sister. We don't get along, never have. I was the center of my parent's world until she came. Then I found myself having to split my parent's attention. Having to share my room, my toys, look out for someone other than myself. I hated the bitch until we got to middle school and I realized she had a little problem," I crossed my arms and breathed in deep and out hard. I wanted to know the point of this story but I let her continue.

"Eating. That girl could eat her food, mines, our parents and still be hungry. I realized she was going to be a fat girl. I used to sneak her food and she thought it was because I loved her. No. I wanted to keep that bitch fat. Fat bitches are nothing to take seriously," she looked at me and smiled.

"You see Manny you came along and was the first man I ever loved. We bonded, you saw more in me than just pussy. Like you said, we traveled, had a deep passion for the arts. I was the center of your world," her eyes got watery as she smiled big at me and said. Then she pointed to my arm tattoo. It was a portrait of Erin's baby picture with her name and birthday.

"But then she fucking came and stole you from me. You stopped wanting to travel, you changed on me. But worst of all, I stopped being the center of your world. A son, I knew you wouldn't be weak over. I knew you would still be hard and still look at me as everything. But a girl would have made me fade in the background. I couldn't do like I did my sister. I couldn't make Erin unlovable. Every fucking body just loved that damn girl," she stood there with tears in her eyes.

"I never wanted to cheat on you, Manny. Hell, I would have died for you but what I will never do. I will never play second to any fucking body," I looked her in her eyes as I walked closer to her.

"You disgust me. I can't even say I hate you or regret you because you gave me one of the best things I will ever have. Erin is smarter than you, she's beautiful inside and out which is something you're not. And as far as your sister goes you were wrong. Big bitches are definitely winning. Ya sister wins first prize in riding my dick and sucking it on more than one occasion," I looked at Josey and smiled big. I wish I had a camera to show her the face she was making. Tears fell and her mouth was open.

"You're lying," she whispered looking in my eyes with so much sadness.

"I swear on my daughter's life. More than I can count on both our hands combined," I laughed and she tried to knee me in the balls but I pushed her making her stumble.

"YOU MUTHERFUCKER! MY OWN SISTER!" she shouted at me making me laugh harder as she stood back up on her feet.

"You were wrong Manny. I don't dislike Erin. I fucking hate that little bitch. I wish I would have drowned her in the tub like I wanted to do so many times," when she said that I lost it. I walked up to her and slapped her with the back of my hand.

"Naw, don't ball up. Look at daddy," I said with disgust in my voice as I picked her up and punched her twice in the face.

"I got something for you 'mommy dearest'," I yelled 'yo' loud and you could hear walking upstairs. Josey's eyes got big as she looked and Delon carry her punk ass son down the stairs.

"Oh my God Manny! What the fuck did you do to him!" she yelled at me with a swollen eye and a bloody mouth. Delon dropped her beat up ass son right next to her.

"Shit he had a run in with my son-in-law. It ain't my fault. Turns out you were right about everybody loving Erin," me and Delon started laughing as Josey took the tape off her son's mouth.

"Mommy! They killed Dad, he told me they did," he said pointing to Delon. This fool was cracking up.

"You think this is FUNNY! Your fucking cruel Manny and you are nothing but your brother follower. Always have been," she said to Delon as she tried to spit blood at him. That was a mistake because he had the temper between the both of us.

PHEW!

"AHH!" Josey screamed as Delon put a bullet between her son's eyes.

"God damn Delon. I wanted to do the honors!" I laughed at my crazy ass brother.

"My bad but that bitch talk too much she always has," his mean ass put his gun up in his waist.

"Oh well," I hunched my shoulders and said as I pulled my gun out and put two bullets in Josey's chest and one in her head.

"Murder-Suicide it is," I said as I put my gun up. Me and Delon started getting to work on the bodies. We had to get them back to Josey and her husband home so we can set the shit up. The perks of being a cop is having the training of knowing how to make this shit look right.

"Let's hurry up and get this shit over with. Lonell upstairs waiting," Delon said and I nodded my head. We were almost done out the dark.

***

"This shit feels like old times with all the killing, set-ups and shit. My fucking dick hard," I said as me, Delon and Lonell rode in an unmarked Yukon.

"Nigga we didn't need to hear that last part but you right though. This shit does feel like old times," Lonell said while driving. We were on our way to Havoc's crib about to deal with him.

"You know this shit can start back up. The money, drugs, set-ups, killings," Delon said from the back seat.

"Naw, I got Erin to think about. She doesn't know this side of me and I don't know if she ever would want to. The weeks and weeks gone away from her ain't what's up," I shook my head no looking out the window.

"Yea you might be right about that. Dreka doesn't know this side of me neither and with Angelica coming home soon. I ain't even trying to be gone like that and have both my ladies mad at me," me and Lonell looked back at him.

"Both?! Don't tell me you getting back with Angelica crazy ass? You know that's my sister and I love her but bruh she nuts," I joked and Lonell started laughing.

"She is crazy as fuck but she bad as hell and the mother of my child. Plus, I kind of love that crazy shit," Delon confessed.

"Tell Angelica to keep that shit away from Juziel. Them two used to run wild as fuck in high school back in the day. How many niggas did we have to fuck up?!" Lonell laughed as we all started reminiscing high school days.

Pulling up to Havoc house in Southfield we all got out a few houses down. The good thing about being in Southfield was the lack of street lights. You'll get some but luckily Havoc block didn't have any. It was humid as hell tonight and we were in all black from head to toe. Alaric had already made sure the house wasn't bugged and he took care of the street security cameras. He also was able to get us Havoc security system code for us. I swear that nigga could clean up hacking and all that tech shit he was good at.

"A'ight my tracker says Havoc should be about ten minutes away. I'm so ready to get this nigga. Twenty-years plus of friendship down the drain. I just want to know why and then we can get this shit done. I'm ready for a nice ass vacation with my wife after this," Lonell said and me and Delon agreed.

We had shoe covers over our shoes, black leather gloves on caps on our head. We didn't want to leave any DNA behind. With Havoc being a snitch for the police. They are going to check every inch of this apartment to make sure there is no foul play. That's why we didn't sit down or touch anything. In minutes, we heard the front door unlock. Me and Delon stepped in the dining room hallway. Lonell stood out the way as well so Havoc would walk all the way in his house. If he sees any of us he might try to run or make a lot of noise alerting people. Havoc walked in closing and locking the door behind him.

"What's good nigga," Lonell said as he stepped from a nook in the corner next to Havoc bookshelf. Havoc face was of one who had seen a ghost. Me and Delon didn't move yet.

"D-Damn Lonell why are you hiding in my house and shit?" Havoc tried to put on a fake laugh but it was fear all in it.

"I just had to holla at you for a minute and I know we both been busy. I was busy handling shit and you were busy being a fucking rat," Lonell jumped right into it catching Havoc off guard. He did another nervous laugh and said.

"What the hell you talking about man? You know me, I'm a lot of shit but I ain't no rat," he stepped backwards to the door and that was me and Delon que.

"Stop moving muthafucka," I said as me and Delon walked out his dining room. Havoc looked at me and Delon in shock. He waited a while and then looked at Lonell.

"I didn't want to man. I swear I didn't want to, but they made me Lonell. I can't go to jail man I ain't built for the shit. B-B-But I told them tonight I was out," I looked at Lonell and could tell he was ready to attack.

"Don't do it Lonell, remember the plan," I said and he kept a death stare on Havoc.

"You were family nigga. You at ate at my table, at my fucking house," swear Lonell looked like the killer he was.

"Lonell you put those fucking kids ahead of me. It was our operation and then you brought Yatta and his two friends on. You started only listening to them and letting them little niggas outrank me. I was tired of that shit." Havoc confessed and at the point, I pulled the bag out my pocket and gave it to Lonell. It was time to do this before Lonell popped off and everything would be fucked.

"Fuck what he saying bruh. You know he a rat and that's all that matters so let's get it done," I said as Lonell took the bag out my hand.

"Havoc if you don't want your little boy and baby mama to die you will do exactly as I say," Lonell said to him.

"Please don't kill me Lonell. Like you just said, I have a family," Havoc started crying and my annoying ass brother started laughing. I nudged his ass and he hunched his shoulders.

"Sorry nigga but this shit is funny. Issa full grown bitch," Delon laughed and me and Lonell chuckled and shook our head at his crazy ass.

"Walk in your bedroom and put whatever you sleep with on," Lonell instructed Havoc and he looked confused.

"What?" he asked and Lonell pulled his phone out and showed Havoc a video of his baby mama house.

"I didn't stutter nigga," he said and Havoc walked with all three of us following him. He went in his room and undressed. Unfortunately, we had to watch so he wouldn't try any funny shit. He put his gym shoes and dirty clothes in his closet. He put on some pajama pants and a white t-shirt.

"Good, now go in the kitchen and get something to eat," Lonell said and Havoc once again looked confused but he did it. He walked in his kitchen and pulled out a bag from White Castle burger place. We stood in silence as he microwaved it and ate the three burgers in silence. He washed it down with a beer.

"A'ight, move to the living room and cut your TV on. Go to whatever you normally watch," Havoc did it and went to HGTV channel.

"Now sit on your couch and take everything in this bag," Lonell gave Havoc the bag and when he opened it and looked inside. He looked at the three of us like we were crazy.

"Come on Lonell please----"

"Nigga I'm being cool as a breeze right now. Do what the fuck I say or I swear I will kill my Godchild and you know I will," Lonell said that shit and believe you me, he meant it. Havoc started crying as he ate the Mushrooms in the bag. When we made the drop to German's dealer we bought some from him and something else as well. Havoc ate all the mushrooms and then he pulled out an unmarked medicine bottle.

"What is this?" he asked.

"Absinthe, drink up nigga. All of it," Lonell said with a smile on his face. Havoc cried like a baby making Delon laugh his ass off.

"If you spill anything or throw up you have signed your son death certificate," Lonell said as Havoc finished up the bottle.

"There," he said as he put the empty bottle in the bag. Delon came from Havoc kitchen with a knife from Havoc set. He gave it to Lonell.

"Now, since you a snake ass rat I want you to cut your tongue out and then slit both your wrists," This time I joined in the laughing with Delon. This punk ass nigga balled his eyes out and started begging.

"Pleaseeee Lonell. I'm fucking begging you man I swear I told the police I was out. I'll disappear, you n-n-never have to worry about me again. Just let me live for my son," Havoc pleaded.

"Nigga I'm doing your son a favor. You shameful as fuck to have has a father. Now you are wasting time. Cut nigga," Lonell gave Havoc the knife and I promise I have never seen a person cry so bad.

The drugs started kicking in because Havoc became slurry and his eyes got dilated as fuck. He grabbed his tongue and started cutting. Shit, I have heard some shit out mushrooms and absinthe especially with being on the police force. Some white teens got caught dealing with this shit and even using. The shit makes you illuminate, makes everything around you seem unreal. You can't separate reality from fiction. And I guess you can't feel either because Havoc didn't even scream as he cut his tongue out. This nigga cut and started laughing with blood coming out his mouth and tears running down his eyes.

"Shit turning my stomach,," Delon said. We kept our distance so we wouldn't get any blood on us. Havoc was sitting on his couch laughing. This nigga started making small slices in his wrists while still laughing. He had blood on his clothes and his couch. Good, the shit looked real as fuck. Looks like the nigga got high and was on a trip off the mushrooms and absinthe. That was our plan to make the shit look real. Havoc started losing a lot of blood out his wrist and fell over on his couch still laughing and eyes dilated even bigger. Looked like they were about to pop out his face.

"Let's roll," Lonell said as his phone rung while we walked out locking the door. Now we were finally out the dark with all this bullshit.

"What the fuck! I'm on my way," Lonell yelled while we got in the truck.

"What happened?" me and Delon asked in unison. I thought about Erin and I'm sure Delon was thinking about Dreka.

"Some shit went down with Yatta and his baby mama. We gotta get to Children's Hospital," Lonell said as he pulled off. I pulled my phone out so I could call Erin. Damn, now I need a vacation.

Erin

I cannot believe this shit right now. I feel like I just want to go to sleep and start today over from scratch. Eliminate all this bullshit with Jamie, Cleo, and my crazy ass mama. I went from having fun with my boos at a foam party. To be set up and almost killed by my own brother. Now I'm walking through Children's Hospital hallway trying to get to Kenyatta and K.J. I don't know much. Cassidy called me crying saying Cleo was dead and K.J was in the hospital. Hell, I broke down crying as if he was my son. Cleo was a lot of things but I didn't want her to get killed. I don't even know what is going on all I know is I need to get to Kenyatta and K.J.

"Erin!" I looked to my left and Dreka, Cassidy, Alaric, and Z ran in my direction. Then the elevators dinged and Lonell, my uncle D, and my daddy stepped off the elevator.

"What the hell is going on?" Lonell asked. My dad hugged me and kissed the top of my head along with my uncle D hugging Dreka.

"Erin, he won't let anyone in the room until you he sees you. The nurses and police won't tell us anything so please go back there and then let us know," Dreka said and I could tell that she had been crying.

"Ok, I'll be right back," I said as I walked towards al the police officers and nurses.

"Ma'am, I'm sorry but the parent does not want any visitors at this time," a police officer in a suit walked up to me and said. Before I could say anything my dad walked up and told him who I was.

I was granted access and I walked slowly to the door. I knocked light as hell and as easy as I could I opened the door. I wasn't sure what I was walking into but I spoke to God on the way over and I'm trusting in him and his word. The curtain was pulled out but I could hear machines and beeping. Walking past the curtain Kenyatta was sitting in the chair holding K.J's hand with his head down.

"Get the fuck out," he said not looking up. I swallowed my lump in my throat and said.

"It's me, baby," I spoke low and soft because if he still wanted me to leave I wouldn't have felt anyway. This was his son and Cleo was dead so I would have gave Kenyatta his space. He looked up at me and slid his hand out of K.J's and pulled the chair behind him next to him. I walked over and sat down. Finally looking at K.J he still was so chubby and cute. Even with tubes up his nose and an IV in his arm. He had a little hospital gown on and his gorgeous curly hair was out. I couldn't help the tears that came to my eyes but I didn't let them fall. I grabbed Kenyatta's hand in mine and kissed it. We sat in silence for like fifteen minutes until he finally spoke.

"I can't believe this bitch man. I swear on God I feel like getting that bitch cold body and pissin' on it. Look at my fucking boy," when he said that last part his voice cracked. I looked at Kenyatta's face and tears were falling from his eyes. I just kept kissing his hand and squeezing it.

"I am so sorry Kenyatta. I can't imagine how your feeling right now but I want you to know there are more angels in here with K.J right now. The demons that tried to come and end K.J's life couldn't prosper. He will be ok," shit. Now my voice was cracking but I cleared my throat because I needed to be strong for Kenyatta.

"What happened?" I asked lowly because I didn't want to make the mood worse.

"This bitch crushed pills in K.J's bottle. Sleeping pills but enough so he wouldn't wake up. She put her grandma obituary in the crib with K.J. She put one next to her in her bedroom then the bitch hung herself from the ceiling fan. Police said a neighbor called police because it was commotion coming from Cleo apartment. She broke all the shit in there so I guess that alerted neighbors," he looked up and K.J then continued.

"She tried to take him from me for good Erin. That shit would have fucked me up. That bitch was that bitter and selfish that she would kill her own son. Had the fucking nerve to leave a note. I told the police to get that shit away from me," I wiped his face as the tears rolled down it.

"K.J had to get his stomach flushed but the doctors said he will make a recovery. He's just sleeping right now," I sat up and pulled Kenyatta to me so I could hug him. I didn't know what the hell to say. I was stunned if anything because I can't believe Cleo would go this far. To take her own life and almost end K.J's before it barely started. Selfish and bitter doesn't describe her. I pulled away and wiped Kenyatta's tears.

"I'm right here with you. When K.J wakes up I'll be right here with you every step of the way. I know I'm not his mother but-----"

"You are his mother that is if you want to be," he looked in my eyes with such sadness.

"Erin I want this with you forever baby. I know I'm all in bitch mode right now but I am still a man and I still want a life with you cutie pie," I smiled and kissed his lips.

"You are not in bitch mode Kenyatta. This is something serious that could have had a different outcome. You're showing you emotions baby and there is nothing wrong with that," I smiled at him and kissed his lips again.

"This shit just puts me in the mindset of my mama. She didn't give a fuck about me when she killed my father and then herself. Knowing I was in the apartment to and I was too little to help myself. If the neighbors wouldn't have complained about me crying so loud I could have died. I was alone and helpless. I never wanted my son to feel that way and for Cleo to do that to him," he shook his head and got a disgusted look on his face.

"That hoe is lower than low. I feel like killing her mama just for birthing that trick," I let him vent as I kept kissing his hand and rubbing it. Sitting there for a few minutes I let Kenyatta's hand go and scooted close to K.J's bed. I grabbed his little chubby hand and kissed it as well.

"I'm new to this so bear with me but I promise to love you more then I wanted from my own mother. If we stick together we can run your daddy," Kenyatta smacked his lips and I laughed when I said that. I kissed K.J's cheek a few times and then grabbed Kenyatta's hand again.

"I got something for you. I really didn't know when I wanted to give it to you but now seems perfect," I unzipped my BEBE bookbag and pulled out a drawing paper. I was so nervous about showing Kenyatta this. I looked at it one time and then turned it facing him. His eyes got big and he took it out my hand. I put my bookbag back on the side of me and watched him look at the drawing.

"I know it seems weird but it's beyond what you are doing in the picture in my eyes. You look effortless and its one of the few times where I really get to see how perfectly made you are. I could have thought about you sleeping or some sex faces but that's not artistic. I started with your lips and chain. That chain gets me every time along with them lips," I got lost in the picture as I explained it to him. He looked at the drawing still with an expression I couldn't understand.

"Damn baby, this shit is fucking dope. You such a beast at this shit I swear its lifelike as hell. And ain't shit weird about this Erin. Nothing you draw or paint is ever weird to me. Imma hold this shit dear to my heart because I know you don't draw people, so I'm honored you decided to draw my ugly ass," he laughed and went back to admiring the picture. I laughed to and ran my fingers through his dreads.

"Ugly? Nigga bye, this face is perfection, a muse, and all mine," I rubbed the side of his face and kissed him again. Looking back at the drawing he smirked and said.

"Damn!" Then he put it on the table next to the hospital bed K.J was laying in. The picture I drew was of Kenyatta when he gave me my belly button piercing. His face had a sternness but still handsome. His lips were relaxed and his eyebrows were furrowed and that chain rested on his hard chest. He was absolutely perfect and the image kept coming to my mind so I had to draw it. His reaction made me feel amazing.

"You know everybody is out there waiting to see you and find out what is going on," I said to him while he now kissed my hand.

"They can come back now but wasn't nobody coming back until you got here. That's how much you got me, Erin. Shit ain't never right until you come around me," looking at me he leaned forward and kissed me. I let his tongue come in my mouth and we just made out for a minute.

"I love you, Kenyatta," breaking our kiss, I whispered on his lips.

"I love you more cutie pie," I smiled at him and gave him a few more kisses before we let everyone in the room. Kenyatta told them what happened, it was anger and a few tears from Dreka and Cassidy. All and all, we were just happy that K.J was going to be ok and have no side effects from the drugs.

"You know you didn't have to stay up here with me baby. You could have gone home and got in my bed," Kenyatta said as I laid on his chest in the twin size cot we were on. It was a little after two in the morning and K.J still hadn't woken up yet. The doctor said tomorrow morning the drugs should be completely out his system and he would wake up.

"Yatta shut up, of course, I was staying," he looked up at me like I was crazy. He was annoying me saying dumb shit.

"Get fucked up Erin, you already in the hospital. I can fuck you up and send ya' ass straight to surgery," I laughed when he said that, he arched his eyebrow at me.

"Stop talking crazy. You know I wasn't leaving you up here alone. I want to see K.J when he first wakes up," I said then kissed his lips. We talked a little about moving together, having K.J full-time and then we watched some YouTube videos until we both fell asleep.

I woke up about twenty minutes after falling asleep. I eased off the cot and walked over to K.J. He was still asleep, so I just kissed his cheeks a few times. Getting some singles out my purse I decided to go to the vending machine by the elevators. I slipped on my flip-flops and walked out the room. When I opened the door the cop in the suit from earlier was at the nurse's desk with some stuff in his hand.

"Excuse me," I called out to him and he answered.

"Um, I was wondering if you still have the letter that K.J's mom wrote when she killed herself?" He looked at me for a minute and nodded his head.

"I'm not supposed to do this, but Emmanuel is my guy so," he said before he pulled a plastic bag out that had evidence on it.

"I have to turn all this stuff in so hurry up," I nodded my head as I sat down and pulled the letter out.

Yatta,

Did you honestly think you could have K.J and not me to? Did you think I would let you run off into the sunset with the next bitch and I sit quietly like a trained baby mama? There is NOTHING that BITCH can give you that I can't. Instead of you trying to do the right thing and make us a family. You'd rather chase behind Erin and her magic ass pencils. Well no, that's not how this works. Me and K.J are a package deal and if you don't want us both then you get neither. In my grandma's arms have always been safe for me anyways. Just know that as you bury our son, YOU DID THIS! Rot in misery.

-Cleo

I scanned the letter with my eyes and just shook my head. I wiped the lonely tear that fell because my heart broke for K.J. His own mother was so wrapped up in what she wanted that she almost killed him. I have no words for Cleo and although she is a lot of wild things. I never expected this. I put the letter back in the plastic bag, walked up to the cop and gave it to him.

"A woman like that deserves to be exactly where she is, in hell," he gave me a smile and walked off.

I didn't even want anything from the vending machine now. My stomach was twisted up. I thought about my own mother as I went back into K.J's room. She never wanted a relationship with me. No matter what I did, how I dressed, no matter what I painted or drew. She just wouldn't love me the way I saw other girl's mother's love their daughters. I tried and she still looked at me like I sickened her. I just don't get it and I honestly don't think I want to. It was clear that she would never love me right if not at all. I need to let it go and let it be. Laying down on Kenyatta's chest his arm went around my waist and he kissed my forehead.

"Love you, baby," he managed to say while still sleep. I smirked.

"Love you more Kenyatta," I looked over at K.J.

"Love you K.J," I said as I laid back down on Kenyatta's chest. Enjoy hell Cleo and good riddance.

Epilogue

6 Months later
Yatta

"Stupid ass people and their non-speaking English asses. All I wanted was some more of them stuffed waffles thangs. They looked at a nigga like I had a bomb on me," I walked in me and Erin's suite mad as hell.

"Baby we are in another country and another culture. You have to understand where they're coming from. Stop being mean and give me them waffles," Erin pretty ass was sitting in the middle of the king size bed with an all-white fluffy robe on. We had our balcony door open so the sun was beaming in our room. Her big ass hair was curly and all over the place but that's because I gave her some morning dick.

"Here greedy ass," I gave her my plate and she took two waffles off of it and put it own her own. I set next to her in my robe that matched hers feeling like a King.

"Can I get some more of that before we get dress and leave?" I pointed to her pussy as I kissed her exposed thigh and she laughed trying to cover it up.

"Noooo. Kenyatta, we have an Uber coming to take us to the museum in one hour. You've had enough," I looked at her and smacked my lips.

"First off I can never get enough of you. Second how many damn museums does this place have," I laughed as I started eating these good ass waffles.

I surprised Erin with a five-day trip to Paris, France as an early Christmas gift. My cutie-pie gave me the ugly cry when December 1st came and I gave her the plane tickets. Me, Z, Alaric, and Lonell decided to go into business with German's connect in Traverse City. We were making triple so why not give my baby a trip to one of her favorite places. Erin had been doing so good with school, work and taking care of K.J. For someone who didn't have kids, she took care of him better than me. I loved having us under one roof. A month after K.J was released from the hospital. I bought me, Erin and him a four-bedroom house in Farmington Hills.

I wanted a big stupid ass house with hella bedrooms and the works. Erin was like naw, that's unnecessary shit. Cutie pie was right though which was why I was happy she was on my team. Our house was five-thousand square feet with a huge ass master bedroom. I had a giant ass basement, outdoor pool, and spacious backyard. Patio, custom marble kitchen, and four car garage. Erin loved that house and decorated it like the Queen of the house she was. I always wanted to keep her and my son happy. K.J was doing great, he turned one-years-old three months ago.

Me and Erin went all out and threw him a Nick Jr. party with all the characters, a D.J. bounce houses, buffets and open bar for the grown-ups. It was a lot for a son but me and Erin didn't give a fuck. Cleo's family tried all the time to see K.J but I told them to die right along with their fucked-up ass daughter and sister. Ain't none of them muthafuckas ever coming near K.J. My uncle and auntie Juziel are doing good as hell. The rented their house out and moved to Texas. Our connect wanted him to run shit down there so they packed up and dipped. I miss seeing him every day but I was happy he got a new scenery. Juziel and Erin had become real close. I think Erin took to her like a mama and Juziel was loving it.

Speaking of mamas, the news flashed a few months back with Erin's mama. It was said that her husband was into some dirty shit with a thief in Detroit. With fear of being arrested and losing everything he went home and killed his wife and son. Then turned the gun on himself. Shit was sad and I was right there with my baby to help her through that. Erin shed a few tears but all and all I would say she was ok now. Shit crazy as hell right. Get this though. The news also said an informant that was working with the dirty cop. Well, that nigga went home and took some drugs and cut his own tongue out and slit his wrists! Tha fuck is this world coming to?!

Anyways, I decided to start small and rent a space inside of Oakland Mall. I was going to eventually have my own building but right now I travel a lot because of business. So space was all I could handle. I loved that shit though and was making some good money from it. I had three other tattoo artists and one other piercer and then myself. Erin hated when I did women tattoos and piercing but she knew ain't shit to worry about. My dick only works for her and that's real shit. Now looking at her beautiful greedy ass tear these waffles up. I felt like the luckiest nigga ever.

Erin still painted and did her drawings I always made sure of that. I never wanted her to let go of her gift. She was still making imitation art for her pops friend. She enrolled in The Art Institute of Michigan in August. I covered the bill for that as long as she was doing what she loved my cutie pie knew I had her.

"Stop staring at me, Kenyatta," her shy ass covered her face as she ate. I laughed and opened her robe and kissed her stomach.

"You see how mean yo' mama is? Get her right for me daddy's baby," I smiled and kissed all over her stomach. Yea, Erin was thirteen weeks pregnant. We found out last month when Erin fainted at work. My ass was nutting up but it wasn't shit but dehydration. That's when we found out she was eight weeks pregnant. Man, I fucking hit the roof I was so damn happy. Her pops wanted to kill me but he knew I had her and our baby.

"I'm not being mean your daddy is just being a creep," she looked down and said to her stomach. I grabbed my phone and went to my Spotify app.

"Kenyatta we have to get dressed," Erin started whining as I went to our song.

"I just wanna kiss on you baby, that's all," I put the phone on the dresser as the song played.

Girl if I told you I love you
That doesn't mean that I don't care, oooh
And when I tell you I need you
Don't you think that I'll never be there, ooooh
Baby I'm so tired of the way you turn my words into
Deception and lies
Don't misunderstand me when I try to speak my mind
I'm only saying what's in my heart
Cupid doesn't lie
But you won't know unless you give it a try
Oh baby, true love
won't lie but we won't know unless we give it a try
give it a try

112 Cupid played as I laid on the side of Erin tongue kissing her soft ass lips. I loved this girl so much and will forever be grateful. Her ass has had me since ninth grade and I just knew eventually she would let this bad boy steal her heart. I kissed her neck while her leg wrapped around mine. Grabbing her left hand while we went back to kissing I rubbed the four-karat engagement ring I put on her finger our first night in Paris. We went to see the Eiffel Tower at night because it lights up. As soon as it did I dropped on my knee in front of a bunch of strangers. Erin cried and managed to get out a yes.

"I can't wait to become Mrs. Erin Bailey," her pretty ass smiled to me and said.

"You already Mrs. Bailey it's just a matter of getting it on paper," I kissed her lips again and before you know it. I was deep inside of her addictive pregnant pussy.

"I love you Cutie pie," I whispered in her ear before biting it.

"I love you too Kenyatta," that shit made my heart jump anytime she says my name. We ended up missing our museum appointment from fucking like rabbits. But it was all good I made it up to her the next day.

Cassidy

"Cass love would you stop crying before these people think I beat on you," Ric was standing next to me hugging me and rubbing my back because I was crying.

"Well, what did you leave me for then?" I cried out and he started laughing.

"Boo, I only went to get you those almond Snickers you love. I promise I said. 'Boo me and K.J going to the next isle' but you didn't hear me," I looked at him crying harder.

"Stop laughing Ric its not funny," I snatched away and started pushing the shopping cart. We were inside of Wal-Mart shopping because my six months pregnant ass was craving some Almond Snickers. Yup, Alaric first time fucking me again after that shit with German crazy ass, knocked me up. We found out three days ago that we were having a boy which made me and Alaric happy as hell. Neither one of us wanted a girl.

"Stop being like that boo. You are the only wobbling, crybaby ass pregnant woman I want," I hit his arm twice when he said that. Him and K.J started laughing. We wanted to get some practice in, so we offered to keep K.J while Yatta and Erin went to Paris. I was so happy for my girl with her pregnant and now engaged ass. I looked down at my engagement ring and smiled. Even though I wanted to kill my soon-to-be husband. I still loved him and my three-karat princess cut ring.

"You think you're being funny until I have yo' ass sleeping on the couch. Did you get the wine for your mama?" I asked him and he rolled his eyes walking down the liquor aisle. I watched my sexy ass man with his dreads on top of his head. He looked so good in his brown Nike sweatpants and matching hoodie. He had some wheat Timberlands on and his diamond earrings on looking like a Snicker that I wanted to bite.

"Come here, Ric," I said as he put the wine in the buggy. He walked over to me and I pulled him by his tan North face coat. I kissed him hungrily and his hands went around my waist and squeezed my booty.

"Yo' moody ass don't know rather to love me or hate me," he said licking his lips and smiling at me.

"Whatever I decide you ain't going nowhere so it don't matter," I rolled my eyes and gave K.J some Teddy Grahams.

"Never that boo that's why I asked you to be my wife. Plus my mama said if I leave you a baby mama for long she was going to kick my ass," I cracked up when he said that.

Me and Alaric's mama got along great. Yea she was salty about me taking her son from her but she really didn't have a choice but to love me. I wasn't going anywhere, and she truly saw that I loved her son. As for my mama, she moved to Vegas with some nigga she met online. Me and Z didn't give a fuck and both were happy as hell she's gone. Alaric's brothers are doing great and June doesn't even know that he was kidnapped. As far as the police know someone tried to kidnap him but once they drugged him they dropped him off to a hospital.

Alaric's mama knew what German did to me and how he took June. All she wanted to know was German handled. Alaric assured her he was and that was all she cared about. As far as the police are concerned German was cheating on his wife with his ex-wife. Some shit went down with Beth coming to German house Ginger shot Beth and German then shit herself. I'm not sure if I said it right but either way, all three are dead. Such a shame.

"So do you think you're ready for fatherhood?" I asked Alaric as we both turned the room light off where K.J was asleep at.

Me and Alaric decided to move to Ann Arbor, Michigan. We found a three-bedroom home with a two-car garage. As long as the backyard was huge and there was a finished basement Alaric was sold. I cared about the kitchen and master bedroom which was huge as hell. It was close to his school. He decided to take his computer loving ass to the University of Michigan and get his bachelor's degree in data science. I had no clue what the hell that was but he did and that's all that matters. But get this, Alaric and Z surprised me and Dreka with a whole two-story building. The upstairs and downstairs was spacious as hell. Alaric knew I hated heights, so I had downstairs. He had it decked out like a nail salon. I had six nail sections with stools, all the nail tools I needed.

Drills, OPI machines and a station where you put your nails and feet under and the fan dried them quickly. The wall was filled with matte polish, traditional polish, crackle polish. Color and traditional acrylic, a price chart waiting for me to fill it in. And I had five leather soft massage pedicure chairs. Alaric had my picture blown up on the back wall and my color scheme was black, turquoise and white. I swear y'all I cried like a baby when I seen it. I never thought I would have a man believe in what I love so much that he would buy me a building. And my baby was upstairs from me which was amazing. I named my shop The Nail Bar and I was in love. I thanked my boo every damn day with more than sex. He was truly the GOAT!

"I'm more than ready. I feel like I need this shit like I need you. I want my son and I to have the best relationship. I get to basically get a do-over of how a father and son should be," I walked up to him and put my arms around his waist. We were in the bedroom taking off our clothes after eating and putting K.J to bed. That little boy was so sweet and so easy to keep.

"You are going to be an amazing father. Are you sure you don't want to make him a junior or at least give him an 'A' name?" I looked up at him and asked. He pecked my lips and shook his head no.

"Naw, I love the name you gave him. And stop worrying about what people gone think or say about me taking your last name. We know why the fuck I'm shedding that name 'Bell' and that's all that matters, Cassidy. Fuck whoever got something to say as a matter of fact send they ass my way if they say some shit to you," I laughed at how quickly Ric got mad. He decided he didn't want his dad last name so when we get married he was taking my last name. The baby name is Codee Ric Collins. I loved it but I always asked Alaric how he felt about it every day. I just wanted my boo to be comfortable.

"Ok, grumpy I just asked," I kissed him again and I could feel his dick getting hard.

"No, I'm tired as hell and your son is giving me gas," I walked away from Ric and went to the dresser to get my pajamas.

"God damn Cassidy!" he waved his hand in the air and covered his nose. I looked at him and started crying hard.

"Stop making fun of me Ric! This is your fucking baby doing this shit to me!" I threw some socks at him.

"Ok boo, I'm sorry. Damn!" he held his nose and coughed because I kept fucking farting. The shit was uncontrollable I swear it was. He fell on the bed laughing so hard his eyes were watery.

"I swear too God you smell like a fat old dead nigga!" I climbed on top of him and was punching the shit out of him.

"You're. Such. An. Asshole!" I said between hits. He was cracking up making me madder and I started crying again.

"Come here boo I'm sorry. You know I love yo' poot-fart ass," he was kissing all over my wet face.

"No, you don't. Your going to leave me for a skinny girl who doesn't fart all day," I balled my damn eyes out. Ric really did hurt my feelings.

"That will never happen Cass love. I'll wear a gas mask and still make love to that sweet pussy," I looked at him and went back to hitting his ass. He took his shirt off and threw it on the floor. Looking at his sexy hard body I started kissing him while still on top of him.

"Swear you hate to love me and love to hate me," he said against my lips.

"So what," I said and went back to kissing him. God this was going to be long three-and-a-half months. But I couldn't wait until we meet our little Codee.

Dreka

"Ugh fuck Zamir. Sss damn daddy," Zamir was fucking me so good on this sink.

I was locking up my salon about to leave and his ass had to start some shit. Cassidy told y'all about the two-story building Z and Alaric got for us. I gotta take my boo words and say my nigga is a GOAT to. I loved everything about this building including Cassidy being downstairs. Our grand opening was next month and I couldn't wait. Zamir had my shop color scheme pink and black with white furniture. I had six salon chairs and six dryers and chairs. My shampoo station was so cute with white sinks and white leather chairs. I had a huge picture of me and Madam C.J. Walker on my wall that I absolutely loved.

I had a storage room and the waiting area was a white wrap around leather bench. I just loved my Mir-Mir so much for this. I had to come tonight and take pictures of the shop so I could put them on its Instagram. Zamir came because I wasn't home yet and now he had my naked ass all in one of my shampoo sinks. My jeans were on the floor and my panties were in his pocket.

"Shit this pussy so good. You love yo' husband, huh baby girl?" God, he has been saying that for four months now and I loved it. Me and Zamir eloped downtown at the courthouse. My daddy and grandma cussed my ass out but they eventually let it go. They love Zamir so much. He asked me to marry him giving me a three-karat oval ring and I said hell yea! The only person who was there when we got married was my mama.

She has been free from prison for five months and its been great. Of course, my daddy moved her right in with him. He got her a job at General Motors and her probation officer wasn't down her neck as much. It was so fun showing my mama the city again. Taking her shopping, to some restaurants and to the movies. I showed her my old job at Greenfield Plaza and everyone met her. Me, Cassidy and Erin took her out to a bar where our men including my dad popped up and blocked our fun. I swear I felt so blessed to have my mama back in my life. No guards around or monitor visits. My grandma was loving having her at the house and they were always cooking and on my daddy's back.

Zamir loved my mama and said he swears I'm going to age like her. I just laughed every time he said that. My mama treated him like a son and he secretly loved it. Like my Mir-Mir brought a building in Southfield for his boxing studio. I was so proud of him! My mama thought the seller was charging Zamir to much for the building. This crazy woman went down to real-estate building with Zamir and cause hell. They lowered the price seven-grand less than asking price. I cracked up when Zamir told me how my mama clowned. Anyway, we got married with her as a witness and she cried more than I did.

I swear I didn't think twice about marrying Zamir. I loved this man more than anything and couldn't imagine being with anybody else. He took a life for me and I would do the same for him. I loved how mean he was to everyone else but so sweet and soft with me. Zamir was my weakness and I would drop any and everything if he needed me. Now, back to this dick.

"Yessss babe I fucking love my husband," he pulled out and dropped his head between my legs. I pulled his band on his dreads out and massaged his scalp while he devoured me.

"God damn Zamir. Shittt," I came all in his mouth and he was still going at it. I know I had to sanitize the fuck out this sink when we were done. He started licking and kissing my thighs. His beard was soaked as he got in my face and kissed me hard.

"I love the fuck out of my wife. And if she ever think for a second she about to be without me," he looked me in my eyes biting his bottom lip and sliding his dick back in my pussy.

"I will snap her pretty ass fucking neck. This shit forever Dreka, gimmie a kiss," he put his hand around my neck looking crazy. I was so turned on that I started squirting. I loved that crazy ass talk he would do. I kissed his big lips biting on his bottom lip that I loved.

"You mine Zamir, huh daddy? Are you mine?" I moaned while looking at him which I knew drives him wild. He licked that bottom lip and smirked at me.

"You tryna make me nut quick, you think you fucking slick huh," this nigga had me in a 'V' shape sucking the hell out of my toes. I was cumming all on his dick and in the sink.

"Fuck!" Zamir came all in me and I was right with him. I was still on the depo shot so he could come in me all day. Yea me and Zamir were married but we just were not ready for kids right now. We did, however, move into a new condo in Canton. I just wanted a new start and a new place that was ours. It was a two bedroom with a garage and a nice fitness center, pool, and sauna. We loved it and trust me we both want to be parents just not right now.

"Damn baby girl that shit was so good. Come here," he pulled me to him just as I put my jeans on and kissed me.

"Zamir you can't be coming up here bending me over. This is a place of business," I laughed as I put my UGG boots on.

"Shut that shit up Dreka. I'll bend ya ass over, spread you eagle and fuck you against whatever wall I want to. You my fucking wife," he grabbed my neck and hand me against the wall.

"Look at'cho freak ass getting wet," he said right before he kissed me. He was right I was so wet with how ruff he was with me.

"I am wet but I'm also ready to go home and have my husband fuck me all over our condo," I said in my sexy low voice.

"Then let's wrap this shit up wife. I feel like having you sit on my face while you call me ya' King," I laughed at his crazy ass talked shit while we walked out the shop and I locked up.

On our drive home I thought about all the shit that took place these last few months. Me, Erin and Cassidy managed to tame the fuck out of these three wild Detroit niggas. All the drama and stupid ass bitches that just wouldn't let go. Tia and Cleo didn't have to have the outcome they did. It was sad because they were young and all they had to do was move on. Cleo had me happy as hell she was dead. To try and kill your own son because a nigga doesn't want you is sick. I am so happy God was with K.J and gave him a second chance at life.

Alaric's dad did some fucked up shit to Cassidy and had to die at the hands of his own son. And let's not forget my boo, Erin. Her fucked up ass mother and brother tried to mess my cousin life all up. I was so happy Josey crazy ass husband killed her and their son. Hell, then he did extra good by killing himself to. Erin was such a good girl and didn't deserve to be done wrong from her own fucking mama. Speaking of fucked up mamas. I was glad Zamir and Cassidy's mama was gone to Vegas. That crazy ass fucked up woman was a mess and needed to put more miles between her and her kids. All and all I'm just glad all the toxic is gone from all of us.

Drama free and happy lives is what we all deserved. Looking over at Zamir sexy ass as we drove the freeway I grabbed his right hand that was on his leg, interlocking our fingers I looked at our hand together and then kissed his.

"I love you Mir-Mir. You know that right?"

Looking at him trying not to smile was so funny.

"You better," his smart ass said, and I smacked my lips.

"I'm playing, I love you to baby girl," he kissed my hand a few times and we talked all the way home. I love the fuck out of my bad boy. Hell, we all did!

The End

☐